BACKRUSH

NEW YORK TIMES BESTSELLING AUTHOR
JANA DELEON

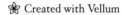

For my husband Rene', my hero.

Tidal Wave

"You're not a wave. You're part of the ocean." – Mitch Albom

CHAPTER ONE

New York City, New York

ALAYNA SCOTT LOOKED OUT FROM THE ROOFTOP PATIO AT the city sprawling before her. It was close to midnight but lights from the buildings, streetlights, and the holiday decor filtered through all but the darkest alleys. She pulled her coat tighter around her body as a cold December wind touched her face. A few seconds later, tiny snowflakes began to fall. It was beautiful and yet still somewhat overwhelming. The people, the businesses, the constant rush to be more tomorrow than what you were today. Even after years of staying ahead of the curve, she was still intimidated when she thought about the vastness that was this city. And the small-town Florida girl in her felt that standing there, with the glorious view, was somewhat surreal.

"It's getting chilly." His voice sounded behind her and Alayna turned to smile at the attractive, well-polished man as he put his arm around her shoulder. He smelled of spice, and she knew the bit of cologne he'd applied that night probably cost more than her entire outfit. Warren Patterson III was considered by the New York social scene to be one of the most eligible bachelors in the city. He came from an old-money New England family. The kind with a summer home on Martha's Vineyard, a villa in Italy, and political ties.

He was Harvard educated and at thirty-five years of age, ran one of the most successful hedge fund firms in the city. But the list of attributes didn't end there. Warren was handsome and never missed his gym workout. And he was charming. Everyone who met him liked him, which meant his party invitation list was almost as long as the list of women looking to land him.

When he'd asked Alayna out, she'd been shocked.

She knew the women on the social registry who'd been gunning to add Patterson to their last name thought their relationship was a fling. One of those things that rich boys did—dating beneath them for sport or entertainment value. No one took it seriously. To be honest, neither did Alayna. Not at first.

But here they were, eight months later, and they'd been exclusive since that first date. Alayna saw the smirks every time they attended one of these events, and she saw the whispers and knew they were all about her. How she wasn't suitable. After all, she wasn't from a prominent New England family. She wasn't even from a prominent Southern family. She had no social standing, no connections, and Alayna knew that everyone thought she was only after Warren for his money.

They were wrong.

Alayna enjoyed Warren's company. He was funny and preferred active entertainment, like bike riding through Central Park, over sitting in a movie theater. And even though he often had to attend social engagements because his clients expected it, he never complained that her working hours didn't allow her to accompany him often. Nor did he take another woman because she couldn't attend. Alayna knew the women in Warren's social circle didn't like her. They put on a good show in front of Warren, of course, but he saw right through it and they often laughed later about the shallow attempts to appear to be friends.

The press, however, had the opposite view. They loved Warren and Alayna as a couple. It was the classic tale of the prince and the commoner. Plus, Alayna was a top-notch chef who'd just opened her own up-and-coming fine dining restaurant in Manhattan that year. She was young and pretty and was conquering a market that many never even got to try their hand at. They were a modern-day fairy tale.

"I've made the rounds," Warren said. "Heard all the boring stories that I'm required to hear. Shaken the hands I'm supposed to shake. Agreed to far too many golf dates—"

"And skirted how many offers from eligible women?"

He grinned. "I didn't count. Are you ready to get out of here?"

"Since my face feels like it's turning blue, I'm going with yes."

"A rooftop party in December...not the best idea, although the view is spectacular."

She nodded and they worked their way toward the double doors that led back into the building. Warren paused along the way to shake hands and acknowledge promises made, and it was another twenty minutes before they finally got into the elevator. Alayna, who'd worked closing at her restaurant the night before and had finally fallen into bed at 3:00 a.m., had been fighting back a yawn all night. She finally gave in once the elevator door closed.

"You didn't get to sleep late this morning?" Warren asked.

"No. I had to go in early to do the food order, then there was an issue with the walk-in and the company was hassling me over warranty work. I finally got that handled and was about to walk out the door when André sliced his hand during prep."

"Ouch. Is he all right?"

"Ten stitches, and he has to take the rest of the week off."

Warren nodded in understanding. "So you ended up filling in."

"Just for the afternoon until Marnie could get there to cover. But by the time I got home, I was too wound up to sleep so I ended up working on the holiday specials I'm adding to the menu."

"What time do you have to be in tomorrow?"

"Midafternoon. I'm working close again."

"Then how about a quick nightcap at my place and we crash? I can have Lawrence drive you to your apartment tomorrow whenever you wake up."

It was tempting. Warren's penthouse was only a couple blocks away, whereas a trip to her apartment in Brooklyn, even at this time of night, was far longer. If she stayed the night with Warren, she could be asleep before she would be unlocking the front door of her apartment.

"That sounds great," she said. "You sure I won't be in the way in the morning?"

"Of course not. I have a ten o'clock meeting but even if I didn't, your sleeping is hardly hindering me from going to work. Just give me a call when you're ready and I'll send the car."

Alayna smiled, still slightly in awe of the lifestyle that Warren considered normal. A car with a full-time driver at his beck and call. A penthouse with a prime location near Times Square. A private jet that, on a rare three days off, he'd used to take her to the Bahamas for a quick stay at the vacation home his parents had just purchased. Vacation home, they called it.

Alayna would have called the ten-thousand-square-foot home with servants' quarters and full-time staff an estate.

Warren's car, a new Rolls-Royce, was waiting for them up front. The driver, an older Italian man named Gino, stood beside it waiting to open the door. He greeted them both with a nod and then proceeded to drive the short distance to Warren's building. He let them out in the drive where the building valet opened the car door and the door to the building, then pressed the button on the elevator. The level of service that Warren received always made Alayna slightly uncomfortable, but Warren, who'd grown up with it, never seemed to notice.

The elevator opened into Warren's penthouse condo and, as she did every time she entered, Alayna took in the incredible view of the city that the wall of glass windows offered. It was even more stunning than the rooftop view she'd had minutes earlier, and much warmer.

Warren headed into the kitchen. "Would you like a glass of wine?" he asked. "A shot of bourbon to warm up, maybe?"

"Actually, I think I'll just take water and get changed out of this dress. I haven't taken a deep breath in hours."

He poured S.Pellegrino into a beautiful red crystal glass and brought it to her where she stood in front of the window.

"The shallow breathing was worth it," he said. "You're stunning. Every man at the party was green with envy when I walked in with you on my arm."

"And every woman was plotting how to trip me near the balcony."

He smiled and leaned in to kiss her. "Probably. Can you blame them? You have it all, Alayna. You're beautiful and talented. And you have a mind for something other than the latest fashion or what a Kardashian did this afternoon."

"One of them had salad and champagne at an outdoor café in Beverly Hills. But I don't know which one."

"Which outdoor café?"

"No. Which Kardashian. I always remember the restaurant."

He laughed. "Of course you do. I've been thinking. Once the holidays are over and things settle down, maybe we could take a trip to Italy."

"Seriously?"

"You've been wanting to add some Italian dishes to your menu. No better way to make the perfect selection than going straight to the source for an extensive taste test."

"That would be incredible. I mean, assuming we could both get time away."

"We'll make it work. I'm going to take a shower before I turn in."

She nodded and as he started to turn, she heard the ding of the elevator. That was strange. Who would be accessing Warren's condo at this hour? Warren went completely still, and as Alayna turned, the elevator door opened and four men wearing suits and brandishing firearms rushed in.

"Hands up where I can see them," the first man ordered.

Alayna dropped the wineglass and it shattered on the white marble floor, scattering shards of red glass across the pristine surface. She felt the sting on her legs as some of the glass connected with her bare skin, and she threw her arms in the air, completely panicked. Were they being robbed? By men wearing suits? How had they gotten past security? She looked over at Warren and saw him standing there, his arms up and his expression completely blank. What the hell was going on?

"FBI Special Agent Kurt Davies," the man with the gun said. He pulled ID out of his pocket with his free hand and showed her before looking at Warren. "Warren Patterson, you're under arrest for money laundering and fraud. You have the right..."

Alayna swayed as the FBI agent's words all ran together. She stumbled a bit as a wave of dizziness washed over her, and one of the other men grabbed her by the shoulders and assisted her onto the couch.

FBI? Money laundering? Fraud?

Those words kept playing through her mind like a broken record, but they made no more sense after the hundredth repetition than they had when the agent first uttered them. It must be a mistake. They'd made a mistake is all. Warren wasn't a criminal. He was a successful, educated businessman from a well-respected family.

"Ms. Scott?" Agent Davies's voice sounded above her. "I'm afraid you're under arrest as well."

She bolted upright and stared at him, not understanding what he'd said.

"What? I've done nothing wrong. This is all a mistake. It has to be a mistake."

"No mistake," Agent Davies said. "Alayna Scott, you're under arrest for accessory—and..."

She swayed again and this time, everything went black.

CHAPTER TWO

FIVE MONTHS LATER.

FBI SPECIAL AGENT KURT DAVIES PUSHED THE DOCUMENT across the desk. "All we need is your signature and this is all over. At least until trial."

Alayna eyed the papers as if they were a venomous snake. And that wasn't far from the truth. It had been five months since the FBI burst into Warren's condo. Five months since she'd learned that the man whom she'd thought was near perfect was as big a fraud as the crimes he'd committed. Five months since her entire life had begun to fall apart, leaving her with even less than she'd had the first day she set foot in New York City. In the city that never forgot, no reputation was infinitely better than a bad one.

She lifted the pen and twisted the top back and forth. The DA had assured her that her testimony was required but by no means the only thing that would put Warren in prison. In his opinion, she was safe from retribution. Alayna still wasn't convinced that the word 'safe' applied, but the DA and the

FBI had been insistent. Warren was a white-collar criminal, not a serial killer. The FBI had accumulated tons of evidence against him. Hard evidence—paperwork, bank transactions, even recorded conversations.

But despite all the reassurances, Alayna still felt vulnerable, as if by signing the document that kept her out of the hot seat with federal law enforcement, she was autographing her own death warrant. Or maybe she was just beyond exhausted and had seen too many movies.

Davies, sensing her hesitation and the reason behind it, leaned forward in his chair. "Remember everything we discussed. We have solid evidence to support the charges against Mr. Patterson. You don't really have much to help our case because you were unaware of Patterson's business practices. I know you feel this puts you at risk, but there are simply too many people he'd need to eliminate to even attempt to save himself, and he can't make the paper trail disappear, so adding a bunch of murder-for-hire charges to his sheet isn't the smart move."

"Laundering money for drug dealers wasn't the smart move, either."

"The smart ones never think they'll be caught. Regardless, there's a whole list of people with more pertinent testimony than what you can offer."

"Yeah, but none of those people were dating him," Alayna said, almost choking on the words.

For eight months, she'd dated a man she didn't even know. She'd thought she did, of course, but when the FBI had led them both out in handcuffs, she'd been made painfully aware that Warren's carefully constructed life was all an illusion and she'd simply been part of the scenery. One of the many items Warren surrounded himself with that made him look normal.

But the FBI and the DA had laid out the facts—Warren

had been laundering money for a Colombian drug cartel, creating shell companies complete with unknowing investors, in order to clean the money. She'd been so shocked she didn't believe it at first. Warren barely even drank and never smoked. He'd never been arrested or even accused of a crime. How could he be involved with something as sordid as drugs? But then the DA showed her some of the evidence against him, and her shock had slowly shifted to overwhelming humiliation.

How had she missed this? She'd shared her life, bed, and dreams with a man who wasn't at all who he pretended to be. The Warren she knew was a hedge fund manager with a stellar reputation for making his clients an excellent return. He was a philanthropist who contributed hundreds of thousands of dollars to charities every year, a patron of the arts, and he attended Mass almost every Sunday. How could that Warren and the Warren that the FBI exposed possibly be the same person?

Agent Davies had assured her that Warren was one of the best he'd ever encountered at presenting a different face. It was one of the main reasons it had taken so long to lock onto him. And even if some cast a side-eye at the speed of his success in the finance industry, she figured they'd put it down to his old-money connections. No one would have guessed that he was laundering money for Juan Rivera, the head of one of Colombia's most notorious cartels.

Warren had asked to speak to Alayna after his arrest, but she'd refused even though the FBI would have allowed it. She figured they probably would have liked to listen in and see if they could get more dirt, but she didn't want to see Warren. At first, she'd been too shocked, too frozen with disbelief, and then later, she'd been overwhelmed with hurt and disappointment, mostly in herself. He wasn't supposed to have any way to contact her, but he'd managed to send flowers—two dozen roses—with a card that read simply, "I'm sorry. Warren."

She'd taken the flowers from the delivery guy, called for a car service, and taken them straight to FBI headquarters, not even wanting the toxic bouquet to cross the threshold into her apartment. Even though she'd purged the unit of everything that had reminded her of Warren, it was still hard to be there —sitting on the same sofa where they'd shared a glass of wine and tales of their workday, dining at the same kitchen counter where they'd discussed one of her latest creations. She hadn't even attempted to sleep in her bed, opting for the couch instead. Too many memories, and none of them real.

Because Warren wasn't real.

His family had immediately distanced themselves from the public following his arrest and issued a statement to the press about the sadness and disappointment they felt over their son's actions. Then they'd gotten cleared by the FBI and retreated to Italy. Alayna didn't know if they'd ever returned to New York. They'd never made an effort to contact her, even when the FBI had made it clear that Alayna was not part of Warren's dealings. But then that was hardly surprising. She'd never spent any time with his parents or sisters except for the occasional charity event and even then, it was all surface level.

She pulled the document in front of her and signed. This was her way out. When Warren was at her apartment, he'd used her laptop to access his email and conduct some of his illegal business, dragging her into his misdeeds. The FBI had cleared her of any wrongdoing fairly early on but had insisted she stick around for a bit longer as they cleared up other things. So she'd waited months for this set of paperwork to freedom. But the investigation and the wait weren't even the worst of things. The worst was when the DA told her that because Warren's company had provided her with an infusion of capital to upgrade her restaurant, it was being seized along with everything else he owned.

Eventually, she might be able to regain control, but what was the point? Closed restaurants didn't make money and without money, she couldn't afford to maintain the lease, the employees, the utilities, or any of the other expenses. And besides, reporters had already descended on her, all vying for the personal angle. Even if she'd wanted to keep the restaurant, it would be forever tainted by what Warren had done. *She* would be forever tainted by what Warren had done. If the DA had wanted to push it, he could have made her life even more difficult. Instead, he'd asked for her testimony on the few things they could use her for, and in exchange, she was free.

Free to find real.

Impact Zone

"The cure for anything is salt water: sweat, tears or the sea." – Isak Dinesen

CHAPTER THREE

ALAYNA PLACED THE LAST OF THE BOXES IN THE TRUNK OF her newly acquired late-model Honda Accord and closed it. She gave her apartment building one final look before pulling the car keys from her pocket. She remembered the day she'd moved in—so excited about the 700 square feet of space that was practically a mansion compared to the tiny studio she'd left. That day, she couldn't wait to get moved in. Now she couldn't wait to leave.

It had taken five months to get cleared by the FBI but only a day after signing the paperwork to prepare to leave New York. She'd had plenty of time to get her things in order, so all that had remained after she left from signing the documents that granted her freedom was packing up a couple boxes of clothes and personal items and handing in her official notice to her apartment super. Everything else had been sold, given away, or wrapped up and boxed months before. The boxes had been stacked against the wall of her bedroom, mocking her every time she entered, reminding her that she couldn't leave this horror behind her.

But all of that was over today.

As she was about to climb into her car, a horn honking down the street caused her to pause, and she watched as a shiny new Mercedes pulled in behind her and stopped. Brad Winston, one of Warren's oldest friends, climbed out and hurried toward her.

"I was afraid I wouldn't catch you before you left," he said.

"You barely made it. Just put my last box in the trunk and I'm about to pull away."

She felt odd talking to Brad, given everything that had happened. Brad had also been completely unaware of Warren's misdeeds and had been reeling ever since the case was laid out in the media. He'd been fortunate that he'd never done business with Warren. Of course, that hadn't stopped the FBI from crawling up his butt with a magnifying glass, and Alayna knew just how painful that could be. They'd never found a smoking gun, so they had no choice but to back away, but by the time they were done poking into every aspect of Brad's life, the damage had already been done.

Brad had retreated to his second home in California as soon as he was free to leave, and Alayna wondered if he'd ever consider New York his primary residence again. Which was why she was surprised to see him now. And because Brad knew that she'd agreed to testify against Warren, she wondered how he really felt about that.

When the news had first come out, Brad was appalled and sympathetic when he realized Alayna had been drawn into the mess. Then the FBI had fixated on him, and he'd withdrawn from everything, trying to deal with the investigation. When they'd talked after he'd been cleared, he'd acknowledged his anger over both of them being drawn into Warren's mess and said he was sorry that it had cost Alayna her restaurant. But more than anything, Brad had been pissed off that the man he thought was his best friend was a stranger. Alayna understood exactly how he felt.

He glanced at her car and frowned. "Are you sure you don't want to fly to Florida? It's such a long drive."

"I'm sure. I can't take my chef's knives with me on the plane, and no way am I shipping them or putting them in checked baggage."

Brad nodded, but Alayna could tell he didn't really understand why she was willing to spend the better part of twenty hours in a car versus three in an airplane. But she didn't expect him to. Her chef's knives had been a gift from her aunt Bea. They were expensive and represented the financial sacrifice of a woman who'd always believed in Alayna. The sentimental value was even higher than their market value, and no way would Alayna risk them getting damaged or lost by an airline or shipping company. It had taken her four months to convince the FBI to return the knives to her after they'd been seized along with her restaurant. They'd finally acquiesced, as if doing her a favor, even though she'd provided clear proof that she'd owned the knives before she ever met Warren.

She was going to need a car in Florida anyway. So she'd bought a used car in a reliable model and would spend two to three days making the trek there. As far as Alayna was concerned, making the long drive from New York was a small price to pay for peace of mind. She'd already lost too much. She didn't know if she could take losing anything else.

"Well, you know my number," Brad said. "If you ever need anything or if you run into trouble along the way, call."

"I appreciate it," Alayna said, although they both knew she'd never call.

He reached into his pocket and pulled out an envelope. "I want you to take this."

She saw the edge of a hundred-dollar bill peeking out and

shook her head. "I can't. You don't need to do anything for me, Brad. None of this was your fault. You have no responsibility."

"I don't feel responsible," he said. "I feel sad and angry and embarrassed...a lot for me but mostly for you, because Warren's fucked-up choices took away everything you worked for. I didn't lose anything except a friend I never really knew and a social standing I never cared about. I want to do something to help you, but this is the only thing I have that you can use. Please. It's a long drive to Florida. You'll have expenses along the way and when you get there. I...I just have to do something. I need to."

Alayna's chest tightened at the miserable tone to Brad's voice that was matched only by his equally miserable expression. She didn't want to take money from him, but she understood the compulsion to do something. Even if it wasn't warranted. She took the envelope and hugged him.

"Thank you," she said. "We're going to be okay. Life will go on and one day, this will be a distant, unpleasant memory."

Brad nodded. "Good luck, Alayna. I hope you find a new, incredible life."

"You too. Goodbye, Brad."

She felt the tears well up and knew she had to get away before they spilled over. She'd managed to hold it together while packing, trying to focus on the drive and not all the dreams that were crushed and the ones that would never be. She jumped into her car and lifted her hand to wave as she pulled away. Brad stood there watching her, growing smaller in her rearview mirror until the bustle of the city obscured him completely from her view.

It was 9:00 a.m. on a Wednesday morning. She'd waited for work traffic to subside before leaving, but getting out of the city would still take more time than she'd like. Once she made it to the interstate, it would just be one long continuous drive, one interstate merging into another, until she arrived in Florida. Given that it was still early May and tourist season hadn't started, traffic near Tempest Island shouldn't have grinded to a halt yet, but the weather coming off the Gulf was unpredictable and could add delays to travel time. But the old car had a new radio with Bluetooth capability, and she'd loaded up her phone with audiobooks the night before, so she was all set.

Unfortunately, it took far longer than she'd hoped to get out of the city. Road construction had added to the traffic issues and by the time she finally got to clear interstate, it was time for a pit stop. She went ahead and topped off the fuel before grabbing her backpack and heading inside for a restroom break. Figuring she'd make up some lost time by driving through lunch, she grabbed a protein shake and banana for the time being as she hadn't been able to manage breakfast, and added a couple of protein bars, some chips, and some peanuts for later. It wasn't the best of meals, but a couple days of eating like crap weren't likely to kill her. Besides, with all the stress, she'd lost weight and was a little thinner than she thought was healthy.

She fired up a book, a fantasy about a kick-ass heroine and her dragon partner, and set off again. As the miles ticked away, her mind drifted from the book to everything that had happened the past year, from her whirlwind relationship with Warren to the utter and complete implosion of her entire life. It was still surreal. Some mornings, she woke up and for a split second, thought the entire thing was a horrible nightmare. Then reality flooded in and the depression she'd barely managed to keep at bay pressed against her, trying to cozy up to her like a warm blanket. But she knew the deception of depression. She'd faced it before and wouldn't allow herself to be enveloped by the promise of no pain, no sorrow. The heartache was bad, but numbness didn't allow for progress. It only kept one still.

By late evening, her entire body was starting to protest. She was used to standing and lots of movement, not sitting in one position for hours on end. The sun was starting to set, and it would be dark soon. Before the sunlight was gone, she wanted to be safely tucked away in a hotel room for the night. She looked at the signs and saw that Roanoke was five miles away. She'd made a list of hotels along the route, from ambitious daily mileage gains to conservative. Roanoke was on the conservative list, but it couldn't be helped. Perhaps she'd be able to make better time tomorrow. And if not, the trip that might have taken two days would take three.

She took the exit for the hotel and spotted a burger place along the service road. Her mouth began to water, and she took that as a sign that the convenience store snacks were long gone and she should grab dinner on the way to the hotel. She pulled into the parking lot and went inside the small but neat building and ordered a cheeseburger and fries to go. A young girl with a big smile took her order and then skipped over to the kitchen to turn it in.

No computer system. Everything still on pads. Your typical mom-and-pop shop.

It made Alayna happy because she loved to see restaurants owned by individuals rather than large corporate chains. The food was usually better and in smaller places like this, the service often was as well. She sat at a table and checked her email and the weather report while she waited. Her email was clear. The weather, unfortunately, was not. It looked as though a thunderstorm was due to roll through early the next morning. She hoped it wouldn't delay her leaving, but she also didn't want to drive in anything severe.

The girl at the counter called out a cheerful "ma'am" and

held up the brown paper sack with her dinner. She collected the bag, left a generous tip in the glass jar on the counter, and headed back out to her car. The hotel was just a half mile down the service road, and it had a single room available on the third floor. She'd ensured that the hotels she'd chosen had one main entry point with occupied reception and required key cards to enter the building at any other point.

Even though the FBI assured her that she wasn't in danger, she hadn't been able to shake the bad feeling that crept over her every time she'd left her apartment. That feeling that she was being watched. And maybe she was. For all she knew, the FBI was still watching her. Although they'd declared they were convinced that she had no knowledge of Warren's crimes, that didn't mean it was true. She knew they sometimes turned people loose in order to watch them. And what if Warren was angry with her for agreeing to testify? With all the other witnesses, it would be business, but with her it was personal. He might be behind bars, but he had connections and probably had money stashed to pay people to do the things he couldn't.

So every day she remained in New York, she was careful.

She'd hoped that when she left the city, the feeling would eventually dissipate, but so far, that same twinge was there. Shaking her head, she unlocked her room and carried her backpack, her dinner, and a small suitcase inside, then pulled the dead bolt. After the long day in the car, she wanted a shower, but the smell of the burger had her stomach overriding her sore body. The shower would wait.

She turned on the television for the noise, grabbed a bottled water from her backpack, and settled in at the writing desk in the corner to eat. The burger was excellent. Or she was starving. Probably a combination of both. But the ground meat was high quality and the seasoning and the sear on the patty were great. Just enough flavor to have a bit of a bite but not oversalted, the way many burgers were. And despite the time lapse between cooking and eating, the fries were still crisp and were home cut, not frozen.

Score another one for the mom-and-pop shop.

She made quick work of the burger and fries, spent a couple seconds wishing she'd added a malt to the order, then grabbed shorts and a tank from her suitcase and headed into the bathroom. She made the water skin-reddening hot, then stood under the strong spray for several minutes just to let her sore muscles unwind. She'd pinned her long blond ponytail up since she'd just washed her hair this morning, and she could feel the fine wispy pieces that had escaped clinging to the back of her neck.

When she looked and felt like a boiled lobster, she climbed out and pulled on her sleeping gear before sitting on the edge of the bed with her backpack. She unzipped it to pull out her iPad, which was tucked next to her chef's knives, and saw the envelope that Brad had given her stuck in between. She'd simply shoved it in the pack before she'd pulled away and had forgotten all about it. Now she pulled it out and counted the bills, then flopped back and blew out a breath.

Five thousand dollars.

Good Lord. She should have looked sooner. She was already nervous about the trip, and that amount of cash had sent her into overdrive. Maybe she'd be able to find a branch of her bank along the way. She shoved the money back in the envelope and stuffed it into a zipper pocket on the inside of the pack. Then she grabbed her iPad to check for the nearest bank branch, shaking her head as she typed in the name.

God bless Brad. Five thousand dollars was a lot of money. She realized it didn't represent the same financial boon to him as it did to her, but it was still a huge gift to someone that he didn't even know that well and was under no obligation to help. Since Brad and Warren ran in the same social circles, they'd spent a decent amount of time together, but usually at events. Alayna was always fascinated with the revolving door of women that Brad maintained. An heiress, a socialite, an actress, a model, and once, a fighter pilot, which tickled Alayna to no end after the run of silly women she'd had to endure.

Alayna had liked Brad from the start. Despite his dubious taste in women, and his absolute refusal to find a suitable rich girl from a good family and settle down—his mom's request— he had always been nice to Alayna and had treated her as if she were part of their circle.

But still...five thousand dollars.

It was a lot of money to give, even from someone who probably wouldn't notice it was gone. She located a branch for her bank in Roanoke that opened at eight. She'd planned on getting on the road before then, but if the storm delayed her, then she'd deposit the cash before leaving town. If the storm moved through early, then she'd find another branch along the way and keep the backpack attached to her with both straps. Between her knives and the money, it was the most valuable item she carried with her.

She yawned and stretched, feeling the stress of the day and the drive washing over her. It was still early, but there was nothing stopping her from climbing into bed and watching some television or playing a game on her iPad for a while. It wasn't as if she had anything to do. No work responsibilities. No apartment to clean. No dishes. No laundry until she got to Florida.

She went to the door and checked the dead bolt. Then she dragged the chair from the desk over and propped the back of it underneath the door handle just as she'd done every night in her apartment. She checked the window to ensure it was locked and made sure the shades covered every square inch. The bathroom light was still on from her shower and it would remain that way. But that was just practical, she told herself. She didn't want to trip if she had to pee in the middle of the night. After all, this was a strange place and she couldn't move through it on autopilot. The fact that it was five clear steps from the bed to the bathroom was irrelevant. She grabbed the television remote and climbed into bed.

You have to stop this.

It was the same thing she'd told herself a million times.

But she still didn't know how.

———

THE STORM MOVED THROUGH QUICKLY THE NEXT MORNING and Alayna took advantage of it and struck out as soon as the sun was up. The banking part of her agenda would have to wait. Right now, she wanted to get as many miles between her and New York as she could because every mile farther from Brooklyn was one mile closer to Tempest Island. And Aunt Bea.

She'd had a missed call from her aunt the night before, having dozed off watching HGTV and playing *Bubble Witch*. By the time she'd awakened and noticed the call, it was already past midnight. Her aunt was usually up early, so Alayna figured she'd just get on the road then give her a call. She yawned as she loaded her suitcase in the car, then went back into the hotel to snag a large cup of coffee and a bagel from the setup in the lobby. Unfortunately, the sleep she'd gotten between *Bubble Witch* and when she woke shortly after midnight had been the only solid stretch she'd managed. The rest of the night, she'd tossed and turned, busy dreams keeping her from deep slumber.

At 5:00 a.m. she'd finally given up and had taken another shower, hoping to prep her muscles for the drive ahead. Then she'd drunk the stingy two cups of coffee provided with the room and gone over her route on her iPad. If everything went perfectly, the remainder of the drive would take eleven or twelve hours. As soon as the sun peeked over the treetops, she headed out.

When 8:00 a.m. came around, she put in her earpiece and dialed her aunt.

"Alayna, thank God," her aunt said. "I was just about to call again. I was afraid something had happened when I didn't hear from you last night."

"Not at all. I just fell asleep watching television and didn't think you'd appreciate my calling back in the middle of the night when I woke up and saw I'd missed you."

"I probably wouldn't have hated it. Well, maybe just a little. Anyway, how far did you make it yesterday?"

"Only to Roanoke, I'm afraid. Traffic was crap getting out of the city and I ran into some construction. I'm hoping to make better time today."

"Are you already on the road?"

"Left an hour and a half ago."

"That's great. I don't suppose you're going to make it tonight though."

"I'm going to try, but it will depend on how things go. I don't want to be driving after dark."

"No. It's best to be cautious when it's an unfamiliar route. Give me a call later and let me know for sure. I was planning on leaving the key for you so you don't have to stop and get it from me. Whether it's tonight or tomorrow, you'll be tired and wanting a shower. There will be time for visiting later on."

"Thanks, Aunt Bea. I'll let you know how things look this afternoon."

She hung up the call and smiled. Just talking to Bea, knowing she was on her way to Tempest Island, made her feel 100 percent better. Her aunt was her rock. Her biggest fan. And Tempest Island was a magical place. A place of belonging and healing. When everything went down in New York and she knew she wouldn't be able to stay, it never occurred to her to go anywhere else.

Some might consider it giving up.

Alayna considered it going home.

She pressed the accelerator down and smiled as the miles ticked off behind her. At lunchtime, she stopped to refuel and checked the time and the app that reported traffic. Everything ahead of her looked clear and she'd made excellent time so far. Maybe even good enough to get to Tempest Island before dark. Which meant no time to waste on things like eating. At least, not eating in a restaurant. So she grabbed a hot dog and chips from the store while the fuel pumped and promised herself that she'd do a purge from junk food once she was settled in.

By 5:00 p.m. she was roughly two and a half hours away from her destination, assuming the roads remained clear and the Gulf didn't kick up a surprise storm. She'd lost a little time stopping at the bank to deposit the cash, but she'd felt better knowing the funds were out of her backpack and safely tucked away in her checking account. Now she was stopped again, this time for fuel, and stood staring at a motel across from the gas station. Did she risk it and continue? If she didn't run into trouble, she'd arrive just before sundown. She rolled her head around in a circle, then twisted from side to side, trying to loosen up her stiff body. If her muscles could vote, they'd be standing in a hot shower in about twenty minutes. But her desire to be home, in her own space—well, her space for now —was greater than the discomfort she'd have from another two to three hours on the road.

Mind made up, she went inside to grab what she hoped would be the last of her convenience store meals, then jumped in her car, ready to get back on the road. As she snapped her seat belt in place, she felt the hair on the back of her neck rise. She looked from side to side, then checked her rearview mirror, but didn't see anything odd. Just normal-looking people going about their everyday business.

She pulled out of the gas station and merged onto the interstate. As she drove, she checked her mirrors but didn't see anyone enter the road behind her. She took a deep breath and slowly blew it out. It was just her imagination. Because of everything that had happened, she was on edge. And traveling alone just made things worse, but when Bea had offered to fly to New York and drive back with her, she'd refused.

Bea had already done enough and was continuing to do for Alayna. She had a bookstore to run and didn't need to pay people to cover for her just so Alayna had someone to talk to on the drive. And then there was the other thing—the dark possibility that Alayna didn't like to think about. If someone was watching her, waiting for an opportunity to exact revenge for her agreeing to testify, then having Bea with her would only put her aunt at risk. No way Alayna was doing that. If anything happened to her aunt because of her bad decisions, she'd never forgive herself.

She checked the mirrors again and felt her back relax when the only vehicles behind her were a school bus and an eighteen-wheeler. Letting out a sigh of relief, she queued up the book she'd been listening to and tried to concentrate on the story. In a couple more hours, she'd be on Tempest Island.

Where her new life awaited her.

———

MATEO RUIZ WATCHED AS THE HONDA ACCORD disappeared over a rise in the interstate, but he didn't bother to accelerate. He preferred not to lose sight of her, but it wouldn't be the end of the world if he did. He already knew where she was going. If she managed to elude him, he'd simply proceed to Tempest Island and acquire the target again. When she'd stopped in Roanoke the night before, he'd hoped she'd check into a hotel, then go out for dinner, giving him an opportunity to search her room. But when she stopped at the burger joint and left with a bag, he knew she was going into lockdown mode.

He'd managed a search of her car that night, but the boxes of personal items and clothes contained nothing of interest. He figured anything important was in that backpack that never left her side. He sped up a bit and inched from behind the eighteen-wheeler he'd been trailing in order to take a look up the highway. The Accord was ahead of him by probably a half mile and showed no sign of exiting. He slumped a bit in his seat and grabbed the coffee he'd picked up at the diner across the street from the convenience store Alayna had stopped at. The waitress had warned him that it was old and probably lukewarm at best, but he didn't have the time to wait for a fresh pot to brew, so he'd taken it anyway.

He took a sip and cursed. It wasn't even lukewarm. More like cool, and it tasted burned. Disgusted, he rolled down his window and tossed the entire thing out. Only a couple more hours and then he could settle in with all the hot coffee he wanted. Or better yet, a cold beer.

He always liked a cold beer after a long day on the job.

CHAPTER FOUR

ALAYNA LIFTED THE GIANT CONCH SHELL IN THE landscaping and pulled the key out of it. Trust Aunt Bea to keep her word and leave the key where Alayna could let herself in to get settled rather than insisting on meeting her there, thus forcing her into an awkward conversation that she wasn't quite ready to have. It was coming, that conversation. But not yet. Maybe when she felt more normal.

You'll never feel normal.

Too exhausted to go down that road again, she pushed the thought from her mind as she opened the door and stepped inside. The cottage was smaller than she remembered, the way structures always seemed with childhood memories, but the feel was exactly the same. The walls were still painted a light turquoise with white beadboard ceilings. To the left of the entry was a wall with two doors. One led to the tiny laundry room. The other to a small but serviceable bath.

To her right was the compact but efficiently constructed kitchen, with its white cabinets and turquoise sea glass back-splash. It had an eat-in dining area comprising a window seat on one side and a weathered table and chairs. The cushions in the window seat and the chairs had been updated since the last time she'd visited and were now both white-and-turquoise striped.

The kitchen was open to the living room, which was located at the back of the cottage. The entire back wall of the room contained two sets of sliding glass doors that led onto a deck and allowed a ton of natural light into the room. But this room was all about the view.

A most magnificent view.

White sand that felt like powder cascaded in sweeping mounds from the edge of the deck all the way down to water that matched the paint on the interior walls. Gentle waves swept in from the Gulf of Mexico, tiny whitecaps dotting the tips as they rolled onto the pristine sand. Sea oats adorned the dunes that stretched on each side of the cottage, blocking the view of her cottage from the one some fifty feet away. No matter how many times she'd seen it, this stretch of Tempest Island never ceased to amaze her with its beauty. And this time was no exception.

The Accord sat in the driveway, waiting to be unloaded, but she ignored it and dropped her backpack on the couch before opening the doors onto the deck. The sound of the water rushed through her. She closed her eyes and took in a deep breath, letting the warm salt air pass through her nose and mouth. A gull flapped overhead, and she opened her eyes to watch it glide across the water then dip down to pick up its dinner.

The sun was sinking fast, creating a yellow, orange, and pink glow across the horizon. Soon, it would be dark. That thought had her closing the doors and locking them behind her. She needed to get her stuff inside before the sun went down. She headed outside and grabbed her small suitcase from the car and hauled it inside. The suitcase contained her toiletries and her sleeping clothes, which would get her through the night. That, along with the remainder of the snacks she'd bought at the convenience store, would do until tomorrow morning.

Then she carried the snacks, and what was left of a case of water into the cottage and sat them on the kitchen counter. On the final trip, she opened the center console and pulled out a can of Mace. The last ray of sunlight hovered on the horizon but any minute, it would fade away, and this uncluttered stretch of the island would be pitched into darkness, with no streetlamps or illumination from other structures to cast a glow around it. Only the porch lights and the moon, if it didn't storm, would penetrate the dark.

She locked the car and hurried inside, pulling the dead bolt on the front door, then grabbed the suitcase and backpack and headed for the only bedroom the cottage contained. The walls were still the same turquoise as the rest of the cottage, but the old yellow bedspread with seashells on it had been replaced with a bright white one with a mermaid in the center and turquoise scalloped edges. The matching pillow shams were perfectly propped up against the driftwood headboard. The only window in the room shared the same awesome view as the living room.

She flipped the blinds closed to shut out the night, placed the suitcase on the bed, and pulled out the change of clothes and toiletry bag. After so many hours on the road, her sore body ached for a shower, but she'd wait until morning when this little space in the world was filled with sunlight again. She shed the tennis shoes, jeans, and tee she'd been wearing since before daylight and let out a sigh when she pulled off her bra. She tugged on shorts and a tank, then grabbed the toiletry bag and carried it to the bathroom.

As she moved through the rooms, she did a quick check of the windows, ensuring they were all closed and locked, then checked the doors once more. She closed the blinds as she went and completed her rounds by shoving one of the kitchen chairs under the front doorknob. Then finally satisfied that she was secure for the night, she unpacked her snack bag, placing the meager contents on the counter. Finally, she grabbed the remaining bottled water and headed for the fridge, deliberating between potato chips and a candy bar for dinner. Both had looked good when she'd picked them up hours ago. Now, neither did.

She opened the refrigerator to put away the water and found a loaf of bread, butter, ground coffee, condiments, eggs, sliced ham and cheese, and a container of potato salad. A bottle of wine completed the menu. A piece of paper taped to the wine bottle read simply, "Love you, honey. See you tomorrow. Aunt Bea."

Alayna smiled and pulled out the bread, ham and cheese, and potato salad. Leave it to Aunt Bea to think of everything. A sandwich was a sight better than what she'd brought with her, and even breakfast was covered. Eggs and toast with a cup of coffee...sitting on the back deck. There were so many worse ways to spend the morning.

Like sitting in FBI headquarters.

She shook her head. Those thoughts had no place here. That part of her life was over. She was going to have a new beginning on Tempest Island. A new life. She'd done it twice before, so it ought to be easy, right? Most importantly, no more being scared. The island had been her sanctuary once before and it would be again. But just the same, it wouldn't hurt to leave the lights on tonight. It was a small place. It couldn't possibly burn that much electricity.

She grabbed her cell phone and sent a quick text to her aunt.

I'm here. Thanks so much for the food! Lifesaver.

The reply came quickly.

I know my girl. Get some rest. I'll see you tomorrow.

Alayna smiled as she made a sandwich, poured a glass of wine, and headed into the living room. As she put her plate on the end table next to the couch, she remembered the Mace. She hesitated, trying not to give in to her fear, but she knew she wouldn't be able to relax knowing her one item of defense was out of her reach. She headed back into the bedroom and grabbed the canister, then placed it on the end table and plopped down on the couch.

She snagged the television remote and turned on the TV. She'd never been one to spend a lot of time in front of the screen except the occasional movie when she had a night off and Warren was out of town. But ever since that night the FBI had erased her dream world, she'd spent a lot of time alone in her apartment and the noise of the television had been her companion, even though often, she wasn't paying attention. Before that night, books had always been her preferred way to relax when she'd had some rare free time, but lately, she'd found she couldn't concentrate well enough to get into the story. Even while listening to audiobooks on the drive to Florida, her mind had constantly wandered. But television didn't require a lot of effort, especially if you didn't really care much about what was on. And the sound filled the silence that she'd grown to hate.

She located the Weather Channel first to check out the forecast. The weather had been great on the drive into Florida, but it was the Gulf Coast, and thunderstorms were common. She frowned when she saw the big red blotch moving from the Gulf inland. Letting out a sigh, she changed the channel to HGTV. It looked as though the tiny island was in for a rough night. It was called Tempest Island for a reason. But that meant sleep would be at a premium.

She shook her head. Who was she trying to fool? Sleep had been at a premium since the FBI had taken her out of Warren's building in handcuffs. But she still held out hope that it would eventually change. That sleep would allow her the escape she so desperately needed.

She had to hope. It was all she had left.

———

ALAYNA BOLTED UPRIGHT WHEN THE BOOM OF THUNDER shook the cottage, and she fought back the initial panic that rushed through her before she remembered where she was. Between the cracks in the patio blinds, she could see lightning flashing. A couple seconds later, rain began to pound on the roof. She hadn't realized she'd fallen asleep on the couch, but the stiffness in her back and neck told her she'd been there for some time. She checked her watch: 5:00 a.m. The last thing she remembered from the night before was checking her email around 10:00 p.m. She'd been asleep for almost seven hours and probably hadn't moved an inch. Between that and all the hours she'd spent in her car the day before, it was no wonder she was sore.

It was no use trying to go back to sleep. Even the comfort of the bed wouldn't drown out the storm or slow her racing heart. The sun would be up soon. She might as well start her day. She rose from the couch and headed into the kitchen to make coffee. First, two cups at least, then a shower, then breakfast. She got the coffee maker set up and smiled when the smell of the fresh brew wafted up a couple seconds later. She located coffee mugs and was pleased to find packets of artificial sweetener next to them. As she pulled the items from the cabinet, she heard a noise outside the cottage.

Like something had scraped down the side of the house.

She stiffened, then grabbed one of her chef's knives from its pouch on the counter. She peered out the kitchen window, but the porch light didn't reach that end of the house. In the living room, she pulled back the vertical slats that covered the patio doors and looked out. The light illuminated the deck and a small portion of the dunes beyond, but she didn't see anything untoward.

It was probably something blowing in the storm.

The silhouettes of the palm trees swayed just beyond the cottage, their giant fronds whipping around like sails in a gale. The marsh grass lay almost flat on the ground. That must have been it. The wind had lifted something up and it had hit the side of the cottage, scraping against it as the storm blew it past.

She let go of the blinds but as they fell back into place, she saw something move, just beyond the deck. She yanked the blind back again and squinted into the darkness, but nothing was there.

It's just the storm.

That was the logical explanation, because only a crazy person would be out in that weather. Besides, she reminded herself, no one but Aunt Bea, Brad, and the FBI knew she was here. She supposed anyone who'd known her well enough would assume she had headed back home, but none of those people concerned her. And since the FBI had repeatedly assured her that Warren had no reason to pursue action against her, that left no one who would care.

She was safe here. Her mind repeated that mantra again and again.

But her pounding heart didn't buy it.

CHAPTER FIVE

LUKE RYAN LOOKED OUT HIS BACK WINDOW AND SURVEYED the damage. The storm hadn't lasted long, but it had been fierce. Palm fronds had been ripped from the trees and littered the deck. Patio chairs had made a solo trip across the dunes and now rested haphazardly on the side of the house, a row of sea oats the only thing preventing them from continuing on to Alabama. He chided himself for not putting the furniture in storage the night before or at least flipping it over so it wouldn't catch easily in the gusts, but the weather report hadn't called for anything so strong. Still, it was Florida and the Gulf of Mexico, and all bets were off when it came to coastal weather.

He knew that better than most people.

Now the clouds were gone, leaving a clear blue sky with the morning sun sparkling off the water. He opened the front door and headed outside, not bothering with shoes or shirt. Or shorts for that matter. The cottage next door was empty, and his patio wasn't visible from the other cottage anyway. Since there were no other residences close by and tourist season hadn't kicked in yet, there was no one around to see him. And even if someone happened to walk by on the beach, boxers looked like a bathing suit from a distance.

He stepped onto the soft, cool sand to retrieve the lawn chairs and carried them to the deck at the back of the house where they belonged. Then he headed inside to make another pot of coffee and figure out what he was going to do with the rest of his day. He'd already watched the news and read some more of it online, answered email that needed addressing, started a load of laundry, eaten breakfast, and cleaned the bathroom. Picking up the palm fronds would take all of twenty minutes max and nothing else appeared to need attention.

Which meant he had an entire day to himself. Again.

He poured a cup of coffee and blew out a breath. He'd never heard of anyone dying from relaxation but if it was possible, he was fairly certain he'd be the first victim.

Go to the beach, they said. Rest is what you need to recover, they said.

After only two weeks, he'd decided that *they* were completely full of shit. Sitting around with nothing to do wasn't relaxing. You didn't burn any energy that way. You weren't tired enough to work up to a good night's sleep. You weren't even tired enough to work up to a catnap. He headed back outside and sat in one of the patio chairs. Without realizing it, he rubbed his right knee. The line of scar tissue shook him out of his stupor, reminding him why he was there in all his sedentary glory.

He pulled his hand away and sighed. There was no use going down that line of thought again. He'd already done it a million times, and doing it a million and one times wasn't going to change facts. The reality was, his knee was better than the doctors thought it would ever be, but it would never be good enough to resume his position with the Navy. SEALs couldn't be 95 percent. It was 110 percent or nothing. Other men's lives depended on the physical conditioning and ability of every member of the team.

At thirty-five years old, he was being forced to give up the only job he'd ever wanted.

There were other duties he could take on, of course. But none of them would compare to the thrill of a five-mile swim to infiltrate enemy territory. Nothing would ever be as exciting as a drop from a helicopter into a churning ocean or a HALO jump with his team. Nothing would ever be as fulfilling as successfully completing a mission. The closest he could get to being a SEAL again would be training other men to do the job he wanted to do.

He let out another sigh, then shook his head, mad at himself for indulging in yet one more pity party. It was time he stopped lamenting the things he couldn't do and started figuring out which of his options he wanted to pursue. The problem was, he was having trouble working up even a flicker of enthusiasm for any of them.

Maybe it was time to retire. If he couldn't do what he wanted to do with the Navy, then what was the point of sticking around and watching other men do his job while he rehashed that last mission and every step he'd taken before that fateful shot had taken away his present and his future? If he was a civilian, the constant reminders wouldn't be there. He wouldn't have to see the eager faces of the new recruits every day. He wouldn't think about everything he'd lost. About how being part of his team was the only time he'd felt like he had a family.

He shook his head. Who was he kidding? He didn't need outside visual reminders to know what he'd lost when all he had to do was look down at his own leg.

A noise off to the left had him bolting up. The wind was long gone, so there was no chance that it had caused the clanking he'd heard. And the cottage behind the dune next to him was empty. It belonged to Beatrice Shaw, the nice, somewhat quirky lady who owned the bookstore downtown, as well as the cottage he was renting. But she'd assured him when he signed the rental agreement that the house next door was for her personal use only. He wouldn't have to worry about vacationers disrupting his rehabilitation.

But Bea would be opening her bookstore about now.

So who was over there messing around? He and Bea had passed each other on the road the day before when he was on the way back from his grocery run. She'd waved and given him her pleasant smile as she drove past, and he'd assumed she had been next door doing one of the check-ups she did every week or so. There was no reason for her to be back so soon, especially since she had all her patio furniture for the other house locked up in the shed. There was nothing out to blow around in the storm.

He hurried inside and grabbed his pistol off the kitchen counter, then slipped quietly through the sand around the dune. The sea oats on the side of the house provided the camouflage he needed to approach unseen. He slipped along the back side of the grass, crouching low and stopping periodically to listen, finally pinpointing the noise to the shed. He followed the row of grass until he was directly behind the shed, then moved through it and to the back of the building. It was clear from the noise inside that the trespasser was still there. He crept down the side of the shed and checked the front. It was clear.

He ducked around the corner, then pivoted in the doorway, his gun leveled at what would be center mass on most people. "Stop right there," he demanded.

The woman holding a lawn chair screamed and dropped the chair on her foot, causing her to yelp. Clearly panicked, she scanned the shed, looking for either a weapon or an alternate way out. But neither was to be found. He sized her up, a bit confused. With her blond ponytail, white shorts, and turquoise tank, she didn't look like any thief he'd ever seen. Her bare feet with bright pink toenail polish confirmed his assessment.

"Who are you?" he asked.

"Alayna Scott," she said, her voice shaking. "I have a hundred dollars in my purse inside, but that's it. Please don't shoot me."

He blinked. "Alayna? Bea's niece?"

She nodded.

He dropped the gun and shook his head. "I'm so sorry. I didn't mean to frighten you."

Realizing now that he wasn't a threat, her expression shifted from fear to outrage. "You didn't *mean* to frighten me? Are you kidding? You came onto my aunt's property and cornered me with a gun leveled at my heart. Any normal person would be terrified out of their wits."

A flash of guilt coursed through him. "I really am sorry. I'm renting the house next door, and Bea told me this place would be empty. I thought someone was breaking into the shed."

"And you planned on shooting them for stealing old patio furniture? Seems a little extreme. Or are you in the habit of accosting women while brandishing a gun like you're James Bond?"

Her words should have made him mad. It was clear by her tone that they were meant to be insulting. But instead, he found himself doing something he hadn't done in a very long time. He laughed.

She stared at him as if he'd lost his mind. Then she shook her head and pushed past him.

"I'm so glad you find me amusing, Mr....?"

"Ryan. Luke Ryan. And I don't find you amusing at all, but I can appreciate the absurdity of the situation."

"I'm glad *you* can. If you'll excuse me, I need to call my aunt and verify that she actually rented her house to a crazy person."

"Crazy? I told you I thought someone was robbing your aunt. How is protecting her property crazy?"

She raised one eyebrow and gave him a look up and down. "Do you always parade around other people's property wearing nothing but your boxers and a firearm?"

Shit!

"I was outside on the patio when I heard the noise," he said, trying to explain. "I didn't think—"

"Not thinking seems to have occupied a large part of your morning. Maybe you should call it a day before someone gets hurt."

She walked into the house, closing the sliding glass door behind her, and he heard the lock click into place before she closed the blinds. He stared at the house for several seconds, wondering how his day had gone off the rails so quickly. Since he was short an answer, he headed through the dunes and back to his own stretch of sand.

Bea had told him that her niece owned a restaurant in New York City. That she was a superb chef and had saved to open her own place in Manhattan, then found the financial backing to expand. Luke didn't know anything about the restaurant business, but he understood that was no small feat. And Bea's voice had been so filled with pride when she'd told him about Alayna. But the sultry blonde with the terrified turquoise eyes didn't look at all like someone who stood in a hot kitchen all day.

He shook his head and went into his house. It was too early for a beer, but a shot of whiskey in his coffee wasn't the worst idea. In fact, given his choices so far, it was probably the best one he'd made today.

————

ALAYNA SNAPPED THE BLINDS SHUT, CAREFUL NOT TO LOOK out at the man with the gun. Then she staggered over to the couch and sank down on it, trying to control her breathing before she launched into a full-on panic attack. When she'd heard his voice and saw the pistol, she'd thought it was over. That the FBI and the DA had been wrong, and Warren was about to exact his revenge.

What in the world had he been thinking—creeping around with a gun? What if she'd been armed? Of course, her Mace wouldn't have been any match for the pistol he'd been holding, but that wouldn't have stopped her from trying to get a shot in. She'd taken self-defense classes. One of the first things the instructor stressed was to fight, claiming it was better for the family to have a body than a missing person. It was a cold way to view things, but she couldn't argue with the logic.

She concentrated on her breathing several more minutes and when she could no longer feel her heartbeat in her ears, she picked up her cell phone to call Aunt Bea. What had he said his name was—Luke something?

"Alayna," Bea answered, her smile sounding in her voice. "I'm so glad you got in last night. Is everything good at the house?"

"Everything is wonderful, and thank you again for the groceries. You saved me from a chips-and-candy-bar dinner."

"I figured you'd drive straight through, only stopping for gas. I didn't want you starving before I had a chance to visit with you."

"I'm afraid starvation isn't the biggest threat around here."

"What? I don't understand. Did the storm cause some damage?"

"No. But your tenant next door almost gave me a heart attack. At least he *claims* he's your tenant. I was getting the patio furniture out of the shed and apparently, he mistook me for a thief. He confronted me in the shed...with a gun."

"Oh no!" Bea said, clearly distressed. "I was going to call Luke yesterday and tell him you were coming, but I completely forgot. He wasn't at home when I dropped off the key and the food, and I didn't have time to wait because Nelly was covering for me at the store and she needed to leave. Then I forgot to call. I am *so* sorry. The misunderstanding is entirely my fault."

"It's not your fault. You're not the one who accosted me with a firearm. What do you know about him?"

"He's military, on medical leave. He's under doctor's orders to rest and relax, although he didn't look pleased when he delivered that bit of information as I showed him the property. I get the impression he's used to being a bit more, uh, physical. Sitting around doesn't appear to be in his makeup."

"Clearly. He was so ready for action, he didn't even bother to dress before he left."

Bea sucked in a breath. "He was naked?"

Her aunt's voice sounded a little too hopeful and not nearly enough dismayed.

"No!" Alayna said. "He had on boxers, but that was it. Boxers and a gun."

"Sounds like the beginning of a Hallmark movie," Bea said.

"Don't even go there. Romance and I are not a good mix. I'm going to get my life together, then I'm getting a polite golden retriever and calling things done."

There was a slight pause. "That's it?" Bea said finally.

"You're only thirty-three years old, and you plan on sharing the rest of your life with a dog?"

"No. I might get a bird, too. I've always wanted a parrot, and since they talk, all my needs would be fulfilled. Someone to cuddle with. Someone to talk to. See? I have it all figured out."

"Not *all* your needs would be covered."

Alayna felt a blush run up her neck. "I'm sure I'll manage."

"I'm sorry, dear. I don't mean to push. It's probably my own lack of male company that's driving me to romantic notions."

"I thought you were dating a guy from the post office. Sam, right?"

"I was, but he moved to Pasadena to be near his daughter."

"I'm sorry to hear that."

"Oh, it's no big deal. We weren't that attached, but it was nice to have a man to go out and do things with. Sometimes I get tired of hearing a bunch of women bitch."

Alayna smiled. "Well, then don't come visit me. I'm afraid I haven't had much to be happy about lately."

"You've been through a rough time, but all that's going to change now. You're home. Sun, sand, and a nice ocean breeze will fix everything."

"I hope you're right."

"I'm always right. So how did he look in his boxers?"

———

BEA HUNG UP THE PHONE AND NELLY, HER BEST FRIEND, employee, and sometimes fill-in manager for the store, stared at her, one eyebrow raised.

"Just hearing half of that conversation has me interested," Nelly said. "Spill? The most exciting thing I've had happen this week is the grocery store put raspberries on sale. Words like 'boxers' and 'naked' might give me a hot flash."

Bea laughed. "I think we're both a bit beyond the hot flash days. Thank God. Who needs more heat when we live at the beach?"

"Lord, isn't that the truth. So about this naked thing..."

Bea recounted Alayna's story to a completely entertained Nelly.

"That *was* exciting," Nelly said when she was finished. "Although I wish she'd have doled out a little more in the description department. Concerning the boxers, not the gun. I've seen plenty of guns."

Bea frowned. "You know, I'm wondering if maybe she didn't notice as much as she would have otherwise. I mean, a strange man holding a gun on you would scare anyone with some sense, but given what she's been through..."

"Oh no!" Nelly's expression shifted from amused to distressed. "I didn't even think about that. Do you think she's worried that awful man will send someone after her?"

"I don't know. The FBI and DA assured her that she was way down on the list of people that scumbag would have to eliminate in order to help his case, but I think she's still worried about it. She's always been careful about things, you know? My girl is no fool. But this is different. I'll bet she didn't come out of that apartment of hers except for lawyer appointments and such. And she refused to drive after dark on the way here. I know that's probably smart, but it's not at all the Alayna who left here. That Alayna was fearless."

"But the FBI and DA think she's safe, right? That other witnesses are bigger fish?"

"That's my understanding. But none of the others were in a personal relationship with Warren, so..."

"Of course," Nelly said. "It makes sense she'd still worry. I would. How bad do you think things are? Do you think she'll go back to New York?"

Bea shook her head. "I don't know. She hasn't talked much about it. I know her restaurant closed back when this all went down because I saw the notice on the website. But I figured that was because of the investigation or the media blitz that was following her around. I don't know if that was a temporary requirement or not. She didn't offer up any details about it, and I didn't want to ask."

Nelly nodded. "I think that was probably best."

"I suppose, except for the part where I don't really know anything and it's driving me crazy. I never pushed because she was there and I was here, and no way in hell she was letting me go up there to look after her. I was praying every day that when she got free of all that, she'd come home. But I didn't want to give her any reason to head somewhere else if she decided to bail, so I didn't pester her with my questions. I offered money but she said she didn't need it and several times, I said I'd go up there and help her handle things, but she wouldn't hear of it."

"Probably mortified by the whole thing and didn't want you to see it all firsthand."

"Perhaps, but what does she have to feel bad about? She didn't know what that man was up to. No one did. Not his parents, his employees, or his lifelong friends. Alayna only knew him for eight months. From what she told me they were still in that party and fancy-dinner stage. How was she supposed to figure out what all those people who'd known him his entire life never saw?"

"I know that, and you know that, but you also know that as women, we're always harder on ourselves than everyone else is. I'm sure she blames herself for getting tied up with such a questionable sort, even if there was no way she could have been aware just what kind of person he was."

Bea nodded. "It's been brutal. Every day when I woke up for the past five months, the first thing on my mind was what I could do to help her. And every day, I came up with nothing."

Nelly reached over and squeezed her hand. "You're doing it. You've been doing it. You're here for her. She's got a place to come home to, surrounded by people who care about her. And now that she's going to be in your sight, you'll be able to see better what else she needs."

"I hope so, because God knows, she won't ask."

"She was always independent."

"You say independent. I say stubborn."

Nelly smiled. "Well, she came by it honest."

"What the hell are you talking about, you old coot? I'm the easiest person in the world."

Nelly snorted and started looking around behind the counter. "We got any rubber boots in here? Because shit's getting deep."

"If you're so worried about it, then grab the stepladder and put those new displays on top of the bookcases."

Nelly gave Bea a quick hug. "She's going to be fine. You're going to make sure of that. And I'm going to be right here to help you. Anything you need. You just ask."

"Thanks, Nelly. I can always count on you. Even though you ruined my plans for us growing disgracefully into our sunset years by marrying Harold."

Nelly waved a hand in dismissal. "You know he'll die before me. We'll have plenty of time to embarrass those who love us."

Bea grinned at Nelly, but the grin faded as her friend walked off with the stepladder. She didn't want to admit just how worried about Alayna she was. The last time her niece had closed up this tight was when she was fifteen and her parents were killed in a car accident. It had taken a lot of time for Bea to earn Alayna's trust and tear down the wall she'd erected around herself. This time was different in that Bea already had Alayna's trust.

But she'd bet that wall was ten times taller and thicker.

CHAPTER SIX

LUKE GRABBED A TOWEL AND HEADED OUTSIDE WITH A paddleboard he'd found in the storage closet. His doctor had specifically forbidden him to surf, but he hadn't said anything about paddleboarding. Not that Luke had mentioned that particular activity. He supposed it probably fell under the general umbrella of avoiding things that might twist his knee in a harsh manner, but the Gulf was calm and as long as he didn't fall, there was no twisting involved.

At least, that's what he told himself to dash away that tiny bit of guilt he felt.

He glanced back at Bea's cottage next door and shook his head. His morning had definitely started differently than he'd expected. It had been years since he'd been on the receiving end of a butt-chewing by a good-looking woman. And the worst part wasn't even that he'd probably startled a young woman out of ten years of life or that he'd done so in his underwear. The worst part was that it was the most excitement he'd had since his injury, and there was a part of him that had not only enjoyed it but had also derived a certain level of satisfaction from it.

Great. If he couldn't figure out a spot in the military that interested him, he always had a bright future scaring women in their storage sheds. The pay was lousy and the threat of lawsuits was high, but the thrill was there. He let out a sigh as he took his first step into the Gulf. It was as calm as the Sound today, not even a trickle of air to cause a ripple on the water's smooth surface.

Just what the doctor ordered. Calm. Relaxing.

Boring.

"Ryan?" A man's voice sounded off to his left. He looked over to see an old Navy buddy strolling toward him, a black Lab walking contentedly at his side.

Luke smiled and moved forward to clutch Pete McCord's outstretched hand, then leaned over to pet the dog.

"Man, I didn't expect to see you here," Pete said. "I figured you'd be under the surface somewhere, saving the world."

"Yeah. Long classified story. This is the short version." He pointed at his knee, the scars even more visible since he'd refused to stay out of the sun. "I'm renting that yellow house back there for a while."

Pete's expression immediately shifted from happiness to concern, and Luke knew that as a military doctor, Pete not only recognized the cause of the injury, but knew exactly what it meant for Luke's career.

"Oh, wow," Pete said finally. "I'm so sorry. I hadn't heard."

"I asked everyone to keep it quiet until I knew for sure how things would shake out. My team doesn't even know yet. I mean, they know about the injury. They were there..."

"But they don't know that it was your resignation letter."

Luke shook his head. "That's my fault. I keep delaying... hoping it will change."

"That's understandable. Did they offer you an instructor's position here?"

"Yeah. I'm thinking it over."

Pete gave him an empathetic look. "I know it's not what you want, but if it matters, I can't think of anyone better to prepare those guys for what they'll face than you. You've got a way with people—the men respect you."

Luke nodded. That was true enough, and it had set him up as the natural leader for the team. But he just didn't see how yelling at men from the side of a boat could ever equal the exhilaration of completing a mission. Granted, being a SEAL instructor was much more than that, but once you'd been the real thing, training other men to do the job you wanted to do seemed almost insulting. He knew he shouldn't feel that way. His loyalty should be to the program and in making sure the best men were 100 percent ready for anything they might encounter. But he couldn't shake that lingering selfishness—that desire to do, not watch.

"What about you?" Luke asked, changing the subject. "Are you stationed here? I didn't realize."

Pete grinned. "I got lucky. One of the old base doctors retired and since I'd spent so much time patching up you guys, they thought it might be good to have me on a training base. Which makes me wonder—why haven't I seen you? Professionally, I mean?"

"I was more or less released by my doctor in Virginia."

"Uh-huh. More or less."

"Fine. So I should have checked in a week ago. I guess I just didn't see the point. I'm still on leave and rehabbing the knee, but we all know the score."

"And you thought paddleboarding would be a good rehab choice?"

Luke sighed. "Are you going to be my buddy Pete or Pete the doctor?"

Pete threw up his hands. "I can take a hint. At least the

surf's calm enough today. Just promise me that if you lose your balance, you won't try to save it. Twisting that knee is not your friend. Give yourself permission to fall. You'll be happier tonight if you do."

"That was the plan."

"Well, if you run into any problems, just give me a shout. I'm renting a house for the week just down the beach a bit toward town—bright blue with pink shutters. You can't miss it. Had some vacation time and figured there wasn't a better place to go than a short drive away to paradise. It's amazing that a completely boring mainland has this stretch of perfection sitting right in front of it."

"You live on base?"

"For now. I just transferred here a couple months ago. I suppose it makes more sense for me to stay there—single, no kids, free rent. But I think I've found my permanent place even after I leave the service. I've been considering buying a house on the island. Something small. I don't think I'll be able to swing beachfront, but there are some great cottages around downtown. Only a block or two and I'm on sand."

"That would be a good fit."

Pete was a doctor, but he was also a Florida native and his first love was the water. He spent all of his time off in it, on it, or around it. They had that in common.

Luke leaned down to stroke the Labrador's head. "Who's this guy?"

"This is Gus. He belonged to a vet who passed away a couple months ago. He didn't have any family who could take him, and I didn't want to see him go to a shelter. I'd been thinking about getting a dog anyway since I got into a permanent situation, so I figured Gus and me could make it work. He gets a good home in a place he knows, and I get a dog who's already trained."

Luke smiled. "That sounds like a good deal for everyone."

Pete nodded, but his head was turned away from Luke and up the beach. Luke looked over to see what had caught his friend's attention and saw Alayna taking a seat in a lawn chair, a bottle of water and a book on a table next to her. She was still sporting the shorts and tank and now that he wasn't trying to take aim, Luke couldn't help but notice that her legs seemed to go on forever and even though she was thin, she was curvy in all the right places.

"Wow. Your neighbor is seriously hot," Pete said. "Have you been over to introduce yourself?"

"In a manner of speaking."

"Uh-oh. I know that tone. I take it the meet and greet didn't go smoothly?"

"Well, considering I thought she was stealing from the woman who owns the house and had my nine on her when I confronted her, I'm going to go with definitely not smoothly."

Pete stared at him a couple seconds, clearly wondering if Luke was joking with him. Finally, he must have decided it was all the gospel because he started laughing.

"Man, I don't mean to laugh," Pete said. "But that's got to be one of the worst ways ever to move in on a girl. You're lucky you didn't give her a heart attack."

"I'm lucky she didn't have a weapon. I got the impression she would have used it even though the odds were against her."

"Sounds like my kind of woman."

"Go for it," Luke said. "You're armed with a cute dog. I have a feeling you'll do a lot better than me."

Pete grinned. "I'm going to take a pass. Being back stateside, I've finally gotten my life shifted from chaos to uncomplicated. And women are the definition of complicated."

"It's just as well. According to her aunt, who owns that house as well as the one I'm renting, the frightened blonde owns a restaurant in Manhattan. Probably just here for a visit."

Pete glanced over at Alayna again and pursed his lips. "If she's leaving soon, that might change things. A vacation fling can be fun. You should try talking to her without your gun."

"Me? No way. I've already got enough on my plate. I don't need to add to the pile."

Pete shrugged. "Whatever you say, but there's more than one way to rehab a knee."

"You're awful."

"What? I was talking about dancing."

Luke grinned. "Sure you were. Hey, do you have your phone on you? I want to give you my number."

Pete pulled it out of his pocket and handed it to Luke, who put in his number and handed it back. "Let's get together one night this week," Luke said. "I bought a couple steaks yesterday. And I keep plenty of beer. We could throw them on the grill, kick back, listen to the surf."

"Steak? Seriously? Man, I wish I didn't have plans tonight." He grimaced. "One of those family things I couldn't get out of."

"You've got family here?"

"An old uncle. My mother's brother. She hasn't spoken to him in twenty years, but he got wind that I transferred here and thinks that means he should get free medical advice."

"Was he military?"

"Please. He's barely held a job. He mostly holds the bottle."

Luke nodded. "Which is why your mother doesn't speak to him."

Luke had met Pete's mother once and she was an old-school proper lady. He couldn't imagine her tolerating poor behavior.

"Exactly," Pete said. "She told me to ignore him, but you

know me. I'll make the trip over there and see for myself. If everything is exactly as my mother expects, I'll give him some rehab information. My guess is he won't call again."

"Probably just wants a prescription for pain meds."

Pete sighed. "Yeah, that's my guess. Well, he's not getting it from me."

"I never thought he would. Sorry you have to deal with that, man."

"No worries. It will probably only be the one time. Anyway, I've got that tonight and dinner with a visiting surgeon tomorrow night. What about the night after?"

"Works for me. Come by around six."

"Great! Can I bring Gus?"

"You're not welcome without him."

Pete nodded. "Then we'll see you at six with our appetites. You want me to pick up anything?"

"Nope. I have it all covered."

"Sounds good. Enjoy your boarding. And take it easy. I'll be taking a closer look at that knee when I come for dinner."

Luke gave his buddy a wave as he walked off. Pete couldn't help handing out medical advice. It was just part of his makeup. He was one of the smartest people Luke had ever met, which made him a brilliant doctor. But more importantly, Pete cared about people and wanted them to be healthy. Which was exactly why Luke didn't get annoyed with Pete's advice. He knew Pete meant it for Luke's own good.

Luke grabbed his board and headed for the water, sending one glance back at Alayna, who had turned her chair to face the sun and was wearing a floppy hat and sunglasses, holding the book in front of her. He felt a twinge that had nothing to do with his knee and snapped his head around. Pete might joke about a vacation fling, but Luke already had enough things to work out. And since he was already in the doghouse, any attempt at even the most casual of relationships with his sexy neighbor had him starting in the negative.

It wasn't worth it. He needed to be figuring out what to do about his sudden career loss and how to get on with the rest of his life. A fling was a distraction he couldn't afford, and a fling with Alayna would be way more effort than he was willing to expend given how things had started. He needed to spend all that energy on figuring out his next move.

———

ALAYNA DROVE INTO THE QUAINT DOWNTOWN AREA OF Tempest Island and smiled as she looked at the brick paver streets and the weathered old buildings that made up the town center. The whole business area stretched along both sides of Main Street. The storefronts were mostly glass and many had awnings in bright shades of blue, pink, and yellow that contrasted against the brick frames. Giant planters with tropical flowers were placed along both sides of the street and the blooms were another burst of color against the faded paint of the storefronts.

Behind Main Street on the north side were two blocks of homes, mostly cottages that looked as though they'd been plucked out of a Disney story and placed on the island. More bright colors abounded there, in both the color of the homes' siding and the gardens that were so well manicured that they looked painted rather than real. The residents of Tempest Island took pride in their town, and it showed with the way they maintained their property. Even the rentals were indistinguishable from the homes occupied by residents.

That half-mile stretch of businesses was it—the entirety of downtown shopping and eating. The neighborhood behind downtown stretched further out along the Sound on the east side of the island another couple miles. In both directions, the road continued along the shoreline with oceanfront homes dotted along the way until you reached protected seascape on both ends. Bea's cottages were on the west end of the island, where houses occupied the Gulf side but not the Sound side, which provided more privacy for the owners.

Due to a very protective city council, Tempest Island had managed to avoid miles of concrete and instead, enjoyed that untouched look for much of its shoreline, which set it apart from other places along the coast. One small two-story motel existed downtown, but the building blended right in with the other shops. There were no high-rise hotels or luxury condo developments. No chain restaurants or retail stores.

It was absolutely perfect.

She found an open spot to park in front of Island Books and smiled when she saw that the Old Time Ice Cream Shop next door was still open and appeared to be doing a good business even though the tourist season hadn't started yet. She made a mental note to stop for a treat before she left, not that she really needed a reminder. The smell of waffle cones wafting around her was enough to tempt anyone.

She opened the door to the bookstore and stepped inside, drawing in a deep breath. She'd always loved her aunt's store. Bea had acquired the old town hall when they'd needed more space and constructed a new building farther down the street. The outside was two stories of weathered red brick that sat on the corner with steps on the back that led to offices upstairs that she rented out. Large glass windows spanned the front of the first and second floors. The inside was even better. A wall of floor-to-ceiling bookcases in the lobby had been part of the town hall design, and Bea had left them intact and found a carpenter who could match them throughout the store. The store always smelled of wood oil, leather, and vanilla.

It smelled like home.

Bea wasn't at the front counter, so Alayna wandered through the store and finally found her in the back unloading a carton of books. The bookstore's cat, a big gray Maine coon named Shakespeare, was sprawled on top of one of the boxes and gave her a sleepy look as she approached. She reached to scratch his head between the ears, and Bea looked back, her face lighting up with a smile when she caught sight of Alayna. She dropped the book she was holding and hurried over to gather Alayna in a tight hug.

"My little mermaid," Bea said as she squeezed. "It's been too long."

Alayna relaxed into the hug, her chest tightening. It was Bea who'd taken care of her when her parents were killed. She'd immediately purchased a home downtown just a block away from her store and moved out of the beach cottage and into a place with enough space for two people. Back then, she'd rented the beach house, but when it was vacant, Bea and Alayna had spent time there, Alayna falling asleep on the couch, listening to the sound of the surf.

She'd been an angry and confused fifteen-year-old. Right at that cusp of adulthood and really needing her parents' guidance. Bea had been patient and kind and somehow instinctively knew when to push and when to draw back. When Alayna had finally realized that Bea was suffering their loss as much as she was, they'd learned to lean on each other. And they'd made it through.

"I've missed you," Alayna said when they finished hugging. "I'm sorry I didn't come to visit more often."

Bea waved a hand in dismissal. "You were busy working on your career. You can't just up and vacation based on an old woman's fancy. Besides, it's not like I don't know what's involved with starting and running a business. No time for much of anything but work and sleep, especially in the beginning."

Alayna nodded. What her aunt said was true, and even more true for Manhattan and the restaurant business. Even after grueling twenty-hour days, she'd go home with the constantly nagging feeling that she'd missed a trick. That there was something else she could do to make her restaurant more popular, to improve the menu, to motivate her staff. The only time she had given her mind a break was when she was with Warren.

She'd have been better served to make more trips back home.

"So have you settled in?" Bea asked. "Is the cottage going to work for you?"

"Why? You trying to get rid of me already?"

"Hell, no! I already told you the place is yours for as long as you want to be there. I'm hoping that's a good long time. We have a lot of catching up to do. I've got years' worth of island gossip to impart."

The doorbell jangled and they looked toward the front of the store as a group of women walked in.

"We can start tonight," Bea said. "I'll pick up Chinese takeout and wine and see you at seven. Get the table and chairs out of storage. Maybe it will be nice enough to eat on the patio."

"Let me cook for you at least," Alayna said.

"There's plenty of time for that later."

She gave Alayna's arm a squeeze and headed off. Alayna watched as her aunt greeted the customers with a huge smile and sighed. She'd come down to the bookstore for a couple reasons. First, she loved it and wanted to see it, and she loved her aunt even more. Second, she knew Bea couldn't grill her while she was working. She'd hoped if Bea saw her in person that it might delay her aunt visiting the cottage, which would postpone the embarrassing talk that Alayna wasn't quite ready to have. But it looked as though her life was going to be on display again that night.

It's just as well, she thought. It wasn't as if Bea didn't already know the basics. Alayna had given her enough information that she was reassured that Alayna's attorney had things under control and there was nothing she could do to help. And since the media were always quick to jump on juicy stories about old-money families with social standing, Alayna guessed her aunt knew more than she'd let on during their phone conversations. If she hadn't seen the stories herself, someone on Tempest Island would have been sure to tell her. It was just the way the island was. Everyone knew everybody and most everything *about* everybody.

She headed for the small toy section that always had a collection of jigsaw puzzles featuring marine life. She'd managed to read a bit while sitting outside this morning, but at night, she had a harder time focusing on the words. A puzzle would be a good way to occupy her mind that didn't require a lot of thought. Between that and the television, she might be able to tolerate nights better.

Ten minutes later, she headed out of the store, clutching a puzzle of colorful seashells and a roll-up mat to hold it so it could be moved out of the way when she needed to use the kitchen table. Since she was already downtown, she decided to do some grocery shopping while she was here. Things were cheaper at the stores on the mainland, but she didn't feel like making the twenty-minute drive over the bridge or dealing with the traffic and crowds of the bigger city. Right now, the island was fairly quiet and she really enjoyed it that way. Vacation season wouldn't go into full swing until kids were out of school. Until then, the island was mostly occupied by locals and day-trippers from the mainland. When summer hit, you wouldn't be able to walk downtown without bumping into someone.

The island market didn't have a huge selection, but what they carried was high quality. Seafood was fresh from the ocean the day before and other meats came from a local butcher. The vegetables and fruit were all organic and many supplied by local farms. It was the same with the canned items —sauces and relishes and candied foods, all supplied by local businesses and individuals. The variety was nowhere near what she could acquire easily in New York, but she certainly wasn't going to suffer eating any of the items in her basket.

She picked up fresh vegetables, chicken, scallops, pasta, good dinner wine, and splurged on a couple of incredible-looking steaks. Then she threw in some baking staples, easy fixings, beer, and snacks and called it done. The next time Bea came for dinner, she'd whip up the steak and some twice-baked potatoes. Her aunt might protest her going to the trouble if she knew ahead of time, but if Alayna was ready to put the food on the table, Bea definitely wouldn't turn it down.

And Alayna loved doing things for Bea—even small things —because Bea had done so much for her. Her aunt had been the one who insisted Alayna had talent and should attend culinary school. Alayna had never thought she'd even get in, but one of the top schools in the country had accepted her. The life insurance her parents left had been carefully managed by Bea and covered her tuition and living expenses while she was in Austin at school, with a little to spare.

Alayna knew that Bea had hoped she'd return to Florida after graduating, but Bea also knew that Alayna's big dream was to be a chef in Manhattan, where she could continue to learn from some of the best and, maybe one day, open her own place. Alayna had put in several years at restaurants in Austin and Dallas to get her résumé strong enough to land a chef's position at a top restaurant in New York. Then Bea had stepped in, even taking weeks away from her bookstore to help Alayna find an apartment and get moved.

Alayna smiled at that memory as she tucked the groceries in the back seat of her car. Her first studio apartment hadn't been much larger than a walk-in closet. She had a foldout couch that served as seating and bed. The wall opposite held a kitchenette with a two-burner stove, tiny oven, and microwave. She'd barely managed to fit a toaster and her blender on the limited counter space. The bathroom had been a tiny square with shower stall, toilet, and pedestal sink. The shower was so small, she'd banged her elbows every time she lifted her arms to wash her hair and there never seemed to be hot water available, no matter what time of day she used it.

The good ole days.

Before she started trying to make a name for herself in the big bad city. Before she knew the stress of working for five-star chefs and managing ridiculous work hours. Before she'd tried her hand at launching her own restaurant.

Before Warren.

The beginning of the end.

She opened the driver's-side door, but as she started to duck into her car, she paused. Something felt off. She glanced around, trying to figure out what was causing the discomfort, but all she saw was people and shop owners going about their business. She gave the street a final glance before climbing in her car and pulling away.

But the uncomfortable feeling remained.

———

MATEO WATCHED FROM A SEDAN PARKED ACROSS THE STREET as Alayna loaded groceries into her car, then drove away. He'd observed her since she'd driven into town earlier. First, visiting the bookstore that he knew belonged to her aunt—the same aunt providing her the cottage she was staying in—then doing some local shopping. Her behavior here on the island wasn't any different than it had been in New York or on the long trip to Florida.

She was definitely cautious. Skittish, to be more precise.

Back in New York, she'd only left her apartment during the day and when she exited the building, she got directly into a car driven by the same service every time. No cabs. No Uber. She was dropped off right in front of whatever place she was going, went directly inside and when leaving, reversed the process. Her blinds remained drawn twenty-four hours a day and if she received a delivery, she had the front desk sign for it. At least, that's what she'd done when he'd attempted to get a closer look at her building by pretending to deliver a package.

On the drive to Florida, she was just as careful. She never stopped anywhere unless it was centrally located and occupied by multiple patrons. She stayed in a hotel with single entry and card access for other doors and didn't stray out of the hotel after dark or before sunrise. She'd lived on convenience store snacks and fast food the entire time, never taking the time to sit down in a restaurant. He'd thought the thunderstorm might delay her and then he'd have more of a chance to observe her. Maybe even a chance to access her hotel room, but the storm was gone by daybreak and she'd resumed her solitary and cautious trek to Florida.

At first, he'd thought her behavior in New York was to avoid the press that had hounded her for weeks after Patterson's arrest. But when the press finally cleared out, she still hadn't altered the way she did things. She was definitely spooked. But was it simply because of everything that had gone down or because she was hiding something? The client seemed to think Alayna had something of value but wasn't aware. Mateo didn't buy that for a minute. If she didn't know what she had, then why was she so scared?

The item he was looking for wasn't in her car or her meager belongings unless it was in the backpack, which he'd never had an opportunity to search. Or maybe it was in the boxes she'd prepared to ship to Florida that hadn't yet arrived. When he saw her go into the grocery store, he could have made a quick run to her house and searched the backpack as this was the first time he'd seen her that she didn't have it on her, but he decided it wasn't worth the risk. Not yet. He'd be patient until the boxes arrived and then wait for an opportunity to get a look at all of it at the same time.

In the meantime, the client claimed he was working another angle and maybe that would pan out. Then Mateo would know exactly where to look. Right now, his orders were to search but stay out of Alayna's line of sight. The client didn't want to tip his hand until he was certain that the prize he sought was in her possession. But sooner or later, the client would grow tired of waiting. Even a patient man would only wait so long.

Then Mateo would be able to put the pressure on Alayna. Force her to tell him what he wanted to know. It was the part of his job he looked forward to the most.

CHAPTER SEVEN

ALAYNA SMILED AS BEA UNPACKED FOUR CONTAINERS OF Chinese food onto the patio table. She'd bought enough for an army and Alayna would bet she'd refuse to take any with her when she left. She'd seen her aunt give her a critical once-over in the bookstore and knew one of Bea's first priorities was going to be putting the pounds back on her. If the food tasted as good as it smelled, it wasn't going to be difficult to go along with her plan.

"When I got there I couldn't decide," Bea said. "So I got several different things. We can pick around at all of them and figure out which ones we like the best for next time."

"Next time, I'm cooking for you. It's been too long. No arguing."

"I'm stubborn. I'm not a fool. I haven't had a great meal here since you moved away."

"That can't be true. There are several nice restaurants on the mainland."

Bea waved a hand in dismissal. "They're nothing compared to your fixings. And way overpriced. The only time I grace the doorstep of one of those so-called fancy places is if someone else is footing the bill. And you know how these old coots are down here—afraid to part with a nickel."

"Maybe they're being frugal because they're retired."

"Please, they're just cheap. The last one I went out with was wearing a watch that cost more than my car and always wears trousers and a tie. I put on my best dress and he expected me to eat burgers at that shack on the beach. I told him he could find a place that took reservations or eat alone."

"So what happened?"

Bea scowled. "Not important."

Alayna laughed. "Sounds like the best possible outcome. Do you really want to date a man who wears trousers and a tie to the beach?"

"It was a moment of weakness. Sam had moved the week before and my weekend was looking rather sparse in the way of fun. I don't know why I thought Trousers-at-the-Beach could change that. Maybe I'm getting senile."

"You're not old enough to be senile."

At sixty-two, Bea didn't look a day over fifty. Most of the time, she didn't act a day over twenty, except when it came to business. It was one of the things Alayna loved most about her. That she refused to grow old gracefully. At the moment, Alayna felt as if life had prematurely aged her personally and without consent.

"Get that wine open and let's dig into this before I get the vapors," Bea said. "I had half a tuna sandwich for lunch, then spent the whole afternoon stocking. I thought I was going to pass out when I walked into the restaurant to pick up the food."

"You should eat a bigger lunch," Alayna said as she poured the wine. "At least bring a whole sandwich and not just half."

Bea threw her hands in the air, then plopped down in a chair. "I *did* bring a whole sandwich. That damn cat snatched the other half while I was trying to explain to Agnes Paulson that the true crime section is not providing serial killers with instructions. That woman is like a broken record."

"I'd spend less time beating my head on that brick wall and more time guarding my lunch." Agnes Paulson had been crazy as long as Alayna could remember.

"Or I could just get rid of the cat. Not like I was looking for a cat when he wandered in and refused to leave."

Alayna opened the cartons and spooned out a little of each item onto her plate. "You know Shakespeare isn't going anywhere. I don't know why you pretend you don't love him."

"Fine. The furry nuisance can stay, but he needs to keep his paws off my lunch."

"Then I suggest you stop bringing tuna."

"Tuna's easy. I like easy when it comes to the kitchen."

"I know you do. So bring me up to speed on some of the local gossip. What's the biggest thing that's happened lately?"

Bea grimaced. "Well, the word 'biggest' doesn't really factor into this story, but Old Franklin decided he'd take up boogie-boarding last week. Had his bathing suit ripped right off of him, and does he have the good sense to use the board to block those-that-shouldn't-be-seen? No. He strolls right out of the Gulf wearing nothing but what he was born with and dragging the board by its cord."

Alayna gasped. "Oh my God!"

Bea nodded. "Nelly was there with her niece's daughter and said it was fairly horrific. She threw her straw hat over the child's eyes."

"Did he walk all the way home like that?"

"No. Young Franklin was there and almost had a heart attack running down the beach with a towel. Nelly said he was praying as he ran."

Alayna choked and grabbed her drink. Old Franklin was

ninety years old if he was a day. His son, Young Franklin, was the island preacher, having followed in his father's footsteps.

"Sunday's sermon was about modesty," Bea said. "The whole congregation sounded like they had whooping cough."

"I imagine so," Alayna said as she broke into laughter.

"Everyone except for Old Franklin, of course. He's adamant that the Lord made him that way and if it was good enough for God then the rest of the island can get over it. My poker group has a pool on when Old is going to give Young a heart attack. Buy-in's twenty bucks, if you're interested."

"Let me think on that one."

They talked freely while they ate, Bea bringing Alayna up to date on all the gossip that one small island could produce. Most of it was harmless stuff, but there was the occasional scandal of an affair and the robbery of the pizza place, although Bea claimed everyone knew it was the owner's son who did it, including the owner.

When they'd eaten far too much food and polished off the entire bottle of wine, Bea pushed her chair back and studied Alayna for several seconds.

"So," Bea said. "Are you done with this business in New York?"

"No. I still have to testify at the trial."

Bea frowned. "I thought they had a ton of evidence against him."

"They do. The only thing I can attest to is some of the dates when Warren was out of town and that he used my laptop a couple times when he was at my apartment. They lifted evidence off of it. I agreed to testify in exchange for no charges."

"Charges for what?" Bea asked, clearly frustrated. "Letting the man you're dating use your laptop? Good Lord, it's not like you were hauling bags of money around the city for him."

"I know. And my attorney said we could fight it if they pushed the issue. But he also said it would be faster and cheaper to take the deal. Fighting it could have taken years and tens of thousands of dollars."

"That's crap. The whole thing is crap."

Alayna nodded. She couldn't disagree.

"When will the trial be?"

"I don't know. They wouldn't say, but my attorney said it could be months or even years."

Bea shook her head, clearly disgusted. "More crap—leaving you on hold for that long. Well, when that day comes, I'm going back with you."

"That's not necessary."

"Of course it's necessary. You're not going to do this alone. You've already kept me at a distance on all of this and I respected your wishes then. But I'm done being respectful. From now on, I'm your pushy aunt and the woman who helped raise you."

Alayna felt her chest tighten. "You're more than just my aunt and we both know you didn't just *help* raise me. You stepped into a big hole in my heart and somehow managed to fill it up."

Bea sniffed and her eyes reddened a bit. "You and I can handle anything this world throws at us. You're a strong woman, Alayna. Stronger than you probably think."

"I used to feel that way."

"And you will again. What are you going to do about the restaurant? Are you going to reopen?"

"No. A big chunk of the expansion capital was a loan from Warren's company. The FBI seized the restaurant along with everything else."

Bea's eyes widened, and Alayna saw her jaw flex. "That's ridiculous! You put your money in as well. How can they just take it like it's nothing? Good Lord. I had no idea. I wish you would have told me."

"Why? So both of us could be angry and upset and unable to change the situation? The truth is, even if the FBI hadn't seized the restaurant, it was still over. In the beginning, the press crucified me. Tried to find the angle that indicated I was part of what Warren had been doing. They came up with nothing, of course, but that didn't stop them from speculating. And that's all it takes to tank a restaurant and my reputation. At this point, I probably couldn't even get a job in New York as the french fry girl at McDonald's."

Bea's face flushed with anger and she reached over and squeezed Alayna's hand. "I am so sorry, honey. I know how hard you worked and how bad you wanted your own place. And you deserved it. You've got the talent and you put in the hours. I wanted it for you so much. To think that all of it could just disappear like that...well, it's hard to take in."

Alayna felt tears well up and struggled to keep them from spilling over. Once the initial shock was over, Alayna was certain that losing her restaurant and her reputation was the worst thing to come out of all of it. The truth was, that hurt far more than losing Warren. She supposed that was because the restaurant was real, and Warren was a carefully crafted image with her as an unwitting accessory. And if she was being honest with herself, she was never as invested in Warren as she was in her business. She'd cared for him and enjoyed him, and it was possible she would have eventually felt more, so while the timing of his takedown was crap for her career, it was good for her heart.

"I know you wanted it as badly as I did," Alayna said. "You've supported my dream from the beginning. I feel guilty for letting you down."

"Don't you ever say something like that again," Bea said,

her voice firm. "You could never let me down. Warren managed to fool law enforcement, his clients, his friends, and even his own family for years. What is it you think you should have seen that they didn't?"

"But none of them were romantically involved with him. I believed that the man I saw was the real person. And it was all a huge lie. Am I so foolish or desperate that I couldn't tell he wasn't genuine?"

"You're neither foolish nor desperate. You're simply a good woman who got taken by an exceptional criminal. You're not equipped to deal with someone like Warren. Most people aren't. We don't think that way, so we're not looking for it in the people we care about."

Alayna knew Bea was right. It wasn't the first time she'd heard those words. Her employees, her shrink, and even the FBI agent who arrested Warren had told her the same thing. But it was still a bitter pill to swallow.

"Did you love him?" Bea asked quietly.

"No. But I did care for him. And I considered him my friend. But none of it was real."

"Your feelings were real, and who's to say that Warren didn't feel something for you too? He's a seriously troubled man, but you're a remarkable woman. I can't help but think he was aware of that."

"Maybe." Alayna shrugged. "But if he cared for me at all, how could he involve me with his crimes? How could he lend me dirty money to expand my restaurant?"

Bea sighed. "Because he didn't think he was going to get caught. Oh honey, I wish I could wave a magic wand and take all the pain away. But since my wand is currently in for repair, all I can offer is this house, cheap wine, and really good Chinese takeout."

"Best offer I've had lately."

"Better days are coming. This place heals people. You know that."

Alayna nodded. After her parents died, when Bea told her she'd be moving to Tempest Island, she had dug her heels in, not wanting to leave the only place she'd ever known. Not wanting to have to start over at a new school, make new friends. But every day a bit more of the serenity and beauty of the tiny stretch of sand had trickled into her, until one day, she no longer lashed out over the unfairness of what had happened. Instead, she thought of her parents and smiled, remembering what incredible people they'd been, and knowing how happy they would be to see her and Bea enjoying life again.

When everything in New York came crashing down on her, the island was where she longed to be. To retreat to the one place that could break down her sadness and allow her to heal. The five months the FBI had held her in New York were brutal, with most of her time spent hiding in her apartment. The people she'd called friends had disappeared like fireflies at dawn, but she couldn't blame them. The relationships were all surface level and none of them were willing to risk their own situations over a casual friendship. Guilt by association traveled fast and well in the city.

"Now that we've got this over with," Bea said, "I won't be asking about it again. But if you want to talk, then you know I'm always here to listen."

"And to give out advice?"

"If I've got anything worth giving, you know it's coming out of my mouth. Probably coming out even if it's *not* worth giving. But if you'd like to speak to someone who might know better, I have a friend with a practice on the mainland. She's older, so none of that new age crap."

Alayna nodded. "I was seeing someone in New York. She

lived in my building and offered to see me at my apartment, which worked perfectly for me. But I'm not sure that I want to do that any longer. I'll let you know."

"Good. So now that the serious business is out of the way, I want to hear more about your sexy neighbor and his boxers. Were they the short kind or the longer ones? How are his abs? I've never had the pleasure of seeing him without a shirt, but now that you're here, I might find more reasons to drop by hoping for a glimpse."

The sadness that had enveloped Alayna drifted away and she laughed. "I don't think I even noticed his abs at the time. I was too focused on the gun."

"That's unfortunate. But understandable."

"I did see him paddleboarding later on though. His abs are well developed and very tan. You said he's with the Navy, right? What does he do?"

"I don't know. I asked, but he was a bit dismissive about it. Didn't want to go into his position or the injury. Can't blame him, I suppose. No reason for him to hand out his personal business to a nosy old woman. Maybe you could find out for us."

"Don't even go there. I'm here to figure out how to fix my shambles of a life. I've got no use for, and am no use to, other people, especially men."

Bea looked a little disappointed. "Well, at least snap a picture next time he's out on that board. Give your aunt a little thrill."

Alayna smiled. "I suppose it's the least I can do since I'm living in your house."

"Consider it rent."

CHAPTER EIGHT

THE SHIPPING COMPANY WITH ALAYNA'S THINGS ARRIVED AT 9:00 a.m. the next morning. She'd slept restlessly and had been up for hours before the truck backed into the drive. She'd sold her furniture and donated a lot of other stuff, but she'd still had a good twenty boxes when she was done packing what she couldn't part with. The vast majority of it was kitchen supplies. They were chef quality, and no way was she selling them for pennies on the dollar.

She stepped outside to greet the driver, and he gave her a nod as he verified her name and address. Then he opened up the back of the truck and started pushing boxes to the back edge.

"Need some help?"

His voice sounded behind her and Alayna jumped, then turned around to see Luke Ryan standing there. At least he'd managed to dress this time. And so far, he hadn't pulled a gun on anyone.

Before she could answer, the driver piped up. "I wouldn't turn it down. There were supposed to be two of us on this run, but my partner's wife went into labor early. I'm trying to figure out how to keep my schedule."

"Then let's get you unloaded and out of here," Luke said and grabbed two boxes from the truck. "Where do you want these?"

Alayna hesitated for a moment but couldn't come up with a single argument against his help that didn't make her sound petty. Better for her to let Luke do his manly duty and then get back over to his side of the dune.

"I pushed the kitchen table against the wall," she said as she headed into the house. "I figured on stacking the boxes on the table first, then under and in front of it. I'm afraid there's probably more boxes than space."

Luke put the boxes on the back corner of the table and nodded. "We'll make it work."

Alayna tried not to notice the way his biceps rippled when he extended his arms to place the boxes on the table or his wide shoulders as he walked back outside. Clothes didn't really hide anything that he had to offer and just admitting that to herself made Alayna uncomfortable. She couldn't afford an attraction right now. Or maybe ever. Clearly, her judgment was crap. Luke Ryan might seem like a nice guy—albeit a bit quick on the draw—but she wasn't ready to trust that opinion.

And besides, it didn't matter. He was there to recuperate from his injury. But once he was healed, he'd go back to whatever it was that he'd done before. Luke was temporary, and she couldn't afford to place any effort into temporary. She had an entire life to rebuild, and all her energy had to be focused on her future.

On permanent.

She headed outside to grab a box and passed Luke on the way out. He gave her a broad smile and a wink, and she felt parts of her body that she thought had shut down tingle with awakening. She picked up the pace and grabbed a box, careful to avoid looking directly at him as she carried it inside.

The three of them made quick work of the boxes, and Alayna signed the release and gave the driver a nice tip. He smiled his appreciation and thanked them both for helping him, claiming he might be able to come close to staying on time. He lifted his hand out the window to wave as he drove off, and Alayna and Luke waved back. As the truck pulled away, Alayna stood in an uncomfortable silence.

Then her upbringing took over. Southern manners were required regardless of one's discomfort. If this were any other time—before Warren—and someone had helped her with a sweaty, boring task, she would have tried to repay them. No way was she going to forgo the positive things, even if it meant being slightly uneasy.

"I really appreciate the help," Alayna said to Luke. "Can I offer you an iced tea or beer—I know it's a little early for that. I made fresh lemonade this morning, if that interests you."

"Fresh...like from actual lemons?"

"That's the generally accepted method."

"I haven't had fresh lemonade since I was a kid."

"Then let's have that. I'll pour up some big glasses and we can sit on the patio and cool down in the breeze. Unless you have something you need to do."

He smiled. "My schedule is clear."

"Good," she said as she glanced back at the truck to avoid the smile. "I made some cinnamon rolls this morning as well if you'd like one. Those, I'm afraid, are not fresh. They came out of a can."

"I'll take anything you're willing to offer."

She whirled around and hurried inside.

That's exactly what she was afraid of.

———

Luke watched as Alayna hurried to the refrigerator and prepared the lemonade. He made her uncomfortable. Yesterday, he figured it had been the gun, but the way she'd avoided his eyes as they unloaded the boxes told him it was something else. She wasn't scared of him or she wouldn't have invited him into her house, but there was something going on with her. Something below the carefully polite surface.

He'd made the suggestive comment without thinking and then could have kicked himself for it. He blamed being out of practice. It had been a long time since a woman had sparked his interest. And wouldn't it just figure that the one who did was carrying so much baggage she couldn't even manage a simple exchange without looking away?

She plopped a cinnamon roll on a paper plate and handed it to him before heading to the back patio with the two large glasses. He sat at the small patio table, took a huge bite out of the cinnamon roll, then sighed his approval.

"Tastes great," he said. "You're not having one?"

"I've already had two. If I have another, I'll make myself sick."

He nodded. "I wouldn't have figured you for a disposable calories sort of breakfast. Your aunt told me you're a chef."

"I have yogurt and fruit, but sometimes you just feel like saying to hell with it."

He smiled, surprised at her statement. Most of the good-looking women he'd met were obsessed with diet, afraid to gain a pound. Although he thought Alayna could stand to gain a few. She had that gaunt look about her that implied long-term physical or emotional distress. And the dark circles under her eyes were indicative of lack of sleep.

"I'm happy you said to hell with it today," he said and lifted his glass. When the first swig of lemonade rushed into his mouth, his eyes widened. He took two big gulps before putting the glass down and realized she was studying him.

"Well?" she asked.

"That's incredible. Just the right balance of sweet and tart. If you bottled this, you could sell it and make a fortune."

"The unit cost would be so high, it would never sell. And acquisition of suitable product would be an issue as well as labor. There's a reason companies use machinery to pump out the cheap stuff."

Food business, Luke reminded himself. "Bea said you own a restaurant in New York."

"I used to. Not anymore."

The way she said it implied it wasn't up for discussion. Maybe the restaurant had failed. The boxes inside indicated she was here for more than a visit. Maybe that was the reason for her physical decline.

"You thinking of opening something here?" he asked.

"I don't think so. Real estate on the island is expensive, and start-up costs for even a small venue are high. Besides, the hours are brutal when you're just the chef. When you're the owner as well, they go straight past brutal and into absurd."

He didn't know anything about the restaurant business except what he'd seen on reality shows, but what she said made sense. He imagined the competition in New York made it even worse. But she hadn't given him an outright no. She'd said, 'I don't think so,' which meant she either wasn't sure or simply had no idea what she was going to do. He understood that state all too well.

"I can see how the hours would get old," he said. "And I imagine it was a lot of stress running a restaurant in New York. The competition has got to be fierce."

A flicker of something crossed her face. Aggravation? Anger? He wasn't quite sure.

"It is," she said finally. "Look, I really don't want to talk about my restaurant. Things went well until they didn't. And then they went horribly wrong. It's something I don't want to revisit."

"I can appreciate that."

"So what about you? Bea says you're on medical leave. How's your recovery going?"

He frowned. "You know how you don't want to talk about your restaurant?"

Her eyes widened. "Ah. Got it."

"Let's just say we both seem to be at a crossroads and neither of us seems overly happy about it."

She gave him an empathetic look. "Probably why I stocked up on disposable calories."

"I'm always happy to help you out with those. You know, so you don't get sick eating them all. And if you want to fix lemonade, hell, I'd pay for everything. Even the labor."

He managed to coax a smile out of her, and he felt his heart tug. Two wounded warriors. That's what they were. He didn't know what Alayna's injuries were or how she'd gotten them, but he could recognize a kindred spirit easily enough. Life had beaten Alayna Scott down. But it hadn't taken her out. That spark was still there. Maybe his was as well.

He just had to find it. And maybe douse it with gasoline.

———

BEA LOOKED UP FROM THE DISPLAY SHE WAS WORKING ON when the door chime went off. One look at the woman who stepped inside ruined her previously decent mood. Veronica Whitmore was the resident rich bitch on Tempest Island and thought everyone who lived there should bow to her as though she were the Queen of England. Bea had no use for her on any given day, and since Veronica never came into Bea's bookstore, Bea knew the reason for her visit. Forcing a blank look on her face, because pleasant just wasn't going to happen, Bea approached the woman who was standing in the entry as if waiting for trumpets to signal her arrival.

"Veronica," Bea said. "You looking for a book?"

Veronica gave her a derisive look. "I prefer musical theater for my entertainment."

"Then you must not get a lot of it."

Given the perpetual stick up her ass, Bea had decided long ago there were lots of things Veronica probably wasn't getting. Especially since her husband appeared to like her about as much as everyone else.

"I just thought I'd check in on you," Veronica said. "Since Carlson is on the city council, I figure it's my duty to make sure the businesspeople on the island are doing well."

"I'm doing as well as I always have, and if you don't need a book, I'd like to get back to my display."

Veronica frowned. Most people on Tempest Island showed her deference. She wasn't used to being dismissed, but then she didn't talk to Bea that often.

"I heard that Alayna moved back," Veronica pushed on. "I suppose after the scandal she had no choice."

"We all have choices. In fact, Carlson was asking me a couple weeks ago about security cameras for the bookstore. Would you please let him know that I priced them out but for now, I'm just sticking with that nine-millimeter I keep under the register?"

Veronica's eyes widened and she took a step back. "Well, I can see your manners are as good as ever."

"And I can say the same. Have a nice day, Veronica."

Bea turned around and walked back to her display, not even glancing behind her. A couple seconds later, she heard the door chime again and assumed the Wicked Witch of Tempest Island was off to find someone to gossip with.

"Why was Veronica Whitmore in here?" Nelly's voice sounded behind her, and she jumped.

Bea turned around and sighed. "Why do you think?"

Nelly shook her head. "Good Lord, Alayna and Melody graduated from high school over a decade ago. When is she going to drop this stupid one-sided rivalry?"

"When she's dead, which could happen sooner than she expects if she keeps coming in here trying to pump me for information on Alayna."

"Maybe you'd better take the rounds out of the gun and get a can of Mace. Just for a couple weeks."

"I could take that wimpy, fake-breasted, unnatural blonde with my bare hands."

Nelly laughed. "True."

Bea blew out a breath. "She'd better not start flapping her gums and causing issues for Alayna. That girl needs some peace and the time to regroup."

"How long is she going to be here?"

"Given that all her belongings arrived this morning, I'm hoping she doesn't leave again. And if Veronica Whitmore causes it to happen, you're going to be posting bail."

Nelly looked confused. "All of her belongings? What about her restaurant?"

"She lost it," Bea said and filled her friend in on what had happened.

Nelly's eyes misted up and she had to grab a tissue before Bea was finished.

"That's horrible," Nelly said. "Just horrible. All her hard

work gone because she dated the wrong man without even knowing it. It's so unfair."

"It is," Bea said. "And I can tell that's what really has her churned up. She says she didn't love Warren, and I believe her, although I do think she cared about him and she said she'd considered him a friend. I think she feels like the ultimate fool where he was concerned even though everyone and their dog has pointed out why she's not. But I think losing the restaurant is what really brought her to her knees."

"Oh Bea! What are we going to do to help?"

Bea smiled at her friend and reached out to squeeze her hand. "You're the best friend someone could ever have. You know that, right?"

"I'm aware. And I'm also aware that Alayna is like a niece to me and like a daughter to you. So what's our plan? We can't just let her stir around in misery, especially with Veronica Whitmore lurking around, just waiting to rub it in."

"I know. I'm working on an idea. Come with me. I want to run something by you."

———

ALAYNA SPENT THE REST OF THE MORNING AND INTO THE evening unpacking boxes. She managed, with some effort, to wedge all her kitchen items into the cabinets and drawers, although she did have to box up Bea's stuff to do it. She knew her aunt wouldn't mind and in fact, was hoping she had some space in the storeroom at the bookstore to house the boxes until Alayna vacated her beach house.

She supposed it was silly, really, to unpack all her belongings. This wasn't permanent. It probably would have been smarter to ask Bea to store her own stuff until she decided what she was going to do, especially since it was already boxed. But there was something about seeing her chef's knives on the counter next to her KitchenAid stand mixer and blender that made her feel more settled, almost happy. Granted with the toaster and the can opener, that meant there was about a foot of space left for prep, but she didn't care. Once the kitchen table was cleared off, she could use that, or put a cutting board over the sink.

When she finished the kitchen, she moved into the bedroom to unpack her clothes. The tiny closet was designed more for vacationing than full-time living, but Alayna had gotten rid of the fancy dresses she'd worn to events she attended with Warren, along with the designer shoes and handbags. Most had been gifts from him and because of that, she never would have worn them again. But they fetched a great price for her at a high-end consignment shop. It covered her rent for three months, which helped bolster her diminishing savings. Five months of living in New York with no income didn't come cheap. Neither did her attorney. And the FBI was hardly going to cut her a check to help out.

She'd been really frugal and still had some money...enough to keep her afloat for a year or so if she didn't run into car problems or health issues. And then there was Brad's gift, which would add another two or three months to things. Not having rent to pay was a huge help, and utilities on the little house wouldn't be much. She'd paid cash for the car as per her personal finance rule of not accruing debt, which was why she'd gone for a reliable late model. Her friends in New York had never understood her policy about money. Most young people living in the city had jobs that barely covered necessities. They lived their lives outside of work mostly on credit. But Alayna had a business she wanted to open, and she didn't want to spend her thirties paying off frivolous choices made in her twenties.

Besides, the one and only time she'd borrowed money, look where it had gotten her.

She wasn't ready to jump into the employment pool just yet, but still, she eventually had to start thinking about what to do for income. Bea had offered her a job at the bookstore, but Alayna knew that she didn't really need the help. Bea never rented her personal beach house anymore, so wasn't losing revenue by letting Alayna stay in it, but her aunt had already done so much for her that Alayna didn't want her doing more. Especially if it meant dipping into bookstore profits to do so. As far as Alayna knew, the bookstore operated in the black, but there was no way it was making her aunt rich, especially with the bulk of the business being seasonal.

Bea had always been careful with expenses and had taught Alayna money management skills that she'd leaned heavily on in New York. Her aunt always said she was planning for her retirement, but Alayna had a hard time picturing Bea slowing down, much less coming to a complete stop.

Sighing, she opened the first box and took out a stack of clothes. She was unlikely to restructure her entire life standing in front of the closet with a pile of shirts to hang. Everything would come with time. That's what Bea kept telling her, and she really needed to believe her aunt was right. Because so far, she'd been unable to think past the next couple days, and even that was fuzzy.

When the last of the empty boxes was broken down and stacked in the storage shed, her stomach began to rumble. She checked the clock and was surprised to see it was a little past 7:00 p.m. She hadn't eaten since she'd consumed the cinnamon rolls early that morning. No wonder she was hungry. Unfortunately, the last thing she felt like doing was preparing a meal, which would mean cleaning her currently pristine kitchen all over again, and a sandwich just wasn't calling her attention.

She glanced outside and tapped her fingers on the kitchen counter. The sun would set in about thirty minutes, but if she hurried out now, that gave her time to pick up something downtown and bring it back for dinner. Restaurant prices on the island had a premium attached to them, but she decided she deserved a splurge. Now that all her kitchen items were in place, she'd make a trip to the grocery store on the mainland soon and do a bigger stock-up on groceries. Then she could get back to cooking. Maybe even remember the joy it used to bring her.

She grabbed her purse, locked up the house, and headed out.

CHAPTER NINE

ALAYNA GLANCED NEXT DOOR AS SHE CLIMBED INTO HER car, but Luke's truck wasn't in the drive. He'd surprised her, she thought as she drove into town. It was easy to be so focused on her own problems that she missed other people struggling. And even though he did a good job of downplaying the seriousness of his situation, Alayna hadn't missed the clenched jaw and the involuntary flex of his hands when she'd asked about his recovery.

She'd seen the scar on his knee, even though she'd made sure he didn't see her looking. The scar was still red and raised and it ran right across his kneecap. It couldn't be that old but even though she'd watched closely, she'd never seen him limp. Since he was on medical leave, the injury must have been serious, so either Luke healed quickly and was just waiting for a doctor to agree with him or he was so hell-bent on not showing any weakness that he was careful to appear as if nothing was wrong.

Even in the short time she'd known him, she could see him doing that.

Still, he'd said they were both at a crossroads. Did that

mean his current position with the military was in jeopardy if he didn't get a medical release soon? Or was the injury itself the problem? That would account for the frustration she'd felt he had. She'd thought about asking him what he did with the Navy, but if he hadn't been forthcoming with Bea, Alayna doubted he would open up to her. She didn't even have a house to rent him.

There was an open parking space in front of the pizza joint, so Alayna took it as a sign and pulled in. Pizza in Florida didn't compare to pizza in New York but fortunately, Alayna had never developed snobbery on that front. Very few things that contained marinara and cheese could be bad. And just in case the marinara wasn't to her taste, she'd double up on the cheese.

She went inside and was pleased to see that things hadn't really changed inside. The red-and-white-checkered table-cloths still adorned the tables. Pictures of the beach hung on the wall. Bea had told her the original owner had retired a couple years before and sold the place, but apparently the new owners were smart enough to leave things alone. *If it's working, don't mess with it.* General rule for all businesses, but definitely for the restaurant business. Changes in what appeared to be the most insignificant things could cause a shift in clientele.

She headed for the counter and that's when she noticed Luke standing there, talking to Melody Whitmore. Well, maybe 'talking' wasn't necessarily the correct word. They were standing so close together that they could be dancing, and Melody was gazing up at him, wearing that sexy pout that had landed her the captain of the football team in high school.

Alayna hesitated, then started to turn around and leave. For reasons Alayna had never really understood, Melody had taken an instant disliking to her when Bea moved her to the island. Jill, a girl who befriended Alayna the first day of school, claimed that Melody was just jealous because Alayna was as pretty as she was, but Alayna never really believed that. Whatever the reason, Melody had gone out of her way to poke at Alayna at a time when she was so tender, a gentle breeze hurt. The last person she wanted to see now was Melody, when that gentle breeze would be just as painful.

But before she could turn, Luke caught sight of her and motioned to her with his hand. "Alayna," he said. "I was just about to get us a table."

She stared at him for a moment, completely confused, but then caught the pleading look and realized what he was up to. The last thing she wanted was a potential confrontation with Melody, but her conscience wouldn't allow her to walk away and leave Luke in the other woman's grasp. Taking a deep breath, she plastered on a smile. Melody gave her a critical eye as she approached, the sexy pout now replaced with a frown.

"I didn't realize you were visiting," Melody said.

"I'm not visiting," Alayna said. "I moved back."

"And after all that unpacking you did today, you must be starved," Luke said. "Are you ready to eat?"

Alayna nodded but Melody refused to take the hint.

"I suppose it makes sense that you'd come back here," Melody said. "I mean after everything that happened in New York you could hardly stay there. The media coverage was so harsh. You must be crushed by all of it."

Melody's words were conciliatory, but Alayna could tell by her tone that Melody was totally relishing Alayna's epic failure and embarrassment. Unbelievable. High school had been over a decade ago and Melody was still a total bitch.

"I'm fine," Alayna said, forcing herself to remain calm. "But thank you so much for your concern. Now, if you'll excuse me, I owe this man a pizza. He lifted a ton of boxes today."

Alayna pushed past Melody and waved at a server, who

indicated she could pick any table. Luke gave Melody a nod and followed Alayna to a table in the back corner of the restaurant. She could feel Melody glaring at them as they walked away, but when she turned to sit, she saw the front door slamming shut.

"I'm sorry for putting you on the spot," Luke said. "You don't have to stay. I just figured the quickest way to get rid of her was to be meeting someone else. Not exactly the most heroic of moves, but I didn't realize you two had history."

"Is that what you call it when someone sets their sights on you in high school with the hopes of making you miserable? Apparently, high school never ended for one of us."

He frowned. "I guess some people never grow out of it."

"Melody was spoiled by her rich parents and taught to believe that the entire world should cater to her. And since most people proceeded to do exactly that, she was never disabused of that belief."

"I take it you weren't interested in being one of her followers?"

"I never got the opportunity. When I was fifteen, I moved here to live with Bea after my parents were killed in a car accident. Melody didn't like me from the moment she set eyes on me. Apparently, that hasn't changed."

"I'm guessing she didn't like the competition."

"Ha. You sound like Jill."

"Who's Jill?"

"My best friend from high school. Only friend, really. We lost touch when she went off to college and I went to culinary school."

"That happens," he said. "I'm sorry about your parents. I didn't realize Bea had raised you. Well, at least partially."

Alayna nodded. "Bea has always been my rock. I suppose that's why I'm back here to regroup."

"Well, the good thing is, a place like this isn't exactly a compromise and I imagine Bea's a great person to have your back. But seriously, you don't have to stay and eat. You probably had plans and I don't want to disrupt them. I've already messed up your evening by placing you in the line of fire."

Alayna glanced at her watch. It would be dark by the time they finished eating, and that bothered her more than she wanted to admit. But she'd promised herself that she'd work on normalizing things again when she came here. Maybe now was the time. Besides, Luke lived right next door. With any luck, he'd be going straight home afterward and if anything was amiss, he and his gun were only a yell away.

"No way I'm leaving now," she said. "Our luck, Melody would see us and the jig would be up. Unless, of course, you think you might want to make a play for her later on."

Luke grimaced. "God no. Stop scaring me. I ran into her in the island grocery right after I rented the cottage. Let's just say her moves were more than obvious and, since I'm not even remotely interested, made me a little uncomfortable. I faked a doctor's appointment to get away, but that one wasn't going to work tonight."

"She's very pretty and has a nice body." Alayna continued to rub it in.

"Women like Melody don't have relationships. They have conquests. I've been caught in that kind of aftermath before, and no way am I doing it again. The Middle East is easier to navigate."

Alayna couldn't help smiling. She hadn't wanted to like Luke. Hadn't wanted to like any man, really. But he was hard not to like. He had a relaxed way about him, which was surprising given the intensity she'd seen at their first meeting. Despite having his own issues to deal with, he still seemed to be able to derive pleasure from life. Even the simple things, like fresh lemonade and cinnamon rolls from a can. Maybe she could take a lesson from him. Start focusing on the little joys that filtered through every day, and then maybe one day, that feeling would take over.

A server stepped up to the table and Luke looked over at her. "You up for pizza or were you planning on something else?" he asked.

"Definitely pizza."

"What do you like on it?"

"Everything but the kitchen sink."

He nodded and looked up at the server. "You heard the lady. One large pie with everything you've got on it."

They both ordered sweet tea and declined a salad, and the server hurried off with the order.

"How long were you in the Middle East?" Alayna asked.

A flicker of something, sadness maybe, flashed over him and she chided herself for asking the question. He'd probably been injured in the line of duty, and since he didn't want to talk about it, he wouldn't want to talk about the place it happened, either.

"I've been in and out for the past ten years," he said. "I'm a specialist, of sorts, so I'm rarely in one place for a long length of time."

"That must be hard on your family."

"Never married. No kids. No family."

He'd delivered the statements so matter-of-factly that she stared for moment, not sure how to respond.

"No family at all?" she asked finally.

"The military is my family."

There was something about the way he said those words that made her heart clench. She might have lost her parents, but at least she had Bea. It sounded as if Luke didn't have anyone he could rely on outside the men he served with, and that was sad.

"I saw you paddleboarding yesterday," she said, changing the subject. "I've been thinking about trying it. Is it hard?"

"With a decent-sized board and calm waters, you shouldn't have any problem with it if you've got good balance," he said, looking relieved that the conversation had shifted to something other than personal. "I'm surprised you've never tried it given that you lived here before."

"It wasn't really a thing back then, but now I see it everywhere...people really seem to enjoy it."

He nodded. "I prefer surfing, but that's off the table for a while. But paddleboarding can be interesting, especially when you've got clear water to do it in, like here. You can see so much more standing than you can from a kayak."

"But you can store beer and snacks in a kayak."

He laughed. "You've got me there. If you want to give it a try, I'd be happy to show you the ropes. The board came with the house rental and it's meant for those with little to no experience. You look like you're in good shape. You should be able to get up and go in no time. If the Gulf is too rough, we can walk across to the Sound."

She knew she should refuse the offer. The last thing she wanted to do was give him the impression that she was available for anything beyond being casual acquaintances. And if she was being honest, she liked Luke far more than she wanted to. The more time she spent with him, the harder it was to ignore the attraction. But even if she was ready to invest herself in a relationship—and there was absolutely no way that was the case—Luke was the last person she should take a chance on.

Whenever he got medical clearance, he'd go back to duty and based on his description, that meant leaving the country often and for who knew how long. Alayna knew women managed relationships every day with that complication, but she didn't think it was something that would work for her. It was better to leave things as they were now. Surface level. That way the attraction she felt couldn't turn into hurt later on. She'd had enough loss to process, both recently and in the past. But instead of issuing the 'no' she should have, her mouth completely betrayed her common sense.

"I might take you up on that," she said. "If you have the time, I mean."

"All I've got is time. If you're free tomorrow and the weather's good, just come over and we'll give it a go."

"Thanks, but I hate to just pop in. If I could get your phone number, then I could call first if I decide to go for it. I mean, if you don't mind my having your number."

"Of course. I should have offered it already anyway."

She handed him her phone and he put in his number, then she called it and he logged hers.

"Now that you have my number, if you run into any issues over there, give me a call," he said. "I know it's Bea's house, but if I can save her the aggravation of a leaky sink or weatherstripping on a door or whatever, I'm happy to help out. She's a nice lady, though I got the impression she was kinda hitting on me when I signed the rental agreement."

Alayna laughed. "She is nice, and she probably was flirting with you. Bea has never had a problem going for what she wants."

"It was flattering but a little unnerving."

"You should have heard her when I told her about your gun and boxers."

He groaned. "I don't think I want to know."

She smiled and relaxed back in her chair. It had been a long time since she'd enjoyed a meal out with good company. She hadn't even been certain she was capable. And really, what could it hurt to share some lemonade and a pizza, or let him show her how to paddleboard? It wasn't as if she were making promises. She wasn't even making passes.

She'd leave that to Aunt Bea.

CHAPTER TEN

As soon as Mateo saw Alayna drive away, he called his associate. Aboard a boat anchored in the Sound, Mateo had a decent view of the front of the beach cottage. He'd seen the moving truck arrive this morning with the boxes and had spotted her through the kitchen window, unpacking. That meant everything she'd brought from New York was now inside. If Alayna had what the client was looking for, it was in the house.

"She left a couple minutes ago," Mateo said when his associate answered. "Do you have eyes on her?"

"Yeah," his associate Carlos said. "I've got a clear view from the motel window. She just pulled in. Parked in front of the pizza joint across the street."

Mateo frowned, weighing his options. If she'd called in an order, she wouldn't be gone long enough for him to access the house. And while he preferred to do that sort of thing under the cover of night, her habit for sticking inside after sundown made it difficult. At least as long as his orders were to maintain secrecy.

"Can you see inside?" Mateo asked.

"Sort of. She's standing at the counter talking to a man and a woman. The guy is the one who lives next door. I don't recognize the woman."

"Are they waiting to be seated or is she picking up an order?"

"No one has addressed them yet. Hold on. It looks like the other woman is leaving and the target and the guy are moving to a table."

This was it. If he was going to make a move, he had to do it immediately.

"Call me when she leaves," Mateo said. "And I mean the second you spot her near the door. Don't move from that window. Don't even blink."

Carlos would follow instructions. That was the advantage of having a young associate who was still afraid of you. While he couldn't yet pull his weight in some ways, Mateo didn't have to worry about Carlos questioning his orders or simply choosing to do something different. He shoved the phone in his pocket and hurried down the ladder and to the back of the boat where the WaveRunner was secured.

The remote location of the beach house had both positive and negative aspects to it. On the positive side, there were fewer people around to observe something out of the ordinary, like the same boat cruising the Sound. On the negative, it was harder to blend and he couldn't stay anchored across the way from the cottages without someone eventually noticing.

The marina had available slips and they offered a clear view of the main road. He'd be able to sit on the deck and see if Alayna drove into town and if she accessed the bridge to go to the mainland. It was something he'd look into first thing tomorrow because that way, he could dismiss his associate in the motel. Mateo preferred to work alone.

He boarded the WaveRunner and headed for the shore. It

was a short walk across the dunes and the road to Alayna's house. If she was eating dinner, he figured he had at least an hour, maybe a bit more. But as soon as she left the restaurant, he had to get out of the house and back across the dune before she spotted him. That was another downside of the location— no place to hide.

He beached the WaveRunner and grabbed a small towel from the storage box before hurrying across the dune to the house. He wiped the sand and water from his feet and tucked the towel in a palm bush close to the front door. He'd procured a copy of the house key long before Alayna left New York. The client figured as soon as the FBI turned her loose, she'd head home. It had been child's play to sneak into the aunt's house and make a copy of the keys to her two beach houses, her own home, and her business.

He opened the door and let himself inside, figuring he'd start in the bedroom. Her closet displayed a surprisingly meager amount of clothes for a woman her age, but then he supposed the fashionable wear he'd seen her sporting in the city didn't have much place on the island. He started with the boxes on the shelf but found only old birthday cards and photos. Then he went through each garment, inch by inch, feeling every seam to see if something could be hidden inside. Afterward, he checked her shoes.

He felt the back of the closet for any movement, just in case there was a secret cubby, but the walls were solid, as was the floor. When he was satisfied that nothing was hidden there, he turned his attention to the dresser and started his search again, even removing the drawers and looking for something taped underneath. The client was convinced that if Alayna was in possession of the item, she had no idea about it. Mateo didn't agree. The client didn't think Patterson had been stupid enough to let his girlfriend in on his crimes, much less ask her to secure anything for him, especially something so important.

Mateo, on the other hand, thought Patterson was plenty stupid. At least stupid enough to get caught. But until he could convince the client otherwise, his orders were to treat the girl-friend as an unknowing participant. The less she knew, the better, which meant his directive was to procure the item, assuming it was there, with her being none the wiser. Mateo felt the direct approach would have been more efficient and witnesses could always be dealt with. But it did attract more attention and ultimately, it wasn't his call.

He searched the dresser and the nightstands and was checking between the mattresses when his phone buzzed. He pulled it out and answered.

"She just walked out of the pizza joint," Carlos said.

"Got it," Mateo said, and shoved the phone back into his pocket, cursing. The hour he'd had wasn't enough. He'd made some progress but every time he had to leave and reenter, he had to spend some time revisiting each location to ensure things hadn't been moved around. What he needed was a large block of time. Surely she'd leave the island at some point. All of the big retailers and grocers were on the mainland. She had to make a trip there sooner or later.

He hurried out of the beach house, locking the door behind him, grabbed the towel out of the bush, and headed across the dune to the WaveRunner. The sun was mostly down, so he didn't worry about her spotting him on the Sound. The noise carried, of course, but plenty of locals fished at night. An engine running on the water wouldn't alert anyone and since sound carried far over water, the fact that someone could hear the vehicle but not see it wasn't an issue either.

By the time he boarded the boat and headed up to grab his binoculars, she had pulled into the drive. As she got out of her car, she gave the neighbor guy a wave and went inside. The neighbor lingered a bit, watching her enter her house before going inside his rental. Mateo frowned. The neighbor could be a problem. He had that cadence that only military sported and if he attached himself to the woman, protector mode could kick in if he thought she was threatened.

The potential for complications frustrated him, although he should have anticipated this. Alayna Scott was an attractive woman. The neighbor would have to be blind not to notice. Time to do a bit of research on him, just to determine the level of the threat. Luke Ryan. He had a name. It was time to get more.

He pulled out his phone and dialed. The client answered on the first ring.

"I managed an hour inside," Mateo said. "But no luck. She returned before I could cover the entire place. I need more time to do a thorough look. If you're ready to let me handle things differently—"

"No," the client cut him off. "If you go that route and don't find what we're looking for, you alert the FBI to start looking at her all over again. I want this to happen without her ever knowing you were there."

"If she's hiding it for Patterson, she's going to notice if it's missing."

"I'm not convinced on her culpability. And even if that's the case, she's hardly going to report it to the FBI if it's gone. And she has no access to Patterson. I'm working on something that should give us better information."

"And if she's in on it?"

"Then we'll do things your way. But for now, you're a ghost."

Mateo slipped the phone back into his pocket and stared out at the tiny bits of light creeping through the blinds of

Alayna's house. His way was better. Faster. He hoped the client figured that out soon. The money was really good, but there were other jobs. More interesting jobs, where he was allowed to handle things his own way.

———

As soon as Alayna stepped into the house, she knew something wasn't quite right. She started to turn around and rush back out to the safety of her car, but common sense won out and she pulled her Mace from her purse. The door had been locked and upon inspection, showed no sign of tampering. She knew the windows were locked. Even though she never opened them, she checked the locks every night and before she left the house.

A quick glance told her that nothing appeared out of place, so what had set her off? She walked slowly through the house to the bedroom, the Mace held out in front of her, then let out a huge sigh of relief when she found the house was completely empty. Because she knew she'd never be able to settle down if she didn't check, she did a walk-through and tested all the doors and windows. Everything was battened down.

She blew out a frustrated breath and grabbed a bottle of wine from the refrigerator. She had to stop doing this— freaking herself out. It wasn't conducive to moving forward. In fact, quite the opposite; it kept her mired in the past. Warren wasn't coming after her. All the experts had agreed on that. In fact, they'd been almost dismissive about it. As if she didn't really matter, and perhaps that was true. She hoped it was true. But even the FBI's reassurances hadn't been able to quell the feeling that this wasn't over.

But maybe it was her testimony that still had her on edge. Maybe once she was done with the trial, she wouldn't have these feelings that could never be substantiated. She poured herself a glass, grabbed a container of strawberries, and went to sit in the living room, hoping the television could provide some distraction.

Her cell phone sat on the small table next to her, mocking her with its presence. She took a big sip of wine and sighed. She owed Agent Davies a phone call. Part of her 'release' from New York had been on the condition that she check in once she arrived in Florida and every two weeks after. She should have called yesterday, but she hadn't been able to bring herself to do it. Hadn't wanted to taint this place with the stain of New York.

But it was already tainted. Because she was here.

Before she could change her mind, she grabbed the cell phone and dialed. Maybe she'd luck out and he'd be having dinner with friends or be sleeping or out with a woman. But she wasn't surprised when he answered on the first ring. Davies had struck her as someone who went beyond workaholic into slightly obsessed with his work. She knew the look. She'd worn it for years.

"Ms. Scott," he said in his usual clipped, businesslike voice. "I trust you've made it safely to Florida and have settled in."

"I have. My things arrived today, so I'm as settled as I'm getting."

"Good. Then put this date on your calendar and give me a call again in two weeks."

"Fine. I, uh..."

"Is there something else?"

"Yeah, I was just wondering about Warren. I mean, he's still in prison, right?"

She knew bail had been denied due to the flight risk, but she couldn't help asking.

"Mr. Patterson is locked away and will remain there a good

majority of his life," Davies said. "In the extremely unlikely event that the situation changed, we would notify you immediately. It's part of protocol."

"Of course. I remember you said...I guess I was just...never mind."

"Ms. Scott," Davies said, his voice less clipped, "I assure you that Warren Patterson is no threat to you. If he were, we would have taken precautionary measures. The FBI is not in the habit of getting witnesses killed, even if they only play a minor role."

"Oh, I'm not saying...you know what, forget it."

"I can understand how you might feel exposed, but I'm giving you my word. Patterson isn't making a play for you. If he did, we'd know and we'd cut him off before any plans he made could come to fruition. You've been given an opportunity to rebuild your life. I suggest you focus on that and leave any worry about Patterson to me."

Given an opportunity.

She bristled at his phrasing. As if the DA had bestowed on her some great gift. She hadn't done anything wrong except make a poor choice in dating. It wasn't as though she was the only person in history to have done so.

"Thank you," she finally managed, although it wasn't what she wanted to say.

"Two weeks," Davies said, and disconnected.

She tossed her phone on the table and shook her head. That had been a waste of time. Well, maybe not completely. At least now she was angry instead of frightened.

When Warren had first been arrested, she'd come under heavy scrutiny, sometimes spending an entire day being questioned. She'd been closed in a small room, and often left alone for hours on end before an agent started the questions all over again. At first, it was obvious they thought she was aware of

Warren's dealings, but as the questioning continued and her story never changed, she could see the shift in their expressions. In the beginning, they'd looked at her as if she were culpable. Before it was over, they had dismissed her as just another silly gold digger taken by a smooth-talking criminal.

She wasn't sure which one was worse.

She grabbed the remote and turned up the volume on the television, then took another sip of wine. At least she had one question answered—Warren was still in prison and expected to remain there. She'd known that was the case, but it helped to hear it. Whatever had set her off earlier must have been her fear manifesting. The house was clear. No one had been inside. She had to stop letting her imagination get the best of her.

If only she could figure out how.

CHAPTER ELEVEN

LUKE SANK ONTO THE COUCH AND OPENED UP HIS LAPTOP. He'd had a twinge of curiosity when Alayna had refused to talk about her restaurant but had figured it was as simple as not wanting to relive failure with someone she didn't really know. He couldn't blame her for that. He wasn't exactly begging people to talk about his injury. But then the very pushy and obviously jealous Melody had made a comment that had stuck with him.

The media coverage was so harsh.

A restaurant going out of business in New York City was hardly an uncommon thing, much less something that reporters would waste time on. But the closing had caused enough of a stir to garner attention from the press. And unless Melody had been in the city when it happened, she'd seen the story on a national news channel. So the question was, what in the world had happened at Alayna's restaurant that had national news channels interested?

It took only seconds for the entire sordid story to appear on his screen.

And holy shit what a story it was. Money laundering, drug

traffickers, old-money scandal, and Alayna Scott stuck right in the middle of the takedown. No wonder she didn't want to talk about it.

He continued reading, trying to find out Alayna's connection with the criminal business, but although the media had tried to make something of her relationship with Patterson, they hadn't been able to connect her with his crimes. Even the FBI had eventually stated that Alayna was a witness and an ancillary victim of Patterson's crimes, but that hadn't stopped reporters from hounding her, trying to make a connection between a beautiful, successful woman and all the dirty business Patterson had been up to.

He shut the laptop and shoved it to the side, disgusted.

Had Alayna really been in the dark about everything? The FBI seemed to think so. Or they had given her immunity in exchange for testimony. Patterson was a big fish with the access to several avenues to clean money. He might have made a move to use her restaurant for that sometime down the road, but based on what he'd read, that hadn't occurred prior to Patterson's arrest. But since the FBI had shut it down, Luke assumed Warren had invested in it and they'd closed up shop just as they had all of Patterson's business interests, leaving Alayna with no restaurant.

Had the FBI gotten it right? Was Alayna really an innocent victim? Certainly, she didn't seem to have the makings of an archcriminal, but he knew better than most that appearances could be deceiving. Still, he couldn't reconcile the skittish woman with the likable aunt to money laundering for drug dealers. And he was good at personal assessment. He had to be.

His mind flashed back to their initial meeting and her panic when she saw the gun. Granted, anyone in their right mind would have been scared in that situation, but Alayna's fear seemed to go deeper than that moment. He'd also noticed when she glanced outside and checked her watch before agreeing to have dinner with him. And how she'd checked the dark street before hurrying inside and drawing the blinds closed.

Alayna Scott was scared. The question was, did she have reason to be?

Don't get involved.

The words of his former commander echoed through his mind. He'd gotten in too deep once before with a woman he'd thought was trying to move on with her life after a difficult situation. Her problems were nothing compared to Alayna's, but she'd managed to use him for all she could get, then practically ran him over to move on to the next biggest pocketbook she could snag. His commander had clued Luke in on her game from the beginning, but Luke had lacked the experience and cynicism about women that the older man had gained throughout his years of reading people. So Luke had ignored the warnings and paid the price.

Now those word were coming back to him in waves.

He shook his head, trying to push those thoughts back to that dark place in his memory where they belonged. Alayna wasn't Serena. The FBI had cleared her, and he was going to stick with his intuition. Alayna Scott was an innocent woman afraid of retaliation from her ex. And although he hoped that Alayna never needed his help in a somewhat professional capacity, he was going to make sure he was available in case she did. Patterson might have taken her down, but he wasn't going to take her out.

Not on Luke's watch.

———

ALAYNA WOKE EARLY SUNDAY MORNING, A LITTLE IMPRESSED by how well she'd slept. For the first time in as long as she could remember, she'd managed six comfortable hours and undisturbed. Well, partially undisturbed. She felt a flush run up her neck as she recalled the vivid dream she'd had about Luke. A very active dream. A dream that had no place in her conscious or subconscious.

She stretched and hopped out of bed, pushing all thoughts of her sexy dream and her hot neighbor aside. Luke was a nice guy and a temporary neighbor, and she'd been a little bit surprised by how much she'd enjoyed dinner with him. And while she'd be lying to herself if she said she didn't find him attractive and interesting and nice, she needed to keep things in perspective. She'd returned to the island to sort out her messy life. It was fine to spend a little casual time with Luke... as a friend. But no way could she allow dreams she had while she was asleep to become dreams she had when she was awake.

She headed into the kitchen and set coffee to brew, then popped a couple slices of bread in the toaster. She'd picked up fresh strawberry preserves at the market and couldn't wait to try it. Strawberry preserves on toast had always been her favorite breakfast, much to Bea's dismay. Her aunt had tried everything to get her to eat breakfast when Alayna first moved to Tempest Island. And despite the fact that cooking was the very last thing on her aunt's list of things she loved to do, Bea had cooked omelets and pancakes and even bought a waffle maker.

When Alayna had found an unopened jar of strawberry preserves and declared it the best thing she'd ever had, Bea had been both relieved and somewhat exhausted, then had proceeded to buy six jars of it, just in case the woman who made it decided to quit. No one had been more excited than

Bea when Alayna had formed an interest in cooking and taken over meals a year later.

While she waited on breakfast, she opened all the blinds and pushed open the patio door, allowing the breeze to waft into the house. Then she fixed up her toast and coffee and carried it outside to watch the birds do their morning swoop for fish. The smell of the salt air was intoxicating and the sound of the waves crashing on the beach was hypnotic. Before she'd moved to New York, Alayna had spent several years using her vacation time to travel to other countries just to immerse herself in the food of different cultures. She'd seen some breathtaking landscapes, but none of them made her feel like this one.

While she enjoyed her breakfast and the view, she deliberated over what she wanted to do with her day. The unpacking was done, the beach house was clean, and she had enough groceries and leftover Chinese takeout for another couple meals. Plus she was cooking for Bea tonight, so getting calories in wasn't going to be a problem. She probably should make a run to the mainland to stock up on more food and toiletries, cleaning supplies and the like, but she couldn't seem to find the desire to leave her little piece of paradise.

You've got time.

She tried to keep that in mind, but the workaholic in her kept trying to convince her that if she wasn't working, she was being lazy. That instead of sitting around with excellent toast and jelly and watching birds fly, she should be figuring out what to do with her life. She rose from her chair with a sigh and grabbed the crusts she'd saved and headed for the water.

What she really wanted to do with her day was call Luke and ask him to teach her to paddleboard. But given how much she enjoyed dinner with him the night before and her subsequent dream, she knew it wasn't a good idea. She tossed the bread onto the hard-packed sand near the surf and watched as a couple of the bravest birds landed near her and picked up their prize. Luke was a curveball she hadn't seen coming. After Warren, she'd expected to never look at a man with interest again. To never be able to trust the words that came out of a man's mouth. But yet she was drawn to Luke in a way that she'd never been with Warren. It was almost primal. As if she had no choice in the matter.

That scared the hell out of her. But it also excited her.

The old Alayna had been very deliberate. She researched everything thoroughly, then made a plan and a backup plan and a backup plan for the backup plan. Some had believed her fearless, but she wasn't one to indiscriminately take big chances. When she made a big move, it was only because she firmly believed it was the right time to do so. The restaurant had been her biggest gamble ever—or so she'd thought—but she'd been profitable in the first three months, which was why she'd finally cracked and taken the expansion money from Warren.

Now she needed another plan. And damned if she had any idea what it should be.

"Did you catch the sunrise?" Luke's voice sounded behind her and she couldn't help smiling as she turned to greet him.

"No," she said. "I finally got a decent night's sleep. You know how it is acclimating to a new place."

He nodded. "I've acclimated fine to the place, but my training has ruined sleeping late for me. And by late, I mean beyond 6:00 a.m."

"I can see that. With me, it was the opposite. Restaurant business starts later in the day and runs late into the night, so sleeping late was necessary. My body is still geared for that schedule, so I'm still going to sleep late at night, but not often managing to stay asleep."

"It catches up with you eventually."

She nodded. "About once a week, I find myself head-bobbing in the middle of the day. I crash and catch up, then start the whole futile process over again. But it *is* getting better. At least I slept past dawn this morning."

"Have you made plans for the day?"

This was it. The crossroads. Either she told him she needed to take care of personal items to give herself some space to figure out how to deal with him, or she rolled the dice and went completely against logic. Against her usual nature.

"No," she said. "Nothing except for having Bea over tonight for dinner. She's an awful cook and ends up eating takeout or frozen dinners and sandwiches most of the time. I want to treat her to a great meal since she's given me this bit of paradise to live in while I decide what I want to do next."

He smiled. "An awful cook, huh? Was she ever married? I've never heard her mention a husband or any children, but I never asked. I didn't want to risk bringing up something she'd rather not talk about."

"You would have been safe with that subject. Bea never married. She had plenty of opportunity, mind you. She's always been a spitfire and she's still an attractive woman. But she never found a man who could convince her that he was worth compromising for. Bea is very set in her ways."

"I can see that. She's obviously strong-willed or she wouldn't have a successful business and the two beach properties."

"She's always been a whiz with finance and very careful with her money. I worked at the bookstore with her after I came to live here, and I learned so much from her about accounting and forecasting and managing cash flow. I couldn't have opened my restaurant without the knowledge I gained from her."

"Well, dinner is some time away. Are you interested in that paddleboarding lesson?"

This was it—time to fish or cut bait.

"You know what?" she said before she could change her mind. "I think I am. If you've got the time to show me, that is."

"This lesson will be the most pressing thing I've had on my schedule for weeks. I'm going to thank you ahead of time for giving me something to focus on besides relaxing."

She laughed. "Thinking about relaxing isn't relaxing at all. And when it's forced on you, it's ten times worse. I had my appendix out a few years ago and it was a little more complicated than the usual, according to my doctor. But after the fourth day of lying around, I almost cried with relief when building maintenance knocked on my door to fix a plumbing leak."

"You didn't cause the leak on purpose, did you?" he joked.

"No. But I thought about breaking something else afterward."

His smile faded just a bit. "Your friends didn't come visit you?"

"No. You have to understand, it's a different way of life in the city. When you're young and trying to get things going with your career and your personal life, there's not enough time in the day to get it all in, especially not when you spend a decent amount of your day commuting from a place you can afford to where you work. Everything is fast-paced. Everything has a sense of urgency that you don't have in a place like Tempest Island. And honestly, I never really developed any close friendships. It's hard to. People constantly come and go. It's a difficult place to get your footing. Most people I met early on didn't make it more than a year."

"Sounds lonely."

"It could be at times. I suppose it's completely different from the life you know, where everyone is all together working toward a single purpose and living as a unit. It must be a nice to know that so many people have your back."

"It is," he said but she noticed he almost frowned when he said it.

"So what time do you want to do this?" she asked.

"That's completely up to you."

"Okay. Then how about we meet out here in a couple hours. That will give me time to take care of a few chores. Afterward, I'll make us up a fruit salad and some ham sandwiches."

"Best offer I've had all week," he said and gave her that slow, sexy smile that she'd seen in her dream.

"Great," she said as she took a step back, hoping the heat on her skin masked the blush she felt creeping up her neck. "Then I'll get to work and see you in a couple hours."

"Looking forward to it."

She gave him a half wave and headed back to the house as quickly as she could without appearing as if she were trying to flee. As soon as she stepped inside, she chided herself for losing her cool.

What are you, fifteen years old?

She was acting like a teen with a crush, blushing over a smile. It didn't bode well for the paddleboarding plans. And why now? Obviously, her judgment had been lacking when she'd picked Warren. How could she be sure it was any better now? Especially when she was already under so much stress?

She sighed. Was she going to question her entire life every time she met an attractive man? Was she going to let one mistake define every future relationship? She really didn't want that to happen. More than anything, she just wanted to be normal, doing normal things, with normal stress and normal joy. That wasn't too much to ask, was it?

She knew what her shrink in New York would say—that until you feel normal, act normal. Her therapist believed that if you pushed yourself into the behavior you'd like to feel, eventually the action would take over and your feelings would catch up. So she knew what she had to do. She had to put on her bathing suit and stop second-guessing herself. Luke Ryan was a temporary neighbor, and it was only a paddleboarding lesson. They weren't even exchanging a handshake, much less vows. She could spend an enjoyable afternoon with an attractive man and it didn't have to mean anything more.

She'd just keep telling herself that.

CHAPTER TWELVE

LUKE WAS ALREADY ON THE BEACH WITH THE PADDLEBOARD when Alayna stepped outside. He wore white swim trunks with blue racing stripes, sunglasses, and nothing else, and suddenly, her earlier vow to treat this as an outing between temporary friends seemed questionable. As did her serviceable navy blue one-piece swimsuit that she'd purchased for swimming laps at the gym, not because it presented her in the most flattering light.

She shook her head. This wasn't a date, and she wasn't trying to attract Luke. Her swimsuit was perfect for water activities and that was where things ended...except for the part where she couldn't stop staring at him as she approached. When he'd accosted her in the shed with his gun, the majority of his body had been exposed, but it hadn't registered as heavily as the pistol that had been trained on her. Later, when he was out with the board in the Gulf, she'd gotten another look, but only at a distance.

The closer she got, the more exquisite he became. And with every step she took toward him, her heart ticked up another notch. His skin had that deep, evenly dispersed tan that can only be acquired from spending weeks in the sun. The dark skin enhanced every ripple of muscle on his body, and there was a lot of ripple to take in. She'd already gotten a good look at his legs, and even the injured one hadn't appeared to have lost any muscle tone. The rest of him matched his legs.

His biceps looked as if he were flexing, even though he was standing relaxed, and the flex continued onto his shoulders. His abs were what every guy she saw in her gym back in New York wished he could achieve. Clearly Luke spent a lot of time on his body, but it wasn't something you could achieve by the gym alone. It was obvious that he was made for action and saw plenty of it, which made her wonder again exactly what he did for the military.

He gave her a big smile as she approached. "You ready for this?"

"I think so," she said as she dropped her beach bag, giving her an excuse to divert her eyes for just a second. "I mean, I'm excited about it, but also a little nervous."

"We lucked out. It's a good day for it in the Gulf and the view is better here than the Sound."

"It's nice to have options." She gave the board a hard stare. "Do you want to cover the basics on land?"

"Nah. It's not like surfing. You don't have to snap up into position, so no need to practice it on land. And I'll be there to steady the board while you find your balance. Can I assume you're a strong swimmer, or would you like a life jacket?"

She glanced back at the Gulf and bit her lower lip. She was a strong swimmer, but unconscious people didn't swim all that well. One fall and a blow to the head and then there could be trouble.

"How far out are we going?"

"Waist deep, and I'll be right there."

"Then I'm good." She took a deep breath and blew it out. "Okay. Let's do this."

Luke picked up the board and they headed into the water. Alayna let out a small gasp as the somewhat chilly water soaked her feet and Luke grinned.

"It's still a little cool," he said.

"It is," she agreed. "But give it another couple weeks of this sunshine and it will be nice."

"You'll acclimate quickly enough as long as the sun is out."

From years of swimming in the Gulf as a teen, Alayna knew he was right, but those initial steps were always the worst. Goose bumps rose on her legs and arms as she moved forward, but she was gradually adjusting. When they were waist deep, Luke positioned the board next to them, pointed it at the shore, and stood next to it, facing her. He was so close she could see the gold flecks in his green eyes and the tiny scar on his chin.

"First, you'll hop on the board and get into a kneeling position in the center," he said. "Ready?"

"Just like that?"

"Just like that."

"Okay." Alayna said a quick prayer that she didn't embarrass herself. Then she pulled herself onto the board, scooted to the center, and knelt. The board swayed beneath her with the movement of the tide, but Luke held it in place.

"Okay, here's your paddle," he said and placed it across the board in front of her. "It's best to go ahead and learn to stand with the paddle, as you probably won't have someone around to hand it to you every time."

She put one hand on the paddle and glanced back at the Gulf to make sure it was still nice and calm.

"This part you can do however you're most comfortable," he said. "You can lift one knee and get the foot underneath you so you can push up into a standing position. Or you can put both hands flat on the board in front of you and push up, kinda like a yoga move. Do whatever you think you can maintain balance best with."

Alayna considered her choices and decided to go with the one leg up, then rise. She had never been a yoga person, choosing to burn her calories running or swimming. She lifted her right leg up and got the foot flat on the board, then placed the paddle across her knee. Thank God she'd never scrimped on core exercises, she thought, as she forced herself to stand. She rocked on the board and felt her abdomen tighten as she struggled to maintain her balance.

"Move your other foot forward and spread them the width of your shoulders," Luke instructed.

She inched the left foot up to match the right, then scooted them both a little to the side, clutching the paddle with a death grip.

"Awesome!" Luke said. "See how easy that was?"

She looked down at him. "You and I have different definitions of easy. Apparently, I should have done even more ab work."

"Paddleboarding is definitely good for the core. Okay, now that you're up, grab the end of the paddle with one hand and the middle with the other."

She positioned the paddle as instructed and he nodded.

"I'm going to let go now," he said. "Take a couple seconds to make sure your balance is good, then you're going to gently paddle forward. One stroke on one side, then the other. The tide will help carry you into the shore."

He let go of the board and she swayed first to one side, then the other, her legs and core working in unison to keep her upright. When she finally felt stable enough, she eased the paddle into the water and gave it a little push. The board moved forward, and she shifted the paddle to the other side and pushed again. Luke stayed nearby, moving with her toward the shore.

"That's it!" he said. "You got it. First time up and you're doing great."

She smiled and felt her body relax just a tiny bit. It wasn't as easy as people made it look, but it wasn't as scary as she'd imagined, either. And really, what calamity could befall her when she was in waist-deep water and Luke was standing right there ready to assist? With her newfound confidence, she gave the board a larger stroke and quickly shifted again, pushing it forward.

"Okay," Luke said. "Now you need to turn or you're going to get in too shallow. Unless you're ready to quit."

"No. I'm good. How do I turn?"

"Paddle on one side until you get the board facing the direction you want to go. I'd suggest turning all the way around. Then you can go out a ways, turn again and head back in, and repeat the process until you're ready to take a break."

She nodded and shifted the paddle to her right side. That felt like the best option. She gave it a good shove, then another and another, and slowly, the board turned until she was facing the Gulf.

"I did it!" she said, unable to keep from grinning. "It's so cool up here. I can see everything in the water—the fish and seaweed. You were right about the view. It's a totally different perspective than the kayak."

"So worth the additional effort?"

"Definitely," she said, and started to paddle out.

And that's when she saw the tide in the distance.

"Oh no," she said. "There are waves coming."

Luke looked out and frowned. "Don't panic. Just head

straight for them and try to ride them out. You can still touch bottom, so you're fine."

She knew he was right but that didn't stop her from clenching as the first wave reached her board. Which had the exact opposite effect of what she desired. The stiffness caused her balance to shift more. She wobbled to the right, then left, and thought she'd saved it when the second wave hit and she tumbled off the board and into the ocean, crashing right on top of Luke.

The chilly water encompassed her as she flailed about in a tangle of arms and legs, trying to get back into a standing position. Strong arms circled her waist and pulled her up and she broke the surface, looking right into Luke's smiling face. Another wave hit her from behind and pushed her forward until every inch of her body was pressed into his. His grip around her tightened as they balanced for the next wave, and then everything went calm.

Except for her beating heart.

"Oh my God," she said. "I fell right on you. I'm so sorry."

"I'm not," he said, his voice low.

She knew he was going to kiss her, and she also knew she shouldn't let him. That she should pull away and avoid the letdown that was certain to come if she got involved with Luke Ryan. But her heart and body had pooled their resources to override her mind. His lips touched hers, softly at first, then more insistent. Warmth coursed through her and she moved her arms around him, feeling the muscles on his back rippling as he balanced them in the current.

He tasted of salt water and sunshine and when he parted her lips with his, she felt her whole body relax against his as his tongue touched hers in a slow, erotic dance. This was so much better than her dream. Her chest pressed tightly into his and even with only swimsuits on, the thought ripped through her mind that they were overdressed.

You have to stop.

Her mind broke into the moment, reminding her of the plan. Of her precarious position, especially when it came to emotional involvement and men. She removed her arms from around him and moved back enough to break contact. He released her immediately, sensing her discomfort.

"I'm sorry," he said. "I didn't mean to make you uncomfortable."

"You didn't. That's all on me. Look, I'm attracted to you, but I'm not in a place in my life where I can get involved. I've got things..."

His disappointment was clear, but he nodded. "I understand. And I won't try to change your mind. But I'd still like to remain friends. It seems we both need things to fill our time here, and it's nice to have company for dinner or an activity."

She let out a breath, filled with both disappointment and relief. "Friends. That would be great."

"Let's head in and get a drink of water to get rid of the salt," he said. "Then you can decide if you want to give it another try. The paddleboard, I mean."

"Of course. Sure." She reached down to release the paddleboard lanyard from her ankle and handed it to Luke, who secured the board.

As they walked to shore, she lagged a tiny bit behind, needing some time out of view of his piercing eyes and ready smile. Unfortunately, the view from the rear was just as tempting as the one from the front.

Keep your mind on the game.

And the game did not include frolicking with Luke Ryan.

No matter how much she wanted to.

———

Bea pushed her chair back from the table, looked over at Alayna, and let out a satisfied sigh. "That was the best meal I've had on this island in years. Hell, the best meal I've had since you moved."

Alayna smiled. Pleased that her aunt had enjoyed it so much.

"Seriously," Bea said. "Between working on my lawn today and eating three times what I should have, you might have to cart me home in a wheelbarrow. But I couldn't bring myself to stop. That was incredible."

"It wasn't a big deal," Alayna said.

Bea waved a hand in dismissal. "You're being modest. Seared steak with that rich buttery sauce and scallops, creamed corn—*real* creamed corn, not that shit in a can— those twice-baked potatoes that were so good they made me want to cry, and then you bring out blackberry tarts for dessert. I keep having to pinch myself to make sure it's not a lovely dream. You have a gift, Alayna."

Alayna warmed under her aunt's compliments, even though she hadn't been exaggerating about the ease of preparation. The meal had been a simple one for her, although she did recognize that wasn't the case for most people.

"You were always my biggest fan," Alayna said. "Have I told you lately how much I appreciate everything you've done for me? And everything you're doing for me now?"

Bea smiled. "I love you, honey. There's nothing I wouldn't do for you."

"Nothing?"

"Well, I probably wouldn't eat escargot or have a bikini waxing, but everything else is pretty much open."

Alayna laughed.

"It's good to hear you laugh," Bea said. "And I see you've got a nice tan starting. The pink part anyway. Can I assume you spent some time today enjoying this glorious weather and that beautiful water?"

"I did." Alayna fidgeted just a bit, not really wanting to get into her day with Bea because she knew right where her aunt would head with that information. But as Bea was also Luke's landlord and might find out through other means, she relented.

"Actually," Alayna said, "Luke taught me how to paddleboard."

Bea perked up. "Really? How did you like it?"

"I'm a little wobbly and I fell several times, especially when the waves picked up, but I can see why so many people are doing it. It's fun and it's great exercise. Plus there's the bonus of getting to work on my tan. How often do you get to say that?"

"Seems to me there's more of a bonus than tanning if you have Luke teaching you."

"Don't even go there. We're just friends."

"Good Lord, girl, no one's saying you have to hitch yourself to the man. Looking is still free, last time I checked. And if I had a partially clad Luke Ryan in front of me, I'd probably be looking so hard my eyes would bleed."

Alayna laughed. "Oh my God, Aunt Bea, you kill me."

"If you haven't noticed how good-looking that boy is, you might already be dead. Come on, take pity on your old aunt and tell me how he looks in swim trunks."

"Fine, but then you have to stop. I'll go with one word —perfection."

Bea sighed. "I haven't had a date in months and all I get out of you is 'perfection.' You're a real disappointment in the sexy-man-talk department."

"I don't see him that way."

"Were you blindfolded while you were paddleboarding?"

"Of course not. But I meant what I said. We're just friends."

"Uh-huh. I was reading an article in one of those trendy lady magazines at my hairdresser's the other day. It was talking about 'friends with benefits.' Sounded like a good deal to me."

The blush rushed up Alayna's neck and onto her face. "There will be no benefits to being friends with me except maybe the occasional good meal."

"That's *his* benefit. I was thinking more about what you're getting out of the deal."

"I got paddleboarding lessons. That's all I want."

Bea shook her head. "I'm still not convinced we're related. If I was thirty years younger…"

"Anyway," Alayna said, changing the subject, "since I enjoyed it so much, I was thinking about buying my own board. I need to keep up some regular exercise. The island doesn't have a gym and I'm not interested in driving to the mainland just to work out. I can run now but in a couple months, it will be a lot hotter and I won't want to."

"Paddleboarding *is* great exercise. I tried it myself a couple times."

"Really?"

"Yeah, didn't stick though. Too much effort for me, so I'll stick to my kayak. But if you want your own board, then talk to Mark at Island Surf Shop. He can recommend what's best for you, and he has new and used boards. You might be able to find a good used one and make a deal on it."

"A bargain sounds perfect about now. I'll check with him tomorrow."

Bea nodded and stared out at the surf for several silent

seconds. "When you come into town, stop by the bookstore for a minute. There's something I want to show you."

"You don't have a sexy new stock boy, do you?"

"Ha! I should be so lucky. No. It's just something I was thinking about doing and I wanted to get your opinion."

"Sure. I'm happy to do whatever I can. Do you need any help at the store?"

"No. It's pretty quiet now. Give it another month and we'll be hopping, but I have my summer girl lined up—just graduated from high school and looking to make some money before heading off to college this fall. Between her and Nelly, I'll be fine."

"I'm surprised a young person wants to spend the summer indoors."

"She's a bookworm, that one. And blushes if a boy passes within twenty feet of her. I'll probably make her cringe on a regular basis with the things that come out of my mouth, but she might as well get used to it. I doubt dorm room talk is rated G."

Alayna laughed. "Probably not."

"How are you doing otherwise?" Bea asked. "I know I said I wouldn't pry, but I want you to be happy here."

Alayna reached over and squeezed her aunt's hand. God, she loved this woman. "I'm getting there. I'm the closest to happy that I've been in a long time, anyway. I felt better as soon as I drove onto the island. And I believe things will continue to get better every day."

Bea sniffed and Alayna could see tears in the corner of her eyes. "That's all I can ask for," Bea said.

"Me too."

———

Mateo lowered his binoculars as the aunt pulled away from the house. He'd gotten bored sitting still and cruised out of the marina several times that day on the chance that Alayna might leave her cottage for the mainland for an outing with her aunt, since it was Sunday and the bookstore was closed. But she'd stayed there the entire day and then her aunt had arrived that evening. When he'd first seen the aunt's car pull up, he'd hoped they'd be going out to dinner on the mainland, which would give him a better opportunity to search the house, but no such luck. Given that Alayna was an elite-level chef, he supposed her sitting down for a long dinner at any of the local spots was more wishful thinking than anything. She could probably whip up better food in her kitchen in less time and for far less money.

He checked his watch and pulled out his cell phone. Time to check in.

The client answered on the first ring. "Anything?"

"No," Mateo said. "She stuck to the house all day. Had her aunt over tonight."

"She'll leave eventually for shopping on the mainland. The island is too expensive to keep buying basics there."

"Probably. There's something else. Something that might complicate things."

"What?"

"Not a what. A who. The guy who's renting the house next door has shown an interest in Alayna. Name is Luke Ryan."

"Some guy at the beach sniffing around a pretty woman is hardly a surprise and shouldn't be an issue."

"Normally, I would agree, but I'd bet anything Ryan is military. He's got a fairly recent knee injury. My guess is he's on medical leave or maybe even discharged, but I'd like to know what exactly his service involves."

"I'll find that out and get back with you. Is that it?"

The client barely waited for him to get the word 'yes' out of his mouth before disconnecting. Mateo could tell the client was irritated with him. He didn't want to waste time or resources on Ryan. But he couldn't see what Mateo saw. The way Ryan watched Alayna as she entered her home, refusing to move until she was safely inside. That wasn't just sexual attraction. If Ryan had developed feelings for her, even just protective ones, that could be a big problem. Especially if Alayna felt threatened. And as skittish as she was, he knew it wouldn't take much to push her to that ledge.

He started the boat and headed back to the marina. Alayna never went out after dark. He was calling it a night.

———

From his seat on his back patio, Luke heard Bea's car start and back out of the driveway. Apparently, dinner was over and Bea was calling it a night. He checked his watch: 9:00 p.m. Still early. He reached into the cooler and passed Pete another beer before tossing a hot dog weenie to Gus.

"He's going to have a stomachache," Pete said.

"Just him?" Luke asked. "You had a rib eye so big it didn't all fit on your plate and at least a gallon of potato salad. I'm not even counting cake slices."

"Yeah, but he doesn't have to clean up after me if I get sick."

"Good point." Luke looked down at the dog. "Sorry, big guy. No more weenies."

He could swear Gus gave him a woeful look.

"How did your knee hold up to paddleboarding?" Pete asked.

"No stiffness. No nerve pain."

Pete nodded. "That's good. Just make sure you don't

overdo, and when you exert yourself, ice it for twenty minutes afterward."

"Yes, Doctor."

"I don't know why I bother. You never listen to a thing unless it's a direct order from a superior."

"Technically, you outrank me, don't you?"

"A doctor versus a SEAL is apples to oranges. Besides, everyone treats you guys like gods."

"I only play one on missions," Luke said. "You're the actual life-or-death guy."

"Then maybe you should listen to me once in a while."

Luke grinned. "I hear everything you say."

Pete snorted. "You just ignore it."

"You just requested I listen. You didn't say anything about *doing* what you said. But stop your worrying. I iced the knee. I always do after a workout. Trust me, no one wants it back to normal more than me."

Pete frowned but didn't say anything.

"Look," Luke said, "I know that's never going to happen. Normal, that is. But sometimes I have this fantasy thought that if I can get it close enough, they'll reconsider."

"They can't take the chance. Every member of your team has to be 100 percent and as the team leader, you have to be 200 percent. There's no margin for error when other men's lives are on the line."

Luke sighed. "You think I don't know that? That I'd put my men at risk just to sate my own ego? I wouldn't do that, man. And I know what I'm looking at. I've read more about this type of injury than probably an entire medical school. I know the score. I'm just not ready to admit that there's never an exception."

Pete nodded. "I get that. And I don't blame you. If something happened that caused me to have to give up being a doctor, I don't know what I'd do. And even though I'd have options, they wouldn't be what I wanted. Everything else would feel less."

"Exactly. I know they'd love for me to be an instructor, but I don't know that I can do it—train other men to do the job that I want to do. It's probably selfish of me, but whatever. I'm not going to make excuses for how I feel about it. The entire situation sucks. I've been sitting on this sandbar for weeks now, and I'm no closer to an answer than I was the day I left Virginia."

"Well, if you ever want to talk things out...go over your options, you know I'm happy to help."

"I appreciate it."

"You have a lot to offer, Luke. Your experience is some-thing that can't be learned from a textbook, and if you can transfer that knowledge to the men in training, you make them better...safer."

Luke nodded. He appreciated Pete's words, and his friend was right, at least about part of it. Experience *was* ten times better than training and with every mission, Luke honed his skills and became a better soldier. But how could he convey that to others when a lot of it was instincts that you developed by being in the heat of the action?

"So, have you hit on that good-looking neighbor yet?" Pete asked.

The change of subject was so abrupt that Luke didn't have time to prepare. "What? No."

Pete narrowed his eyes at him, then laughed. "You have! You old dog. And?"

"And nothing. We're just friends."

"Man, that's sad. Did they remove anything else when they extracted that bullet?"

"Good common sense, maybe. Look, I made a move in that

direction but she's the one who put on the brakes. She's got troubles and she's not interested in additional complications."

"What kind of troubles could a chef possibly have? Ran out of oregano?"

"No. She had serious trouble back in New York." He told Pete about the run-in with Melody at the pizza joint and what he'd discovered with his subsequent internet search.

"Wow," Pete said when he finished. "That sucks. I guess I can't blame her for not wanting to get involved with anyone. Sounds like her boyfriend took her for a real ride."

"And I'm guessing it's not over. The FBI doesn't just let people walk away. Not if they think they can squeeze anything out of them."

"You think she's going to testify when he goes to trial?"

"Probably, although I'm not sure she knows all that much."

"Why do you say that?"

"Because the FBI would never have let her leave if she was a key witness. And they don't have anyone on her here."

"You sure about that?"

"You think I wouldn't have noticed? There's not exactly a lot of places to hide out here. I think I would have seen someone camping behind the dunes or following us on the one main road the island has. It sounds like the FBI has plenty on Patterson without her, but you know how it works. As long as they have her on the line, they can keep going back to that source as long as they need to."

"Even if it isn't yielding anything?"

Luke shrugged. "The Feds don't like to let a lead go, even if it's a dead-end one."

Pete studied him for a moment and frowned, but he didn't ask why Luke held that opinion about federal law enforcement. Luke was glad his friend had such a high level of discretion. He'd rather discuss his knee than explain his feelings about Feds.

"Have you asked her about it?" Pete asked.

"No. She's never mentioned it. Only that her restaurant closed and she didn't want to talk about it. I don't figure it's my place to bring it up and honestly, I can't blame her for not wanting to go over it again. She's probably here trying to get past it all."

Pete nodded. "I imagine the entire thing is mortifying. Especially since it played out in the media. And you know how they'll gloss over facts to go straight for the drama."

"Yeah. I can't even imagine how it was for her living in the city after all that went down. Losing her business and all the speculation about her character. And it doesn't sound like she had anyone helping her out, except her aunt, who was here. It must have been hell."

"Then it sounds like she can definitely use a friend. So I guess it's a good thing you're going to be one."

CHAPTER THIRTEEN

ALAYNA STROLLED OUT OF THE ISLAND SURF SHOP WITH A smile. Mark had been as accommodating as Bea had said he would be and had equipped her with the perfect paddleboard. Even better, it was barely used, but that had gotten her a 30 percent discount over new pricing. Because the board wouldn't fit in her car and she didn't have a luggage rack, Mark had offered to deliver it when he closed up the shop for the night. Since he wore a wedding band and she'd spotted a picture behind the desk of him with a pretty redhead and a cute little girl who looked like a combination of both of them, she took his offer as pure island hospitality or good service. Maybe both.

She crossed the street and headed for the bookstore, wondering once again what Bea wanted her advice on. She'd tried to get more out of her aunt the night before, but Bea had remained close-lipped on the matter, insisting that she needed to see it to understand the question. Maybe Bea was going to finally do something trendy, like add a coffee bar to the store. She had a simple machine on a table next to the front desk so that customers could have a cup while they searched the shelves, but Alayna had been pushing as long as she could remember for her aunt to add an espresso machine and maybe a few baked goods, and charge for it. After the initial investment into the machine, the profit margin on fancy coffee drinks was really good.

The store was quiet when Alayna entered, the bells over the door signaling her arrival. Her aunt was behind the counter, tapping on the computer and frowning. When she looked up and saw Alayna, her frown disappeared. Nelly, who was shelving some books near the desk, beamed when she saw Alayna and hurried over to give her a huge hug.

"Girl, you are prettier than ever," Nelly said. "I can't tell you how happy I am to see you. I've missed afternoon ice cream cones with you."

"We haven't gone for cones since I graduated from high school," Alayna said.

"Then I suppose we have a lot to make up for," Nelly said. "I'll expect you here at least once a week for cone day. Bea can give you my schedule."

Alayna smiled. "How are you, Nelly? And Harold?"

"I'm the same," Nelly said. "He's as ornery as ever."

"He has to live with you," Bea said. "What do you expect?"

"What are you talking about?" Nelly asked. "I'm a walking ball of love and light."

"Lord help," Bea said.

"Anyway," Nelly said, "we're doing just fine. How about you?"

"You look like you're in a good mood," Bea observed.

"That's because I just bought a paddleboard at a 30 percent discount," Alayna said.

Bea broke out into a smile. "Music to my ears. I told you Mark would take care of you. Where's the board?"

"He's delivering it tonight after he closes the shop," Alayna said.

Bea nodded. "He's such a nice young man. Such a shame everything that he's gone through."

"What happened to him?" Alayna asked.

Mark had seemed upbeat and excited about his shop and her interest in paddleboarding. If he had troubles, she certainly hadn't seen any sign of them.

"That pretty young wife of his died of breast cancer a year ago," Nelly said. "She was only twenty-eight years old. Their daughter, Lily, was only four."

Alayna's chest tightened and her heart broke for the store owner and his young daughter. "That's awful."

"He was a wreck for a long time but of course, he put on a good front for Lily," Bea said. "And he needed his business to stay afloat, so he couldn't afford to wallow much. We all chipped in to help, of course. Babysitting, taking him meals. Not me. You know I don't do babies or meals, but I minded his store for him for a bit and got Nelly to cover for me here."

"Since I'm not allergic to a stove, I took some meals," Nelly said. "It was a really hard time for a while."

Alayna shook her head. "I can't imagine. He seems so positive and happy. I never would have known..."

"Oh, he's better now," Nelly said. "Not recovered completely, but then I don't think one ever does recover completely from something like that."

"No. I guess they don't," Alayna agreed.

"But he's a good businessman and a great father," Bea said. "It was a benefit for the island when he decided to open his shop here. He and Lily live in an apartment above the shop. Before Beth died, they had a house on the mainland, but he figured this was a better option. Saves money and he has a sitter who comes in during business hours to keep Lily, but he's right downstairs if they need anything."

"He probably feels better living here after all the support the islanders gave him," Alayna said.

Bea nodded. "We take care of our own."

The bells above the door jangled, and Nelly gave her arm a squeeze before going up to greet the customers.

"So I'm dying to know what it is you want my advice on," Alayna said. "I'm really hoping you're finally going to put in that coffee station I keep trying to push on you."

"No. I'm still not interested in handling anything to do with food. You know me. I can't boil water without there being an issue. Just last week, I caught pizza rolls on fire in my toaster oven."

Alayna stared. "You didn't tell me that!"

Bea waved a hand in dismissal. "What were you going to do about it? The fire extinguisher took care of it and now I have a bit more space on my countertop, although I guess I should find something to cover the scorch mark."

"You're going to be the death of me," Alayna said. "Pizza rolls don't catch fire, you know. When was the last time you cleaned the bottom of the oven?"

"That's not relevant."

"Uh-huh." Alayna shook her head.

"Anyway, this isn't about my sketchy kitchen appliances."

"Or questionable cooking and cleaning skills."

"That either," Bea said. "Come upstairs with me."

Bea motioned to Nelly and the other woman nodded as Bea headed for the back of the store. Alayna fell in step next to her, and when they reached the stairs, Bea unlocked the small gate at the bottom that she'd installed to keep the younger patrons from bounding up. As far as Alayna knew, the space above the bookstore had always been office space leased out to an attorney. She'd only been there once before and had entered the offices through the stairs at the back of the building where there was a larger parking lot, not the inside staircase located in the bookstore. Briefly, she wondered if Bea thought Alayna needed legal representation. She hoped her aunt hadn't been worried about that. Her attorney in New York was handling everything. Alayna thought she'd made that clear.

When they reached the top of the stairs, Bea unlocked the double doors and pushed them open and Alayna could see that clearly things had changed. The office that had once contained rows of filing cabinets, shelves full of law books, and a copy machine that never seemed to stop running was now quiet and completely empty.

"What happened to the attorney?" Alayna asked.

"He bought a building on the mainland a couple months ago," Bea said. "He added a partner to handle real estate law and they needed more space than I had here. And it will be more convenient for clients to not have to make a trip out to the island. This space was fine when he was small and tended mostly to stuff for locals, but it wouldn't do for expansion."

"Have you listed it again?"

"No. I keep thinking I need to get to it. It's not doing anyone any good just sitting here, but then every time I start to write up the listing, I never quite finish it."

"Are you thinking about expanding the bookstore?"

"Not exactly." She gave Alayna a hard look. "I think this island could use a fine dining establishment. An intimate place with stellar food. And I know the perfect person to make that happen."

"Me?" Alayna shook her head. "I don't know that I ever want to own my own place again. And even if I did, I don't have the capital to do it."

"I do, and I can't think of a better investment."

"Bea, I can't take your money. You've already done so much —too much—and you have to think about retirement."

Bea waved a hand in dismissal. "You remember that old uncle of mine?"

"The one who kept a pet pig in his house and fired buckshot at anyone who pulled into his driveway?"

"Yeah, well, the old coot kicked it a couple years ago and he left me everything. I figured I'd be bulldozing that shack and eating bacon for a month, but that miser saved every dime he could. I used what I inherited to buy a property that I flipped, then bought another and flipped again, and well, I just sold off a storage facility last month. Made a good profit on it. I need to roll that money over into something. I can't think of someone better than you. Would have done it before but you insisted on doing it on your own."

Alayna held in a sigh. And look how that had turned out. If she'd borrowed money from Bea and not Warren, then she'd still have a restaurant. Maybe. Well, probably not. Warren's crimes had ruined her reputation to the point that the restaurant probably wouldn't have made it regardless. And then Bea's money would have been lost along with her own, so in the big scheme of things, not letting Bea invest had been the right decision.

Just like it was now.

"I just can't—" Alayna started.

Bea waved a hand in dismissal. "Knowing how your pride is, we could do it all aboveboard. I'd invest for a percentage interest. Then you'd be helping me with my retirement."

Alayna stared at her aunt, overwhelmed. "I don't know what to say. Your offer is incredible, but I can't allow you to take that risk with your money. If you'd invested in my restaurant in New York, it would have all been lost. Instead, you've managed to turn what you inherited into more. I don't want to be the one who ends your winning streak."

"What risk? Jesus, girl, you served me a meal last night unlike any I've had in years and then told me it was no big deal to make. If that was no big deal, then I sure as hell want to see what you come up with when you're putting in some effort."

"But fine dining? On the island?"

"It's high time we offer something besides fried seafood, burgers, and pizza. Sometimes adults want a nice night out where there's table linens instead of paper. And it wouldn't be just the islanders who'd come. Once word gets out, all the mainlanders will be clamoring for reservations. I meant it when I said you had a gift."

"I don't think I'm ready. I don't know that I ever will be."

"That's fear talking. And after all you've been through, I understand. But you're not just a chef. You're an artist. Can you honestly tell me you'd be happy whipping up someone else's recipes for the rest of your life? Following someone else's orders on offerings, presentation, decor, and pricing?"

Alayna frowned. Bea had hit on the very things that had her hesitating every time she thought about contacting local restaurants about a job. Could she follow someone else's menu —just cook the food and never question or ask for change?

Bea gave her arm a squeeze. "Anyway, you don't have to decide today. I paid this building off years ago. It's not costing me a dime for this space to sit here while you think about it. But the storage sale profit just needs to be reinvested by year-end so I can avoid a huge tax bill. So either you get the benefit of the money or the IRS does."

"You're playing dirty."

Bea grinned. "Whatever works. Give it some thought. Take all the time you need. But I'm right about this. It could be a great thing for you, me, and everyone else."

Alayna looked around at the space. It was sectioned off into offices, but the walls weren't load bearing and could be easily removed. The brick from the outside was carried inside and she knew from the exterior view that windows ran across the front and back of the building. The space had character, historical character. The kind that lent itself to a fine dining establishment.

But could she do it again? Put herself out there that way?

And what about her reputation? If Melody Whitmore knew of Alayna's disgrace, then she could only assume that everyone else on the island did as well. Would they believe her innocent, or would they assume she'd been in on everything and simply gotten away with it? And even if they didn't think her guilty, would the taint of Warren's crimes prevent people from giving her a chance?

It was a huge risk. And an expensive one for her aunt.

"I'll think about it," she said, mainly because nothing else would be acceptable to Bea. But she already knew there was no way she could gamble Bea's retirement dollars on her sketchy reputation.

Bea beamed. "Good girl. I knew you'd be intrigued. Now, let's put the *Be Right Back* sign on the door, head out with Nelly, and get an ice cream cone. I've been wanting one all day."

As Bea walked away, Alayna gave the space one last look. It *was* perfect. She could already picture it in her mind. Kitchen on the east wall. Polished cherrywood tables with crisp white linens. Two-tops interspersed with four-tops, with the prime seating lining the windows. No large parties. Just couples and foursomes looking for an intimate meal in a classy setting. A huge chandelier in the center and candle sconces on the walls.

She sighed and pushed the vision aside. It was a nice dream, but that's all it could be.

———

BEA WAVED AT ALAYNA AS SHE DROVE AWAY, THEN WENT into the bookstore carrying a bag of cookies from the ice cream shop. She didn't need the extra calories, but the sugar cookies smelled so good baking that Bea couldn't resist grabbing a dozen on the way out. Despite having just consumed an ice cream cone, Nelly eyed the bag as she walked up to the counter. She pulled a cookie out of the bag and passed it to her friend.

"If it wasn't so hot, I'd hug you," Nelly said.

"You could be standing naked in the middle of the Arctic and still be hot."

"True. And I know I just had ice cream, but boy these smelled so good." Nelly took a bite of the cookie and closed her eyes.

"Yeah, the smell got me too, but why I bought a dozen, I don't know. You're going home with some of these."

"You don't have to twist my arm." Nelly inclined her head toward the stairs. "Do you think she'll go for it?"

Bea shook her head. "I don't know. She said she'll think about it, but I'm pretty sure she was just humoring me."

"You think she's afraid that people are talking?"

"Maybe. Probably. Hell, people *are* talking. Have been since this crap hit the news. You think I haven't seen the side-eye and heard the whispers when I walk in a room? But no one has the balls to just come right out and mention it. Except Veronica, of course."

Nelly frowned. "No one has mentioned anything?"

"Oh, people ask how Alayna is doing, like they don't know anything. Fishing for information. But no one will come right out and ask the question they want to ask, which is was she in on it."

"Surely people don't think so. I mean, even the FBI said she was a victim and a witness."

"And I think that's what most people believe, but there's always a handful of assholes in any community."

Nelly snorted. "There's a handful here just counting the Whitmores."

"That's true enough."

"Come on, Bea. You don't think the gleeful gossip of some hoity-toity snobs would make a difference, do you? People don't even like the Whitmores."

"Maybe not, but they have a lot of pull in this town. Them being against Alayna having a restaurant might be enough for some to stay away in order to avoid crossing them."

"Maybe at first," Nelly agreed, "but once word gets out about the food, don't you think that would change?"

"Of course. I think when word gets out, Alayna would have reservations stretched as far as the calendar would process them. But Alayna is still raw, so the talk matters. This whole mess has taken a real toll on her."

"She's strong enough to handle it. Look how well she did after her parents passed."

Bea shook her head. "That was different. She didn't feel guilty about their death. Didn't feel responsible. She blames herself for not seeing what kind of man Warren was."

"That's ridiculous. He was a con man. Look how long he flew under the FBI's radar. Alayna's smart and talented, but she's a chef, not a cop. What in the world does she think she should have seen?"

"I know and I said as much to her, but you and I both know that sometimes things cut so deeply they hit a vein. It's hard to be objective when you're bleeding out. I think she can be all right after a while, but as long as the trial is hanging over her head, I think it's going to be tough to put it all behind her."

Nelly sighed. "She's afraid the other shoe will drop."

Bea nodded. "And who knows how long it will take to go to trial. It could be years. She can't live in limbo that long. No one could."

Nelly took Bea's hand and gave it a squeeze. "She'll figure that out eventually. And she's going to be fine. You'll see. Everything is going to work out, even if we have to ramrod the whole situation into submission."

Bea smiled. "That's why I love you."

"Of course you do."

Bea studied her friend for a moment. "Do you ever wish you'd done it—had kids?"

"Since Harold and I didn't meet and marry until we were in our forties, I'm going to go with a hard no on that one."

Bea waved a hand in dismissal. "I don't mean specifically. I was just musing the 'in theory' thing. What if you and Harold had met in your twenties?"

"Then he would have still had a full head of hair and I wouldn't have known about that genetic flaw that some poor kid would have had to deal with."

"I'm pretty sure hair comes from your mother. And you're not answering my question."

Nelly scrunched her brow for a bit, then shook her head. "No. I don't think age would have made a difference. You know I love my niece to pieces and her daughter is a joy, but just spending an afternoon with her is enough to exhaust me physically and mentally. I don't think I would have been good at it full time. I'm a much better aunt."

Bea nodded. "I can see that. I like other people's kids in small doses, but I don't think I would have liked someone there all the time, needing something."

Nelly laughed. "You won't have a husband for the same reason. I can't even imagine you with a baby. You're lucky Alayna came housebroken."

"God, isn't that the truth? I can barely get the packing tape gun to work right, and I've been using the damned thing for forty years. I don't even want to know what kind of mess I'd have made of diapers."

"Let's just be glad you didn't have to try. But Bea, you *are* a mother. At least, in your heart, where it matters."

"I suppose I am. But it's times like this I really miss my sister. I keep thinking she would have known better how to handle this or if she hadn't died, maybe it wouldn't have happened at all."

Nelly grabbed Bea's hand and squeezed. "Don't you even think like that. You've done a fine job with Alayna. This mess is no one's fault except that criminal, and when it's all over, our girl will come out on top. I just know it. Your sister was a wonderful woman, but she wasn't a superhero any more than you are."

The bells on the door jangled and Nelly hurried off. Bea took a big bite out of a cookie and looked out the window at the people strolling down the street. They all looked happy, and why shouldn't they be? Some were on vacation. Others were on a day trip from the mainland. They'd left their cares behind and were enjoying their lives in this little strip of paradise.

Bea prayed that one day Alayna could do the same.

CHAPTER FOURTEEN

ALAYNA WAVED AT MARK AS HE DROVE AWAY, THEN TURNED to admire her new paddleboard before hefting it up and carrying it to the back of the house. Mark had offered to tote it for her, but she'd refused, telling him she might as well get used to carrying it around or she wouldn't be using it very often. She placed it on its side against the house, figuring no one would bother it and she didn't want to have to haul it in and out of the storage shed each day. Maybe she'd get some of those brackets that allowed you to hang it on a wall. If Bea was okay with it, of course.

As she turned around, she spotted Luke walking out of the surf onto the shore. It looked like a scene from a James Bond movie. The man was simply gorgeous. And just one glance sent her heart racing into overdrive and other parts of her revving their engines.

Friends, remember?

He looked up, caught sight of her, and lifted his hand in a wave. She waved back because anything else would be rude. At least, that's what she told herself. But the smile as he approached crept involuntarily onto her face and her tingling body belied her carefully laid plans.

"I got a board," she said, gesturing to the turquoise-and-white board leaning against the house.

"That's great," he said and smiled. "So I guess you really enjoyed it. You weren't just saying so to make me feel good."

"Oh, I would never do that."

"Make me feel good?"

The blush crept up her neck and she rushed to explain. "No. I mean, I would never say I liked something when I didn't mean it. Well, that's not entirely true. If you were wearing a completely hideous shirt but were on your way to a funeral and asked me how you looked, I'd say you looked great."

His smile broadened. "You've really thought this out."

"I have a tendency to overthink things. Some people find it annoying."

"Only some?"

"Okay, most. But you don't have to rub it in."

He laughed. "That's a good-looking board. Great brand. And good for flat water or a bit of surf."

"That's what Mark said—the guy who owns Island Surf Shop."

Luke nodded. "I know Mark. I mean, as well as you know someone you've talked to a time or two. I like his shop and he's really informed on his equipment. When it comes to sporting goods, I prefer to deal with someone who has intimate knowledge of his product and he fits the bill."

"He's definitely enthusiastic about paddleboarding and surfing. I think he wishes we had bigger surf here."

"Mark was a pro surfer for a few years and was on the fast track to top tier. Then he had a bad wipeout during a practice and never went back. I don't know why exactly and it's not the sort of thing you ask."

"No. I don't suppose you do. It doesn't surprise me that he was a pro. He sounds wistful when he talks about Hawaii."

"We chatted about surfing at the North Shore for a bit. When the big surf is rolling in, it's definitely a different experience."

"I think I'd be scared to death to get in it. I've seen competitions on television, and I'm amazed at the size of the waves. It's a wonder more people aren't injured."

"Most of the best grew up on the water. They know how to handle getting out of the big waves and they can hold their breath for far longer than the average person. In the pro ranks, at least. But every year, someone who thinks he's ready and isn't gives the big ones a try. The outcome usually isn't what they're hoping it to be."

"I think I'll stick to being a spectator."

"Maybe one day you'll take a trip there. See one of the competitions in person. Maybe even the Eddie."

"That would be awesome, but timing would have to be perfect for me to just happen to be there when the waves just happened to be high enough for the event to be called. Have you ever been?"

He nodded. "I was there in 2016. It's an incredible event. A once-in-a-lifetime sort of thing. Unless you live there, of course. I was stationed there for a while and kept hoping it would happen and I would be able to get away when it did. I got lucky."

"I'll bet that was something to see. If you were stationed there, then you're used to the big surf. You must find the surf here underwhelming."

"If I were cleared to surf, I might, but since that's not an option right now the surf here is just fine. Besides, the beach is beautiful. The sand's the whitest I've ever seen and with the crystal-clear water and lack of tourists, it's bordering on perfect."

"Just bordering?"

"Well, at the moment I could use a cold beer. That would make it a perfect ten."

She laughed. "I could get you a cold beer, but I was about to make myself a frozen margarita and sit outside for a bit, enjoying this afternoon breeze. If you don't have plans for the evening, you could rescue me from drinking the entire blender of margaritas by myself."

"I wouldn't want to put you in danger that way. I suppose I'll have to do my part by consuming a drink or two."

"Would you like to come inside while I make them?"

"No. I don't want to track water and sand all over your house. I'll just wait out here."

"Okay. I'll be back in a few."

She popped inside, her heart beating entirely too rapidly for it to just be the heat. What had she been thinking, waving to him, inviting him for drinks? She'd told him they could only be friends, but she felt as if she were sending mixed signals. No. That was stupid. A woman and a man could have a margarita together without it meaning they were going to jump into bed.

Good Lord! Where had that come from?

She tossed the ingredients in the blender and fired it up, then busied herself by arranging some cheese, crackers, and fruit on a plate. Might as well have a snack with the drinks. The only thing she'd had that resembled lunch was the ice cream, but she hadn't felt like cooking when she got home. Some yogurt and granola would probably top off her night before she called it bedtime. She shook her head. What an exciting life she led.

It could be exciting. If you gave your sexy neighbor a chance.
No. No. No.

That line of thought simply wouldn't do. She grabbed the plate of snacks and hauled it outside, then hurried back in and snagged the pitcher of margaritas and two glasses. Luke was snacking on a cracker and cheese when she stepped back outside.

"This is great cheese," he said. "What kind is it?"

"That one is blue cheese. The island market has a decent supply of groceries, but I still need to get over to the mainland for a bigger shopping trip."

She poured the drinks and pushed a glass over to Luke. He lifted it and took a big drink.

"This is great. Man, before you came, I drank beer and ate chips out of the bag. You've really classed the place up."

She laughed. "I don't think you were breaking any rules with your beer and chip habit. That's sort of the norm here."

He nodded. "It's definitely a casual vibe. The day I arrived on the island, I thought it was beautiful, but the lack of noise bothered me. I was used to hearing men training, planes overhead, equipment moving...not that it's completely silent here but it's quiet, you know?"

"I do. Compared to New York, the island is on mute."

"The better to relax in, right?"

"That's what they say. How's that going for you?"

"It gets a little better every day. A Navy buddy of mine is vacationing just down from us right now and we've been able to get together. And since you've arrived, I've gotten to distract myself with moving boxes and paddleboards."

"And accosting women in storage sheds with a gun."

He laughed. "That story is never going to die, is it?"

"Doubt it. Aunt Bea will keep it going for years. You'll be a legend on the island before she's done. One of those tales told over a campfire and s'mores."

"Not the sort of thing one wishes to be famous for."

"It could be worse," she said, her thoughts flashing to Warren. "At least in that tale, you're not the villain."

"Why not? I could have given you a heart attack."

"The way Bea sees it, you're nothing short of her personal bodyguard, ensuring her property is protected from the nefarious among us."

"That's because it wasn't her that I accosted. She might feel differently if she was the one who'd had a gun held on her."

"She'd feel differently if she was the one who'd seen you in your boxers. I've got news for you—she wouldn't have tried to get away."

He looked a little afraid. "Ah...wow. I'm not sure what to say to that."

"You should be flattered. Bea's picky. It's part of the reason why she's never married. And maybe you should be just a little scared. Well, scared enough to have a shirt handy when she's around. I think she's made me describe that scene to her ten times already."

"Seriously?"

Alayna nodded. "She thinks it sounds like the opening to a Hallmark movie."

He grimaced. "Those cheesy love stories?"

"I can tell by your expression that you've seen one."

"More than one. My doctor loved that channel. She'd turn it on in my room every time she came to change my dressing or do some PT on my knee."

"Why didn't you tell her to put on something else?"

"She outranked me."

Alayna laughed. "I guess recovery in a military hospital gives a whole new meaning to the phrase 'following doctor's orders.'"

"It *is* a different sense of urgency."

"So I guess since you're renting the cottage, you aren't stationed here."

"Not officially. I'm a bit in between at the moment. I've been stationed a couple different places—Hawaii, as I said before, and most recently Virginia. But I'm deployed out of the country a lot of the time."

"That must be hard."

He shrugged. "Not really. With no family to worry about me or count the days until my return, I've got an advantage over most."

She frowned. What he said made sense, of course, but it bothered her. Was there really no one in his life wondering if he was all right? Waiting for him to step onto American soil again? She couldn't imagine being that alone. Granted, she didn't have a husband or kids and no extended family to speak of, but she'd always had Bea. And Bea had managed to fill the shoes of so many people that Alayna had never felt adrift. What motivated a person who had no one standing behind them cheering? And without the voice of experience ringing in their ears, how did they remain grounded? Except for his obvious state of flux because of his injury, Luke appeared to be a man who had his life together. A man who knew what he wanted.

Before she could change her mind, she blurted out, "I was thinking of whipping up a quick chicken fettuccine for dinner. Would you be interested in joining me?"

He looked a little surprised at her invitation but quickly recovered. "There is no way I'm turning down an offer of a home-cooked meal prepared by a professional chef. Especially when my plan was opening a can of chili and dumping it over Fritos."

"I think I can do better, although I do love a good Frito pie."

"I'd like to shower first, though. Do I have time?"

"Plenty. Let's finish the margaritas and then I'll start dinner. By the time you're done with your shower, it will be close to ready."

"Perfect."

He lifted his glass and she clanked hers against it. Thirty minutes later, they'd polished off the last of the margaritas and he'd headed over the dune for his shower. Alayna brought the glasses and empty snack tray inside, got them situated in the dishwasher, and then grabbed the ingredients for the fettuccine. She seasoned the chicken and set it to cook before hurrying into the bathroom to check herself in the mirror.

Her recently acquired sun had turned her skin a light pink that would probably brown nicely over the next couple days. Her hair was another story, though. The Gulf breeze and humidity had the slight wave that she always fought against paying her a visit. That meant shorter new growth whirled around her face without rhyme or reason, making it look as if she'd just spent the past hour jogging or digging a ditch.

She ran a brush through it, then tried to pull it back into a ponytail, but the waves wouldn't cooperate. Instead it looked even messier. Throwing her hands up in surrender, she elected to yank the ponytail holder out, then leaned over and fluffed it all up. The beach-blown look was the island norm, so it would have to do because there was no time for her to wash and style it. She headed back into the kitchen, shaking her head. Her hair shouldn't matter. She wasn't interested in pursuing anything beyond a friendship with Luke.

Who do you think you're fooling?

She stopped short as the words echoed in her mind. What was she doing? Inviting him to drinks, then dinner? Every time she told herself that she couldn't afford to get involved with Luke on any basis other than casually, she ended up spending more time with him. And now, she was worried about her appearance—something she hadn't given much thought to in months.

In a way, she supposed it was a good thing in that she was still capable of these kind of feelings. It showed she was healing. But on the other hand, her attraction to Luke had hit her without warning and also scared the hell out of her. She'd spent years focusing on her training, then on building her reputation as a chef, rarely dating, and when she did, only casually. Then she'd met Warren and had settled into something exclusive even though it hadn't crossed the line into serious. And look how badly that had turned out.

Epically bad.

She went through the motions of preparing dinner as if on autopilot, and she supposed she was. Fettuccine was something she could do in her sleep. Maybe she should have chosen something more difficult. Something that required her to concentrate so that she didn't spend all her time thinking about how much Luke Ryan pulled at her.

A knock on the patio door broke her out of her thoughts and she looked over and waved Luke inside.

"It's almost ready," she said. "I set everything up inside, if that's okay? The breeze has died down and I'm afraid the flies will want to join us if we try to eat out back."

"If that tastes as good as it smells, I'll eat it standing right here," he said as he stepped into the kitchen.

"You can bet it does, but the kitchen table is a sight better than standing. Plus, it has all that extra room to hold things like salad and garlic bread."

"You made garlic bread, too? This might be the best night I've spent on the island."

"Don't take this the wrong way, but you're kind of easy."

He grinned. "I can honestly say I've never had a woman tell me that before. But then, I've never had a woman cook me a meal fit for a king either."

"You might want to hold out on an opinion until you've tasted it. If you'll open the wine, I'll get this right out."

He removed the bottle from the ice bucket and opened it with the corkscrew on the counter. Alayna peeked in the oven and decided the garlic bread was perfect.

"Can you pass me a pot holder?" she asked. "The drawer right in front of you."

He passed her a turquoise pot holder, and she pulled the garlic bread out of the oven and placed it on the stove, the smell already making her mouth water. When she looked over at Luke, he was holding a second pot holder, giving it a once-over.

"This seems a bit out of place in a beach cottage in May," he said.

The pot holder was covered with white, red, green, and gold sequins that formed a Christmas tree and presents. There were a couple of bare spots where some of the sequins had come off and the edges showed definite signs of age.

Alayna stared at it for a couple seconds, then realized she'd never responded. "It belonged to my mother. Every year on Christmas Eve, she pulled out her 'magic' pot holder and we made sugar cookies for Santa."

"Just Santa? Seems like a rip-off."

She smiled. "My dad had a fondness for them as well, which made a lot of sense once I figured out that whole Santa thing."

She took the pot holder from him and ran one finger down the worn sequins. "It was a special day and out of all the years I had with my parents, it's the memory that's always the most vivid. Sometimes I even dream about it."

"That's an awesome thing to have," he said quietly. "The pot holder and the memory."

"It is. And it's gone with me everywhere—culinary school, New York, and now back to the island."

She handed it back to him and he looked down at it and smiled before putting it back in the drawer.

"Are you ready to eat?" she asked.

"You have to ask?"

She plated the fettuccine as Luke poured the wine, and they carried the food to the tiny kitchen table. Luke ignored the salad completely and went straight for the fettuccine, stuffing an enormous bite into his mouth. She watched, waiting for the verdict. He closed his eyes and chewed, swallowed, then looked at her and sighed.

"This is delicious," he said. "The best I've ever had, and one of my Navy buddies is Italian and loves to cook. But don't tell him I said that. He's a sniper."

"Ha. Yeah, I'll keep that to myself."

She looked across the table at him, unable to keep from smiling. Until that moment, she hadn't realized just how important his opinion was. His words had bolstered her confidence in a way that Aunt Bea couldn't. With all his traveling with the military, Luke had probably been able to sample cuisine from all over the world. The fact that he'd proclaimed her fettuccine the best he'd ever had was a real boost to her ego. And right now, her ego could use all the boosting it could get.

"Seriously," he said, "this is incredible. Bea told me you were a gifted chef. I figured she loves you so she had to say that, but she wasn't exaggerating. I can't believe how quickly you put together something that tastes this good."

"Thank you."

"Don't thank me. You earned the compliments. Now, pass

me that garlic bread so I can proceed to make a pig out of myself."

She laughed and handed him the plate. Completely relaxed, she took a bite of salad and they proceeded to work through the food, the conversation light and easy topics like movies they'd seen and her recounting tales of her mischievous fox terrier that she'd had when she was a young child. When they were both stuffed, Luke insisted on helping her clear the kitchen.

"It's a rule," he said. "If you do no work to prepare a great meal, you have to do the cleanup."

"I think that's fair," she said.

They made quick work of the dishes and just as Alayna closed the dishwasher, a clap of thunder sounded overhead. She gave a bit of a start at the unexpected noise.

"I didn't think it was supposed to rain," she said.

"Let's go take a look."

They headed onto the back patio and glanced up at the angry clouds overhead. The wind was already picking up, and she could see a line of rain off the coast.

"Looks like a strong one," Luke said.

Alayna nodded. "Better check the weather report. I might need to turn over the patio furniture."

She went to the living room and turned on the TV to the news. If a big storm was brewing, the local weather station would break in with the details. Commercials were currently playing so they stood there waiting. Luke was so close that she could feel the heat coming off of him. A second boom sounded overhead, and a burst of lightning flashed through the window, causing the lights to blink. She turned to the side and shot a nervous glance out the patio doors.

Luke looked down at her, his eyes searching hers. "I was hoping the night might end with fireworks, but this is a bit more than I imagined. And I know what you said yesterday about only being friends, but you've got to know that my attraction to you is more than just friendly."

Heat coursed through her body. She knew that look. Any woman of a certain age knew that look, and when it was wanted, it set every inch of skin to tingling. And Lord, was it wanted.

He took a step closer to her, so that his chest was practically touching hers. "If you feel the same, just say the word."

"I...uh." What the hell. She tilted her head up toward his and inched closer.

He didn't even hesitate before lowering his lips gently to hers. She leaned into him and he parted her lips with his, deepening the kiss. He wrapped his arms around her and pulled her tightly against him. She ran her hands up his back, his muscles rippling beneath her fingertips. He responded to her touch by dropping his lips to her neck, and she sighed with pleasure.

"Breaking news out of New York." The television cut into her thoughts. "Multimillionaire Warren Patterson III has escaped from FBI custody during a transfer. Three men are dead at the scene, one an FBI agent whose identity has not been released."

CHAPTER FIFTEEN

BLOOD RUSHED FROM ALAYNA'S HEAD AND THE ENTIRE ROOM tilted. Luke's grip was the only thing that prevented her from crashing onto the floor.

"Alayna!" Luke's voice sounded like a distant echo. "Are you all right?"

She felt him moving her across the living room floor and then he lowered her onto the couch and sat beside her.

"Alayna?" He spoke again, his anxiety clear. "I'm going to call for the paramedics."

She shook her head. No paramedics. She just needed to breathe. One breath in. Another out. A breath in. Repeat slowly.

Luke placed his hands on each side of her face and turned her head to face him. His eyes searched her, looking for an indication that she was all right.

"You're white as a sheet," he said. "If you don't say something, I'm going to call."

"Don't," she finally managed, although it came out as a whisper.

"Stay here," he said and headed into her kitchen.

He returned quickly with a small glass of the whiskey she'd picked up because it was Bea's favorite. He lifted the glass to her lips, and she took a sip, then clutched the glass and took another. Her hands shook as she lifted the glass and Luke placed his over hers to steady them. Finally, the room stopped spinning, but her mind was still whirling from what she'd heard.

"I'm sorry," she said. "I didn't mean...I'm fine. I just need to go to bed."

Luke looked at her as if she were crazy. "No way I'm leaving. Look, I know about Patterson. I read it online."

Tears welled up, and she tried to choke them back but couldn't. Mortified, she swiped her hand at the traitorous drops as they ran down her cheeks. She shouldn't be surprised. After that run-in with Melody at the pizza place, Luke had probably googled her. She couldn't blame him. Given the cryptic things Melody said, she would have done the same thing. But it didn't lessen the humiliation.

"I don't want you involved in my mess," she said. "Just go back to your house and forget you ever met me. You don't need this."

"You don't need it either. I already told you I wasn't leaving. So you might as well get used to me sticking around. I'm not the kind of guy who takes off at the first sign of trouble. In fact, it's the opposite. I run right toward it."

Her chest tightened and she struggled with the overwhelming desire to have him at her side while she tried to make sense of this and the right thing to do, which was turn him loose to go on with his life, unencumbered with her baggage.

He must have sensed her issue because he enclosed her hand in his. "Look, I can either go to my house and sit there worrying all night, or I can stay here and help you deal with this. Either way, you're going to be the only thing on my mind, but if you let me stay, at least I won't feel useless."

"I don't know what to say. How to thank you."

"I'm drawn to you, Alayna. I know we haven't known each other for very long, but there's something between us that goes further than just attraction. I don't want your thanks. I want to help. To do what I'm trained to do. You need support right now. I know you have Bea, but take it from the guy who had no one for far too long, more is better."

So many emotions flooded through her that she couldn't think. She wanted Luke there. Wanted his friendship and his support. Wanted his strong arms to prop her up if she buckled. But more than anything, she was filled with fear. What if Agent Davies had been wrong? What if Warren was coming for her?

"Agent Davies," she said. "I need to call him."

"Is that your contact with the FBI?"

She nodded and glanced around the room, looking for her phone. Luke jumped up and snagged it off the kitchen counter, then handed it to her.

Her hands shook as she listened to the phone ring and at first, she thought he wasn't going to answer. Then a horrible thought coursed through her mind. What if Agent Davies was the agent who'd died at the scene? She was just about to disconnect when he answered, and she let out a breath of relief.

"Agent Davies, thank God!" she said. "The news...they said an agent died."

"That's correct. A young agent. Shouldn't have happened."

She could hear the frustration and anger in his voice.

"How did it happen? Did you catch Warren yet?"

"We were intercepted during transport. We suspect the

two other men killed at the scene worked for Rivera. Unfortunately, Warren is in the wind."

Another wave of dizziness passed over her as the very nightmare she'd been praying to avoid came crashing into her reality.

"What do I do?" she asked.

"Stay put," Davies said. "Rivera didn't break Warren out to do him any favors. You don't have to worry about him coming after you."

"I see," Alayna said, still not convinced.

"Look. Everything with you remains the same," Davies said, sounding frustrated. "I'll contact you tomorrow, but right now the doctor is insisting I put down the phone so he can bandage my arm."

"Were you injured?"

"Just a graze. I'll be in touch tomorrow."

The call disconnected and Alayna stared at her phone for several seconds before lifting her gaze to Luke. She gave him the sparse information she'd gotten from Agent Davies.

"He insisted Warren won't come after me," she said.

"He's probably right. I don't think Rivera took this risk to reinstate Patterson as his investment adviser."

She nodded. She'd already known the implications as soon as Agent Davies told her Rivera was behind the escape. "They're going to kill him so he can't give the FBI evidence."

"That would be my guess."

"Then why didn't they just do it there? It would have been easier and maybe none of Rivera's men would have gotten killed."

"Because they'll want to know what Patterson's already told the FBI. See how big the cleanup needs to be."

"Oh." She felt her back loosen a tiny bit. "That makes sense. I'm sorry. It's just that this is the beginning of the recurring nightmare I've had since this whole thing started. Even though the FBI assured me that I'm of no concern to Warren, I've lived in constant fear that he would escape and come after me. I know, it's not rational. I never knew anything about what Warren was doing and don't have much to offer in the way of testimony. I've been told I'm in the clear by practically everyone in law enforcement and the DA's office, but I can't shake the feeling that something is still off."

"To hell with rational, the FBI, and the DA's office. I'd be worried about you if you *weren't* scared."

A small smile crept onto her face. "To hell with rational. I think that's going to be my new motto."

"Look. You went through a horrible thing. Someone you trusted not only betrayed you but cost you your business and landed you right in the middle of a federal investigation. If you feel something, then you feel it. And you shouldn't ignore it. Maybe you're overacting. But what if you're not?"

"You think Warren could come after me?"

"Not necessarily. Based on my understanding of how things went down, I tend to agree with the FBI's take on it. But that doesn't change my advice. If you ever feel uneasy...like something is off, pay attention. Write it down. What you were doing, where you were, how you felt. It never hurts to be careful, even if it's not warranted."

She blew out a breath. "You're right. I've been beating myself up about the weird feelings I get sometimes, putting it down to my paranoia. I just need to give myself more time. Writing it down is a good idea. It might help me organize those feelings so that I can get past them."

Before Luke could comment, there was a loud knock at the front door. She saw him reach for his waist and figured he was involuntarily going for the weapon that wasn't there.

"Alayna! It's Bea!" Her aunt's voice sounded through the door.

"I'll get it," Luke said, and hurried to the door.

Bea rushed in, dripping wet from the storm, some of the curlers in her hair dangling at the end of the now-unwrapped locks. She wore her bathrobe, no shoes, and was clutching a pistol in her right hand. She shoved the gun at Luke before going to gather Alayna in her arms.

"Honey, I saw the news and ran out. Are you all right?"

"I'm okay."

Bea glanced at Luke, apparently not convinced. "Have you talked to those idiots at the FBI?" she asked. "They screwed the pooch on this one."

"One of the agents died," Alayna said. "I'm sure that's not what they wanted."

"Then they should have done a better job," Bea said. "I'm sorry for that agent and his family, but they're supposed to be the experts. What are they doing about you?"

Alayna shook her head. "Nothing."

"Nothing!" Bea jumped off the couch and threw her arms in the air. "What the hell are we paying taxes for? They put you in the middle of their mucked-up investigation and now that they've managed to let that lunatic loose, they're doing nothing? I swear to God no one does their job anymore."

"They said I'm not in danger," Alayna said. "And they're probably right."

"Probably," Bea repeated. "And what if they're wrong? You'll move in with me until they get this mess straightened out. I don't like you out here alone. It's too remote."

"No," Alayna said immediately. If there was any chance that Warren was coming after her, no way was she putting Bea in danger. "I'm fine here. The men that Warren was working for took him. I don't think...it's not good for Warren."

Bea stared at her for several seconds, then her expression cleared in understanding. "I see. Well, I'm still calling tomorrow about getting an alarm system for this house."

"I don't want you to go to the expense," Alayna said.

"It's a good idea," Luke said.

"How is that?" Alayna asked. "Do you really think an alarm would stop someone like Juan Rivera? He just took on the FBI to get to Warren. I'm no challenge at all."

"An alarm would send me over here with a weapon," Luke said. "And I *am* a challenge."

Bea took her pistol from Luke and put it in Alayna's lap. "Keep this."

Alayna shook her head. "I can't take your gun. You need it."

"I've got three other pistols and two shotguns," Bea said. "This *is* the South."

"I keep finding more reasons to like you," Luke said.

"Likewise," Bea said. "Especially if you're going to look out for my niece."

"He was ready to take me down over your patio furniture, remember?" Alayna pointed out.

"Good," Bea said. "But he's off duty tonight. Me and my trusty nine-millimeter are on the job."

Alayna shook her head. "No. You should go home and go to bed. You have to open the store tomorrow."

"Wouldn't get a wink even if I tried," Bea said. "All I'd do is sit there worrying. Might as well sit here where at least I can see you and therefore diminish the worrying part of the equation."

Alayna knew it was useless to argue. Bea had that tone that she took when she had decided no one had a choice. And she also knew her aunt was right. Neither of them was likely to get much sleep, and even though she didn't want to admit it, having her aunt and her trusty nine-millimeter there with her would make her feel better.

"I can stay too," Luke said.

Bea shook her head. "We'll be fine. You're a phone call and a short run away. I'll take care of her."

Luke nodded. "If there's anything you need. Anything at all, call. Doesn't matter what time."

"Thank you," Alayna said. "I'll see you tomorrow?"

"Count on it," he said.

Bea followed him to the patio door and closed and latched the door behind him. Alayna watched as he disappeared into the storm. She'd been all set to drop her guard and let whatever happened between them happen. And now this.

It changed everything.

———

LUKE HURRIED ACROSS THE DUNE AND INTO HIS HOUSE, shedding his wet clothes on his way to the bathroom. He toweled off and pulled on clean clothes, then dried the floor and grabbed a soda. The recliner and television were right there where they were every night, waiting for him to waste a couple of hours until sleep took over. But he knew that sleep would elude him. He stood at the patio door, watching the storm rage over the Gulf, and worried about the storm raging in the house next door. He'd been reluctant to leave but couldn't find a reasonable argument for staying. Not when Bea intended to spend the night. The important thing was that Alayna wasn't alone. The fact that Bea was armed scored high on his approval list as well.

The news of Warren's breakout had shaken Alayna to the core. It had shaken him as well.

And it would only get worse when she processed all the

implications that his mission-trained mind had already run through. Rivera would never have risked such an action unless the stakes were high. The FBI already had evidence of Patterson's money laundering, but Luke's guess was that Patterson was never the real target. He was simply the biggest gun they could use to go after Rivera. The question was, how much did Patterson know?

Was he just the money man? Or did he have more intimate knowledge of Rivera's operations? The news reports Luke had read indicated the FBI had seized all of Patterson's holdings, including ancillary investments like Alayna's restaurant, but made no reference to the money he was cleaning for Rivera. Was it moved through Patterson's system so quickly that Rivera had it all back in his possession? Or was some of it still in transit and squirreled away somewhere that the FBI hadn't yet discovered? Overseas accounts were an easy place to drop money and hard to trace, especially if the funds were bounced around several places before arriving at their final destination.

When Alayna asked why Rivera hadn't killed Patterson on the spot, Luke had told her that Rivera would want to know what Patterson had told the FBI. But he'd hedged on that. The truth was Rivera would have assumed that Patterson gave up everything he knew in exchange for leniency. So Luke had lied because he didn't want to tell Alayna the truth.

That Patterson must have something Rivera wanted.

And it was worth the risk he'd taken tonight.

Luke didn't care one whit about Patterson. He'd made his bed and he could damned well lie in it. But what if Patterson didn't talk? Luke had seen pictures and read the description of Patterson's background. He didn't seem like a man who could sustain the torture he'd likely endure and remain silent, but people could surprise you. If Patterson took whatever secret Rivera was searching for to the grave, would Rivera then move on to others connected with Patterson? And if he did, wouldn't the logical place to start be the woman Patterson was involved with?

Luke ran one hand over the top of his head and blew out a breath. Alayna had made comments about being uneasy and feelings of paranoia, but she'd dismissed them as an aftereffect of everything she'd been through in the same sentence. And maybe they were. After all, who wouldn't be on edge after what she'd gone through? But maybe she'd been mistaken. Maybe the uneasiness was justified. Maybe someone had been watching her this entire time. Waiting for her to receive instructions from Patterson or to make a preset move on a particular date.

And then there was the issue with the FBI, another thing he hadn't gone into with Alayna but would have to soon. The bottom line was the FBI had screwed up badly. Transfers of prisoners like Patterson were so secret that often only a handful of people knew the real transfer vehicle. Route was often given to the driver once in motion. Destination was known to only a couple of people. And there should have been a decoy vehicle. Patterson's transfer had gone so wrong that Luke could think of only one reason why.

The FBI had a leak.

———

MATEO STOOD ON THE BACK DECK OF HIS BOAT, CURRENTLY docked at the marina, clutching his phone. It had been hours since he'd seen the FBI debacle on television, and he knew the call was coming. With three men dead, Mateo could only assume something had gone very wrong. The only caveat was that Patterson had been extracted. Mateo hadn't been brought into that play, but then, Patterson wasn't Mateo's target, and the client didn't have to get his approval.

At midnight, the phone finally rang.

"You saw the news?" the client asked.

"Yes. I assume that didn't go as planned."

"Not exactly. But we still acquired the target."

Mateo recognized the tone of the client's voice and held in a curse. Clients didn't like when people pointed out their mistakes. Mateo had just broken the golden rule of implying failure to the man who currently signed his paychecks.

"Did you get the information out of him?" Mateo asked.

"Not yet. But we will."

"What's my directive?"

"Same as before. If you get an opportunity to search the house without confrontation, then do so. Otherwise, hold back until notified."

"And the neighbor?"

"I have some information. I'll forward it to your email. But I don't want you focusing on him. He doesn't matter."

The call disconnected, and Mateo cursed out loud. They were wasting time. If Alayna Scott had what they needed, then they had to get it now. Patterson's escape would only turn up the heat everywhere. If the FBI took Alayna into protective custody, then things would only become more difficult. Not impossible, but not nearly as easy as they could be now.

If only Mateo was allowed to do things his way.

He grabbed his laptop and opened the file on Luke Ryan. Navy SEAL. Damn it! He'd figured Ryan for military and the guy was in shape, but he hadn't anticipated Special Forces. And since Ryan had clearly taken more than a casual interest in Alayna, he was going to be a problem. Mateo couldn't count on searching the beach house if only Alayna left. Now he had to ensure that both of them were out of the way. Especially if Ryan knew about Alayna's past, because Patterson's escape would put him on high alert. And that was the last thing Mateo needed.

It was one thing to work around a civilian, even a paranoid one. It was completely another to remain in the shadows when a special ops guy was checking all directions. Mateo needed a plan. Because hoping that both Alayna and Ryan would leave at the same time and remain gone for the hours he needed to conduct a thorough search of her property wasn't good enough.

He didn't care what the client said. His bonus didn't come through until the job was complete. And no way was he leaving Florida without that cash. He'd invested over a month in this gig already. The up-front pay was decent, but the bonus was why he'd taken the job.

Accidents happened. Maybe Alayna or Ryan would have one. Something that didn't create suspicion but resulted in an overnight hospital stay. He could arrange something like that. He'd done so before.

CHAPTER SIXTEEN

ALAYNA FINALLY GAVE UP TRYING TO SLEEP AND CRAWLED out of bed the next morning before dawn. Bea was snoring on the couch, so Alayna moved quietly in the kitchen, careful not to wake her. By the time the coffee was finished brewing and Alayna peered out the patio door blinds, the sun was starting to peek over the horizon, sending sparkles across the top of the Gulf. She poured herself a large mug of coffee and eased the blinds and patio door open enough to let herself outside, then slipped into the salty breeze.

She stood for a while at the end of the deck, just staring at the water, wondering how the place that had been so peaceful and made her so happy the day before had now become simply another frightening location. It scared her and made her mad that her little bit of progress had been flung all the way back to the beginning, where everything was a concern. Everything felt life-threatening.

As she stared into the sunrise, trying to process everything and determine what it meant for her—what action she needed to take—Luke walked around the dune.

"You're up early," he said as he approached.

"You're assuming I ever slept," she said.

"Yeah, I don't suppose you managed much."

"Doesn't look like you did, either." The shadows under his eyes gave him away, and she felt a rush of guilt that her personal mess was affecting him. This wasn't his battle. He shouldn't be losing sleep over her.

"I didn't get much," he said. "Part of my training is to be on alert in an emergency situation. You never know when you might be called into action."

"I'm sorry about all of this," Alayna said. "You shouldn't be losing sleep over me. None of this is your problem."

"That's my decision, isn't it?"

"No. It's mine."

He frowned. "Okay. I suppose that's true enough. But I want to help."

"And I appreciate that more than I can even explain, but you have to understand that I can't put more people at risk. It's bad enough that Bea is dragged into this now. I kept her away from New York the entire time I was dealing with it there in order to protect her, and now I've dumped the entire mess right on her doorstep. I don't think you can ever appreciate the amount of guilt I feel over that. Or the shame and humiliation that I'm in this position to begin with."

He drew in a breath and slowly blew it out. "I can't pretend I know how you feel. But I can imagine the hurt and anger that you must be processing. And the fear. I don't know that I can do anything to alleviate those, but I'd like to try."

Alayna felt the tears well up, the events of the night overwhelming her once more. And now, this man whom she barely knew was offering to stand beside her. It was a lot to process and it was a hard offer to refuse. The truth was she wanted Luke's company. In the middle of the night, when she'd been going over everything for the millionth time, she'd realized just how much of a difference he had made in her life already. When she was with Luke, that hope for the future that she thought had been lost forever sparked up again. Feelings that she thought she'd never experience again not only returned but came back stronger than she'd ever felt before.

And she felt safe with him.

But it wasn't fair. It wasn't right to drag him into her problems, regardless of what he said he wanted. Regardless of how badly she wanted him there by her side.

"If you tell me you don't want me around because you don't enjoy my company then I'll accept that," Luke said. "But if you're trying to push me away because you're afraid, that's something I can't accept."

"Of course I'm afraid. I'm afraid for me and Bea and anyone else who gets in Rivera's way. And even if Agent Davies is right, and I'm not in any danger, this isn't over. I still have to testify, and the trial could be years from now. And what happens when Warren gets paroled? And he will. He won't get life without parole. And no matter the sentence, we both know he won't serve it all. He's young. He'll be out again, and regardless of how much time passes and how many reassurances I get that he's not a threat, I don't think I'll ever believe that. I've got a lifetime of looking over my shoulder in front of me. Of constantly wondering when this will come back to haunt me. Bea didn't have a choice of being pushed into this, but I can't, in good conscience, allow anyone else to knowingly step into a lifetime of worry."

She stopped, out of breath. It had been a lot to say but if she hadn't gotten it all out at once, she probably wouldn't have ever said everything she needed to say.

Luke reached over and took Alayna's hand. "You don't have to spend a lifetime in fear. I think Warren's ability to make trouble is about to be cut short, and even if the FBI locate him and take him back into custody, there are things that can be done to protect you. New identities for you and Bea, moving to another country—there are all sorts of options for you to disappear forever from Warren's radar. I know people who can make that happen. And I know places that you and Bea could be safe."

The tears that had been threatening to spill over trickled down her cheeks. "That means Bea would have to give up everything—her bookstore, her friends, her entire life that she loves. I can't ask her to do that, and if I disappear, she'll be the link people use to try to find me. I can't leave her exposed."

"Then stay here and build the life you want and to hell with Patterson, Rivera, the FBI, and everyone else."

"You say that like it's easy."

"It's not easy. It's damned hard and it's scary, but you can do it. You're a strong woman, Alayna. You couldn't have gone through what you have and held it all together if you weren't. You just need to trust yourself. And you need to allow yourself to trust others."

Alayna's chest tightened and she squeezed her eyes shut for a moment, his words piercing her heart. She wanted to believe him. Wanted so desperately to have a future here on the island she loved and near the aunt she adored. And if she was being honest with herself, she wanted to see what was possible between her and Luke. But she was afraid. Afraid of Warren. Afraid of Rivera. Afraid for Bea. And also, afraid of her heart breaking.

"I'm so scared," she said, her voice barely a whisper.

"So am I," Luke said. "Did you love him?"

She shook her head. "I cared about him and considered him a friend. I enjoyed what we had and was mortified by his betrayal, but I didn't love him. Maybe I could have eventually, but I don't know. How do you love something that's not real?"

"Your feelings are separate from his deception. Do you think he loved you?"

"No. Given everything I've learned about him, I wonder if he's even capable. I think I was a good choice. I made things easy for him."

"How is that?"

"I was a career woman and not a socialite. I wasn't looking to land a husband. Wasn't interested in marriage at all. At least, not any time in the near future."

"And that's what all the women in Warren's social circle were after?"

She nodded. "I think I was a good buffer for him. He enjoyed my company, and I was suitable for his image, but I don't think it went any further than that. It's sort of embarrassing to admit. I did care about *him,* but I don't think he could say the same about me."

"If you were only part of Warren's carefully crafted image, that's all the more reason that he wouldn't be coming for you now."

She blew out a breath. "That makes sense."

But even knowing he was right didn't diminish her fear.

"And that's assuming Warren even has the capability to come after you right now," he said. "I doubt that's the case."

Alayna frowned. She knew the more likely scenario was that Rivera had taken Warren because he wanted information. And whether Warren gave Rivera what he wanted or not, his outcome would probably be the same because Warren was a liability.

"I know what I'm asking you to do is hard," Luke said gently. "It means you have to trust someone with your life that you've only known for days. But I promise you, Alayna. I won't hurt you, and I won't let anyone else hurt you either."

She didn't doubt the veracity of his words. Not even a

little. And as much as it seemed absolutely crazy, she did trust him. He was an honorable man, and he was throwing her a lifeline. All she had to do was lower her guard and accept it.

"I...I would love to have your help."

She could see the relief on his face as he moved to gather her in his arms.

"We're going to get through this," he whispered to her. "I promise you."

She pressed her body against his, tucking her face into his chest. His heart beat strong against her cheek and a feeling of absolute calm washed over her. She'd found an ally in the most unlikely way. And now she couldn't imagine going through this without him.

He released her and inched back just a bit. "There are some things we need to discuss. Things I thought of last night that you need to take into consideration. Do you want to bring Bea into the discussion?"

"No. The more I can keep her out of things, the better."

"Good. Then can we talk here? Now?"

She nodded and sat in one of the patio chairs. Luke moved another chair close by and sat where they could look directly at each other.

"The first thing I want to talk about is Warren's escape," he said. "I know I said last night that Rivera would want to know what Warren told the FBI. And I think that's true, but I also think it goes deeper than that."

"What do you mean?"

"It's like you said, it would have been easier to kill Warren on the spot rather than abduct him. Even if Warren told the FBI everything he knew, all Rivera has to do is kill him and he can't testify. Maybe the DA could get Warren's testimony introduced into evidence, but maybe not. And without Warren there to cross-examine, everything he said would be suspect."

"So then why..."

"I think Warren has something that Rivera wants. And he wants it badly enough to risk his men on a breakout rather than a straight hit."

"Like what?"

"Money. My guess is that Warren passed Rivera's funds through several bank accounts across multiple countries before routing it to Rivera. What if Warren was busted in the middle of one of those transactions? He could have millions of Rivera's dollars stashed somewhere that Rivera has no idea how to access."

"Oh!" Alayna stiffened. "I hadn't thought...but I bet you're right. That means when Rivera gets what he wants—"

"He'll kill Warren. My guess is the next report we get on Warren Patterson will be that the FBI has found the body. Assuming they ever locate it."

Alayna shook her head. She knew the likelihood of Warren making it away from Rivera alive was slim, but it felt different hearing someone else state it out loud. And despite everything he'd done, she didn't want Warren to die. She wanted him to pay for his crimes, certainly, but it wasn't Rivera's place to hand out punishment. That wasn't justice. That was revenge.

"What's the other thing?" she asked, not wanting to dwell anymore on Warren's fate.

"The fact that Rivera was able to take Warren at all disturbs me. With a case that high-profile, prisoner transport only happens under very specific circumstances. Only a handful of people are involved in the move, and even fewer than that are actually aware of the who, when, and where."

"What do you mean?"

"The agents on prisoner guard duty aren't told who is being transferred until he's in their custody. There are usually two or more transport vehicles. One for the prisoner and the other to serve as a decoy. The drivers of the transport vehicle aren't told until they're en route to the drop-off location, and they're given their route on the way. Despite all of those precautions, it sounds like the FBI was ambushed."

Alayna's eyes widened as he talked, and then she sucked in a breath. "You think someone at the FBI tipped Rivera off?"

"I don't see any other way for this to happen. Not the way it went down."

"But if someone at the FBI is on the take with Rivera, why didn't they warn Warren before his arrest? You said very few people would know about the transport, so doesn't that mean that whoever told Rivera was part of the takedown?"

"Not necessarily. Sometimes they'll use agents who weren't assigned to the case to handle transport. It's another layer of protection."

"In case someone on the investigative team decided to jump ship for the easy money. Good Lord, do you think Agent Davies knows that?"

"I'm sure he does. You don't get to be in charge of an investigation of that scope without knowing the score."

"But he didn't say anything to me last night."

"And he won't. He's not about to admit they have a traitor among them. And he figures giving you that information will only make you panic."

"He's right about that part. I don't even know what to think. What does that mean for me?"

"I don't know that it means anything for you, especially now with Warren gone."

"So you're saying I shouldn't worry?"

"No. I would never say that. This is a serious situation and until the issue with Warren is resolved, I think you should take every precaution. But I don't want you to panic over this."

"Not yet anyway." She gave him a rueful smile.

He reached over and clasped her hand in his. "If ever there comes a time that panic is called for, I will be right here beside you. You're not alone in this."

Alayna nodded, and the weight that she'd carried all night lifted a tiny bit. Luke was right. She wasn't alone. She had a strong man offering to watch her back and an aunt with a small arsenal ready to go to war for her.

She had everything she could possibly need.

———

"ARE YOU SURE YOU'RE GOING TO BE ALL RIGHT?" BEA ASKED as she fluffed the couch pillows for the tenth time.

Alayna took the pillow from her and put her hands on her aunt's shoulders. "I'm positive. And if you squeeze those pillows one more time, the stuffing is going to come out of them."

"So I'll do something else. You got any oranges to squeeze? I can make orange juice."

"No. I don't have any oranges. What I have is an aunt wearing her robe and half the rollers she put in last night, terrorizing my one-bedroom living space with all the energy she needs to burn off. The best place for you to do that is the bookstore. Trust me, I know the value of distraction."

"But what about you? You need a distraction more than I do."

"I have more experience. And a new paddleboard. If sitting around here thinking gets to be too much, then I'll head out into the water."

"But not alone. Promise me you won't go out there by yourself. Too many things can happen in water. Things that are easily passed off as an accident."

"I promise."

"So you'll call Luke if you decide to leave?"

"No. I'll call Luke if I decide to go into the water. If I leave it would be to go downtown, and I think I'm safe in the middle of town with a bunch of people milling around."

"You could come to the bookstore at lunch. We could grab a burger or a sandwich."

"Not today. Everyone will be talking."

Bea's hopeful expression fled and was replaced with sadness. "They're going to talk whether you're there or not."

"I know that. How do you think Luke found out about Warren? I ran into him in the pizza joint the day my boxes arrived, and that bitch Melody Whitmore brought up all the scandal in New York during a fake sympathy nod while Luke was trying to brush off her advances."

A flush crept up Bea's face. "That family is the worst thing that has ever happened to this island. But you know as well as I do that no one likes them. They can talk all they want and it won't matter."

"Maybe. And I got used to dealing with the comments in New York. But those people were strangers. Islanders are people I've known a good part of my life. They're your friends and customers. I need to process everything that's happened for myself before I'm ready to face other people. Before I'm ready to answer the inevitable questions that are going to come."

Bea blew out a breath. "That's fair. What do you want me to say—because you know the bookstore is going to be twice as busy today as it normally would be."

Alayna nodded. All the locals who were willing to push the boundaries of good taste would flock to the bookstore to get the gossip. To find out what the next scene in the saga of Alayna's drama was going to entail.

"When people ask, tell them the truth," Alayna said. "At

least, partially. Tell them I'm shocked that Warren escaped and that the FBI isn't telling me anything."

"And when they ask if you're afraid the bad guys are going to descend down here to hunt you down?"

"You think they're going to ask it just like that?"

"Of course not. The local gossips are buttholes, but they're not completely mannerless. Still, that's what all the passive-aggressive hinting will be about."

"Then tell them that the FBI says I have nothing to worry about."

"So the truth. Sort of."

"That statement is all factual. I just left out the part where I'm worried myself."

Bea gathered Alayna into her arms and gave her a hug. "I hate this for you. You know that, right? If I could take it all away, I'd give anything..."

"I know. You're the reason I'm here. You, the island—you center me, and buttholes like the Whitmores aren't going to change that. So get going. If you don't show up for work today, you'll just create even more speculation. It's better for you to go about your normal routine. Interest will die off if you don't change your habits."

Bea frowned, but Alayna could tell her aunt saw the merit of her statement.

"Okay. I'll go, but only because I have to fix my hair or it will look like a rat's nest."

"Yeah, what's with the old lady curlers you had in last night? Why don't you just use a curling iron in the morning?"

Bea waved a hand in dismissal. "Too difficult, and there's that whole 'me with a hot iron near my head' thing."

"You're probably right. Go with the curlers. Your hair always looks great, so if it's not broke..."

"I don't think it is, but I best figure out what to do about it this morning. No time to wash and reset. I'm getting a shipment in today, and the delivery guy has been flirting with me. I don't want to miss my weekly ego boost."

Alayna smiled. "Sounds like a full day."

"But if anything happens—anything at all—if a bird tweets and you think it's off-key, you call me."

"I will. But first, I'm going to call Agent Davies and see if I can get an update. When I know more, I'll let you know."

"That's a good idea. And don't hesitate to call Luke. He's right next door and although I hate to admit it, he's probably better protection than I'd be."

"Maybe in hand-to-hand, but you're still a crack shot."

"Got that right. Come to think of it, we need to get you back in practice. We'll head to the gun range first opportunity I get."

Alayna didn't bother to argue. She knew Bea needed to feel as if she was doing something. And if shooting guns was what it took, then Alayna would spend an hour pointing at paper targets. And it wouldn't hurt for her to work on her skills a bit. She hadn't been to the range since she'd moved to New York. She'd been a good shot before she left. And while she hoped she wouldn't have to test that out for real, it would be foolish to go unprepared.

"That sounds good," Alayna said and walked her aunt to the front door. She locked it behind her as soon as she left, then watched her from the kitchen window, waving as she drove away. It was only midmorning and she felt as if she'd been up for a day. But she knew better than to try to sleep. Even if her racing mind allowed it, she didn't want the dreams that would come once her subconscious was free to play.

She wandered into the kitchen and stared at the refrigerator, trying to decide on something to eat. Her aunt rarely ate breakfast, so Alayna hadn't been able to entice her into anything but black coffee. And the truth was Alayna wasn't hungry either. But she couldn't afford to skip sleep and meals, and she'd already lost out on one. She'd missed on both before and it had drained her physically to the point that she'd ended up on the receiving end of a stern lecture at her doctor's office.

So she'd eat because that was something she could control. Sleep had always been more elusive and somewhat of a picky bitch. But nothing on the refrigerator shelves sparked her interest, so she finally pulled out pineapple and milk. A protein shake would do. It covered the basics and would give her the energy she needed to keep pushing through. Maybe sometime later, her brain would ease off the throttle and she'd be able to get some rest. It would probably be easier during the day than at night. Night seemed to amplify everything—noise, fear, worry. It was as if her anxiety went up as soon as the sun went down.

She'd just popped the shake ingredients into the blender when she got a text. She picked up her phone and saw it was from Luke.

You up for some company?

CHAPTER SEVENTEEN

FOR ANYONE ELSE, THE ANSWER TO THAT TEXT WOULD HAVE been an immediate no, but Alayna was surprised to realize she didn't feel that way about Luke. Something about him calmed her. Made her believe that this was just another hurdle she had to get over and then she could find her new normal.

She texted back.

I'm making pineapple protein shakes. Are you interested?

He texted back immediately, and she smiled.

Heck yes. Be right over.

She doubled the ingredients in the blender and set it whirling. By that time, Luke was at her patio door, so she went over to unlock it and let him in. He gave her a lingering assessment as he stepped inside.

"I saw Bea leave and thought I'd check on you, maybe see what your plans were for the day," he said. "How are you doing?"

"That's a loaded question," she said and headed for the kitchen.

"Yeah, I guess it is. Did Bea go to work?"

She nodded. "Only because I made her. Everyone on the

island is going to find a reason they need a book today and if she's not there, it will cause even more talk. Hiding from the situation won't keep people from talking. In fact, it makes it worse. Trust me, I know."

He shook his head. "I'm really sorry. I can't even imagine how hard all this is for you. It was bad enough what happened in New York, and I only know what I read. I'm sure the details of what you struggled with daily were far worse than anything that was reported. I wish coming here had put all of that behind you."

"Me too."

She poured two glasses of the shakes and motioned to the patio door. They stepped outside and she let the cool breeze and the smell of salt air rush over her.

"It's therapeutic," she said. "The ocean. It healed me once and I was hoping it would heal me again."

He studied her for a moment, then nodded. "I didn't think other people felt that way. Ever since I took my first step into salt water, I knew it was something that was meant to be a permanent part of my life. The ocean healed me, too. Gave me purpose."

She gave him a curious look and he sighed.

"I suppose it's only fair that I tell you my story," he said. "I'm asking you to trust me, to depend on me, and you don't really know much about me."

"I was a good judge of character once. But I missed a tidal wave with Warren. So yeah, I would be lying if I said I wasn't curious and that it would probably make me more comfortable to know about the man behind the gun."

"I'll give you the short version because the long one causes me to dwell too much, and dwelling is death to forward motion."

"That's true."

"We'll start with my parents. I've told you before that I didn't have family and that's true. My parents were estranged from their families and I never met or knew of anyone outside of them. They were a typical couple for the era. My father ran an import warehouse, and my mom was a secretary at the elementary school. We had a small house and I played Little League."

"Sounds textbook."

He nodded. "Until the FBI arrested my father for smuggling weapons from the Middle East."

Alayna sucked in a breath and her hand flew up to her chest.

"I was twelve years old," he continued. "They burst in the house and hauled him and my mother out—handcuffed them right on the front lawn in front of all our neighbors. Then the real fun began. They went at my father for a long time, but he refused to talk. Said it would seal his death warrant. So they went after my mother. Surely she knew what was going on. Warehouse managers couldn't afford the new Cadillac he'd given her for her birthday."

Alayna's heart sank. She knew all too well how it felt to be the person who wasn't believed. And she knew how desperate she was to find something, anything, to give them so that they'd leave her alone.

"But she didn't know," Alayna said.

"No. My father told her he'd gotten a bonus and a good deal on the car. As an adult, I look back and think maybe she should have still wondered. And maybe she did, but I don't think so. She was a sweet woman, my mother, but not a strong one. She was one of those perpetually nice people who saw only good and elected to ignore the bad. Unfortunately, that was her undoing."

"What happened?"

"The FBI never relented. They wanted my father's connection in the Middle East, and they refused to believe she didn't know anything. They pushed and harassed until she couldn't take it anymore. So she took a bottle of sleeping pills and climbed into the bathtub."

She could hear the anger—of the boy and the man—as he delivered those crushing words. Tears rushed into Alayna's eyes and her mind whirled with outrage and hurt. She'd lost her parents when she was a teen and it had been a tragedy, but not like his.

"Oh my God!" she said finally. "How awful. And you were so young."

He nodded. "After that, the FBI gave up on my father and he went to prison. He died there two years later in a knife fight with another prisoner."

"But what happened to you?"

"I went into foster care."

Now her tears flowed freely. When she'd lost her parents, her entire world had collapsed, but she'd had Bea to pick her up. To force her to move forward. To not only get on with her life but to thrive. But Luke had no one and that broke her heart.

"Was it as horrible as people say?" she asked.

"I didn't suffer any physical abuse in the system, but the next six years were full of neglect. I had one family that I really liked. Where I felt almost a part of it, but the system doesn't leave you in place for very long. The father got transferred to another state, and I wasn't allowed to go with them. He was a nice man. A good man. He taught me to swim."

"Have you ever tried to contact him?"

He shook his head. "It crosses my mind sometimes, but I was a small blip in his life. I've never seen the point, I guess.

After I was released from the system, I didn't have anywhere to go and had no direction, so I joined the Navy."

"And the Navy became your family."

It made sense to her now, knowing Luke's past. The Navy had provided him with more than just a job. It had provided a home, structure, and a purpose. Then he'd connected with people and had created his own family. Different from the traditional one, but still just as important.

"Does your injury jeopardize that?" she asked.

"Yes and no. I was part of an elite team—the Navy SEALs —and I can't be any longer."

Her heart clenched. "But surely you're fine. I mean, if you didn't have a scar, I wouldn't even know you'd had an injury."

"Unfortunately, it appears better than it is. SEALs have to be 100 percent. Not even 99 percent is good enough. Too many lives depend on perfection. The Navy won't take that risk, and when it comes down to it, I wouldn't allow them to, even if they offered."

"So that's it? They just turn you loose? That doesn't seem right."

"They've offered me an instructor position."

"But you don't want it?"

He looked straight at her. "Would you rather cook or teach other people to cook?"

"Point taken. So that's your crossroads. You're sitting on this stretch of sand trying to figure out what to do with the rest of your life when the one thing you wanted is no longer an option. That sucks."

He gave her a rueful smile. "We make quite the pair, don't we?"

"You know, we sorta do. I mean, we both lost our parents at a fairly young age and to tragedy. And now we're both in limbo with our careers, and they were not only the biggest part of our lives but part of who we are. It's a hard place to be, especially when you never thought you would be there. Maybe that's why I feel a connection with you even though I haven't known you for very long."

"Like recognizing like?"

She shrugged. "Why not? I mean, I'm not into woo-woo stuff or anything, but if we're biologically programmed to pick up on emotions like fear and sadness, then why not uncertainty?"

"And here I was thinking the attraction was because of my big gun."

She smiled. "Let's just say that I'm a much bigger fan of your gun today than I was the day we met."

He tensed just a bit. "Have you heard anything from Agent Davies?"

"No. And since the FBI considers me a non-priority, my guess is that I won't unless I call him."

His jaw flexed. "I don't give a damn what the FBI thinks. They owe you. If they'd turned you loose with no stipulations, then things might be different, but as long as they've got you on the line, then they need to treat you like any other witness to a high-profile crime."

"You're right. Give me a second."

She hurried back inside, dumped the empty glasses in the sink, and grabbed her cell phone from the counter. Then she went back outside and dialed. The phone rang for so long that she thought it was about to go to voice mail, but then Davies answered.

"It's Alayna," she said, shifting the phone to speaker so that Luke could hear what Davies had to say. "I wanted to see if you had more information on Warren."

"Not at this time," Davies said, not bothering to control

the aggravation in his voice. "There's a manhunt for him but so far, we haven't been able to track him."

"And Rivera's men?"

"Rivera is claiming no connection with the men who were shot, but we know better."

"Is there any change in my status?"

"No. And I don't anticipate there will be. Ms. Scott, you have to trust me on this. Juan Rivera wants nothing from you because you have nothing to give. And even if Patterson wanted revenge, he'd have to get away from Rivera to execute it. The likelihood of that happening is slim to none."

"Okay. You'll let me know if you find him."

"Of course."

He disconnected and Luke shook his head. "Jesus, you had to deal with that guy for how long now?"

"Five months. I'd thought when my parents died that was the worst I'd ever feel, but dealing with the FBI proved that theory wrong."

He nodded. "Feds aren't exactly my favorite people."

"I can understand why."

"And as it seems that they're not going to be bothered to do anything where you're concerned, then we'll take matters into our own hands."

"How?"

"Starting with a security system. I have a buddy—retired military—over on the mainland who owns a security business. He'll be able to direct us to the best equipment for the situation."

Alayna frowned. A security system was definitely a good idea, but funds were tight and she couldn't let Bea keep bailing her out.

"I don't think it will cost much," he said. "This is a small house and only one story. You can get a lot of coverage with very little equipment."

"Okay," Alayna said. "See what your friend says and let me know. I'll settle things with Bea. I want to cover the cost myself."

"I understand." He reached over and squeezed her hand. "You're going to be all right. We'll get the security system in place as soon as possible, but in the meantime, you're going to try to act normal."

"Ha. I don't think I even know what that is anymore."

"Then we're going to figure it out."

———

BEA FLIPPED THE *AT LUNCH* SIGN ON THE DOOR, practically shoving customers back as she pulled the door shut. She locked it and headed for the counter where Nelly was pouring them shots of the whiskey they kept on hand in case of emergencies. It sat next to the gun she kept for the same reason.

"I don't think I've ever wanted to scream at people more in my life," Nelly said. "What a bunch of hypocrites. We're supposed to believe that the entire island got the hankering to read the latest romance or learn to cook or knit or develop perfect abs?"

Bea nodded and gulped back the shot of whiskey. "The only thing good about today is the profit."

"I've done more verbal maneuvering today than a politician on the campaign trail. I'm exhausted."

"That's because you're not a sociopath. If we were sociopaths, we could smile and lie all day long, then go out and dance all night in a club with inappropriate men."

Nelly sighed. "I never get the good shit. I just inherited

bad teeth and thin hair. One of those sociopath genes would have come in handy. Not all the time, mind you, but if you could turn it on and off."

"Too many days like today and I'd never turn it off."

"Preach it, woman. Well, I canceled my dentist appointment for this afternoon so I could stick around. If you plan on continuing this circus until closing time, I'll be here."

"You shouldn't have canceled your appointment with the dentist just for me."

"It's the dentist. I was looking for a reason to cancel."

"You just said you inherited bad teeth."

Nelly waved a hand in dismissal. "Another five years and my teeth will be sitting in a cup on my bathroom vanity. I'm pretty sure delaying a cleaning for a week isn't going to speed up that process."

"I don't know what I'd do without you."

"Probably shoot one of these nosy parkers. But seriously, you know I'm here for you. Anything you and Alayna need. Which leads to my next question—what else can I do? I know I'm helping here but it still doesn't feel like much."

"I know. I feel the same way. I stayed with Alayna last night, but she shooed me out this morning, saying I needed to be at the store for the incoming surge. She was right, of course, but I get so frustrated not knowing what to do. Part of me wants to roll her up in Bubble Wrap, surround her with titanium, and ship her off to an unknown destination until all of this is over."

"Leaving might not be the worst idea. Have you suggested it?"

"No. But I'm going to have to bring it up later when I see her. Warren knew where Alayna was from and when she left New York, I'm sure there was no doubt in anyone's mind where she was going."

Nelly's brow creased in worry. "Maybe you can get her to stay at your place. At least there's other houses around. It would be harder for someone out-of-place to stroll around without someone noticing. And you have a bunch of retired insomniacs on your block. They're up all hours."

"I already tried that, but she won't do it. I'm sure she thinks she'd be putting me in danger if she did, and hell, who knows, maybe she would be. Not that I care, mind you."

"Of course you don't."

Bea stared at the people milling around outside the bookstore and frowned. "There is one good thing," she said. "That guy who rented the beach house from me has taken on protecting her."

"The hottie with the boxers and the gun?"

"One and the same. I don't know what he does for the military, but I get the impression he's deadly as hell. And I think he's taken an interest in Alayna beyond just empathy."

"Is she interested in him?"

"I don't know. I think she could be if all of this wasn't coming down on her like a hailstorm. Anyway, when I talked with her earlier, she said he has an ex-Navy buddy who owns a security company on the mainland. He's going to get her fixed up with a good system. That makes me feel a little better. You know I would protect her to the death, but I have the idea that Luke is far more capable of doing that than I am."

Nelly gave her friend a hug. "Well, if you want me to stay with you for a while—just so the quiet at night doesn't drive you crazy—you know I will. Or if you think it's a good idea to get out of your house for a while, you're always welcome to stay with me and Harold."

Bea wasn't the most emotionally demonstrative person. Unless, of course, it was happy or angry. But she felt her eyes mist up as she hugged her friend. She and Nelly had been there for each other since Nelly had landed on the island at eighteen years old. They'd connected immediately and hadn't missed a day of talking except when Nelly went on her honeymoon.

Bea had never been more grateful for her friend than right now.

"I anticipated the drama and brought some grilled chicken sandwiches and potato salad so we wouldn't have to go out for something," Nelly said when she released Bea. "I know you're probably even less hungry than I am, but maybe we can take a couple bites. At least enough to get us through this afternoon."

"Did you cook the chicken or did Harold?"

"I did, so it's not dry."

"Then pass me a sandwich."

Twenty minutes later, they'd made a dent in the sandwiches and the potato salad and were primed for the afternoon round. As they walked to the front of the store, Nelly pulled up short, her body stiff.

"What's wrong?" Bea asked.

"Veronica Whitmore is outside."

"No surprise there. I'm sure she's coming to gloat."

"You want me to run interference?"

"She'd just steamroller over you to get to me. Go ahead and open the door. Might as well get this over with."

Bea went behind the counter while Nelly opened the door. As expected, Veronica marched right past Nelly without so much as a nod and made a beeline straight for Bea.

"Look what you've done!" Veronica demanded as she stepped up to the counter.

"Excuse me?" Bea said.

"Your niece has put everyone on this island in danger. She can't be allowed to stay here."

Bea struggled to keep her temper in check as more locals

made their way into the store. "This is her home. She has as much right to be here as anyone else."

"Maybe legally, but you owe island residents better. You had no right to put them in jeopardy by bringing her here."

"Given that the FBI doesn't think *Alayna* is in any jeopardy, I don't see how anyone else could be. And even if someone was gunning for my niece, why would they bother with you or any other resident? I know you find this impossible to believe but you don't matter. Not to criminals. Hell, not to most everyone on this island."

A couple of patrons snickered, and Veronica glared at Bea.

"I have the respect of everyone on Tempest Island," Veronica said. "Everyone but you, that is."

"That deference you see is fear, not respect. Holding people captive by your husband's position on the city council and down at the bank doesn't create respect. It creates loathing. Most are just good at hiding it because they have to be. I'm not one of them."

"We'll just see about all of this, won't we?" Veronica said. "I might not be able to force Alayna to leave but who knows how zoning might change around here for businesses on Main Street or rentals down on the beach. You might not ever respect me, but I'll be satisfied with fear."

Veronica whirled around and stalked out of the shop, leaving dead silence in her wake. Bea looked out at the crowd of uneasy faces and sighed.

"Everyone," Bea said, "I know you don't all want books, so can we just skip the pretense? I'm exhausted and can't do another minute of this, much less hours. Alayna is fine. The FBI does not now and has never felt she was in any danger. If they did, they'd put her in witness protection. For all of those who actually care about me and my niece and aren't just here for the gossip, there's nothing you can do but I appreciate the offers. Now, if you'll excuse me, I have some orders to place."

Bea turned around, giving the crowd her back, and pulled up the inventory list on the computer on the desk behind the counter. All the activity had led to a sales run on certain subjects that morning and depleted the displays. She needed to replace those books and see what the new offerings were to get her order in.

"Bea?"

Tom Armstrong's voice sounded behind her and she turned around. Tom wasn't just people. He and his wife, Birdie, owned the ice cream shop and they'd been friends with Bea since they moved to the island over thirty years ago. Birdie was a member of Bea's poker group, and she and Tom both regularly stood with Bea at city council meetings pushing against things that they thought wouldn't benefit the island.

"I'm so sorry," Tom said, looking slightly miserable. "I know you said there's nothing we can do, but if you or Alayna need anything, you know Birdie and I are there. If you need to get out of the store for a couple days or even longer, me or Birdie would be happy to help Nelly cover."

Bea reached out to clasp his hand with hers. "I know you would, but I can't just go sit in my house and do nothing. The worry would drive me to drink and you all know how my mouth gets when I drink."

His lips twitched. "The same as it is when you're sober?"

She smiled. "Aside from Nelly, you and Birdie are my oldest friends, and I can't tell you how much I appreciate you. But there's nothing any of us can do right now but wait and hope all of this is over soon."

He nodded. "Well, if you think of anything, you know where to find us. I can always provide you with an endless supply of ice cream or maybe more of those cookies that you like so much. Our new salesgirl said you left with a whole bag of them yesterday."

"I did, and I'm not even telling you how many are left. I might tap you for more, though. You probably just decreased your profit with that offer."

"It will be worth it. You let me know, Bea. Anything at all that you need."

"Thank you, Tom, and you give Birdie my love."

"Always."

Bea watched as he walked out and then Nelly stepped up beside her.

"Your announcement cleared out most of that crowd," she said. "A few still bought books. Probably trying to save face at being exposed."

"How did they take my exchange with Veronica?"

"Most appeared to take it as Veronica being the bitch that she is, but a few looked a little worried."

Bea sighed. "Which is exactly what I didn't want. I don't want people thinking Alayna is going to bring something bad to the island."

"It's not your fault or *her* fault if something happens," Nelly said. "If people want to blame someone then they can darn well place the blame where it belongs—with the criminals and with the FBI, who seem to be chasing their own tail."

Bea nodded. "Now if we could convince everyone of that."

CHAPTER EIGHTEEN

Luke hauled a box of equipment out of the back of his truck and Pete grabbed another one and followed him to Alayna's door. It swung open before he had a chance to knock and Alayna motioned them inside. They placed the boxes on the kitchen counter and Luke pointed to Pete.

"Alayna, this is my buddy Pete," Luke said. "He's a doctor with the Navy and he's going to help me get all this set up. Pete, this is Alayna."

Pete extended his hand. "It's nice to meet you, although I wish it were under more pleasant circumstances."

"Me too," Alayna said. "Thank you for helping, but I don't want to take up your free time. I'm sure you already work hard enough."

"Electronics are easier than patients," Pete said. "Especially guys like Luke."

"Hey," Luke protested.

Alayna smiled. "I can see that. He has a bit of a stubborn streak."

"A bit?" Pete laughed. "That streak is holding his back up."

Alayna laughed, almost surprised that the sound came from

her. She'd been anxious all afternoon but the second she'd heard Luke's truck pull up, so much tension had left her body. Plus, she'd instantly gotten a good feeling about Pete, and if she was being honest, she was glad to have him there. A buffer, of sorts. Her emotions were running high and she didn't want the combination of stress, fear, and attraction to cause her to let things happen with Luke that had no place in her life right now.

"How long do you think this will take?" Alayna asked.

"Two or three hours," Luke said.

"That means four," Pete said.

"Tell you what," Alayna said. "You guys get to it and let me know when you have about an hour to go. Then I'll get started on dinner."

Luke clapped Pete on the back. "Buddy, you are in for a real treat."

"What can I do now?" Alayna asked.

"Nothing at all," Luke said. "We'll be up in the attic and all over the outside and inside if that's okay."

"Of course. Whatever you need," Alayna said. "Since we're working with limited room here, I'm going to take my book and sit outside for a while so I won't be in your way. There's water, juice, beer, and sodas in the fridge. Please help yourself to anything."

"Thanks," Luke said. "Let's go get the rest of those boxes."

Alayna grabbed herself a bottled water and her Kindle and headed outside. She'd briefly considered a run—Lord knew she could stand to burn off some energy—but ultimately, she decided that both the road and the beach were too sparsely populated this time of year for her to feel safe. Same with the paddleboard.

She plopped into the lounge chair and blew out a breath. This was not how she'd hoped her return to Tempest Island would go. Basically, she was no better off here than in New York. She was still clinging to her home and afraid to venture out alone. The view was way better, but in exchange for that, her presence here was putting Bea at risk. She kept trying to tell herself to trust the FBI, but she simply couldn't.

If she was overly cautious and nothing happened, then she'd just lost some free time and some sleep. But if she wasn't cautious and she needed to be, things could go very wrong. It wasn't worth the risk. Once the FBI located Warren, then she could get back to figuring out how to untangle her very tangled life. But for now, she was back on high alert.

She settled into her chair and tried to concentrate on the book, but her mind kept wandering. Finally, she put her Kindle down. It was no use. She needed to do something. But what? She couldn't go downtown because the hordes of gossipers would descend on her. She'd talked to Bea earlier and she'd been correct in her prediction that everyone on the island would suddenly have the urge to read. She'd already eliminated running and paddleboarding, and her house was presently occupied by two hulking men with a ladder and power tools, so it wasn't really a viable place to indulge in diversions.

Her *Occupy Alayna's Mind* space was apparently limited to the patio.

She stared out at the surf and an image of the space above Bea's bookstore flashed through her mind. Common sense told her she couldn't do it, but it hadn't stopped images of a commercial kitchen and crisp white table linens on cherry-wood furniture. She could see the sconces on the brick walls and a huge painting of the sea at the entrance.

Before she could change her mind, she slipped inside, working her way around the equipment and the men, and located a notebook and a pen. Then she headed back outside to work up a menu. It was all a pipe dream, but thinking about menus was the only time she'd been unable to think about anything else. It should have occurred to her before now, but then she supposed when she was in New York, losing her restaurant, the last thing she wanted to think about was food.

So if she was creating the perfect high-end menu for an upscale beach restaurant, what would that look like? Steak, of course. This was the South. And lobster, because, hello, island. But not just broiled. Lobster mac and cheese definitely had to be on there. Shrimp, fish, scallops were all requirements, and another meat source like chicken and maybe also pork, for variety.

Sides had to include sautéed mushrooms, grilled asparagus, scalloped potatoes, and creamed corn. 'High-end' didn't have to be a bunch of items people couldn't pronounce. In fact, things they already knew that were simply elevated in taste would be perfect for fine dining at the beach. Now what about appetizers?

Three hours later, she had pages of notes on everything from the wine list to what the servers would wear. She smiled as it all came into full vision. Bea was right—it could work. It could work really well. Even with prices substantially below New York's, the profit margin would likely be higher. Mainly because the rent was on a whole different level. Not that she wouldn't pay Bea rent or profit share or whatever she wanted, but still. There was no way the cost of operating here could be anywhere near operating in Manhattan, even on the island where things had more of a premium.

"Alayna?" Luke's voice broke into her thoughts. "Sorry, I didn't mean to interrupt you."

"You didn't. I was just doing some wishful thinking."

He glanced down at her notebook. "That was a lot of wish. Anyway, you said to let you know when we were about an hour out. My best estimate is that's where we are now."

She rose from the lounger. "Great. Then I'll get started on dinner."

"We wired everything in the kitchen first to make sure we'd be out of the way. We just have the outdoor cameras to install back here and then we'll be ready to power up the entire system and get it all programmed in. You'll have two keypads for the alarm, of course, but I can also set up an app on your iPad and phone. I can set the cameras up on your iPad, phone, and laptop."

"Wow! That's a lot more than I expected. Are you sure you gave me the right price?"

He nodded. "I explained the situation and my buddy gave me everything at his cost. And since you're paying for labor with dinner, it's a good deal."

"If I wasn't so desperate for the additional security, I'd feel guilty."

"Don't. My buddy was happy to help and so is Pete. I work with a lot of good guys."

She smiled. "Yes. You do. And I best get to working on dinner for two of the best."

———

BEA UNLOCKED HER HOUSE AND WALKED INSIDE, TOSSING her purse on the kitchen counter. Then she grabbed a beer and went and flopped into her recliner. It had been a long, hard day, and she felt as if she'd repeated the same thing so many times that she might not ever be able to say anything else. Some people were genuinely concerned but most were just curious. This kind of excitement simply didn't happen on the island. There was crime, but nothing that captured national news channels for weeks on end.

She'd talked to Alayna while she was closing out the

register and her niece had filled Bea in on the security additions and invited her to have dinner with the three of them. But Bea figured Alayna had a full house already and Luke watching over her. With her complete lack of sleep the night before and all the aggravation of today, Bea was ready to sit and do absolutely nothing. Except maybe drink. And she was really glad she'd stocked up on alcohol the day before, because one beer wasn't going to be enough for the day she'd had.

She got up and headed to the kitchen. Surprisingly enough, she was hungry, but when she checked the meager offerings she had in the fridge, she sighed. Maybe she should have taken Alayna up on her offer. At least she wouldn't have been eating frozen waffles or cereal. She took the milk out and smelled it, then blanched. Okay, frozen waffles it was.

A knock on her door surprised her, then she frowned. Surely there wasn't a person rude enough to interrupt her evening wanting gossip. She stomped to the door, ready to lay into whoever had violated her personal space with their bullshit, but when she opened the door, Nelly stood there holding a covered dish and smiling. Behind her were the other members of the Jokers, their poker club—Birdie Armstrong, Scarlet Southerland, and Isabella Rodrigues, Izzy for short.

"It's poker night," Nelly said as she walked in. "Don't tell me you forgot."

"I guess I did," Bea said. "I don't know that I'm up to it, though."

"Nonsense," Izzy said. "You've had a horrible day and you could use some distraction, some great food, and drinks with friends. Besides, I made cheese enchiladas."

"Well, hell. Why didn't you say so when I opened the door?" Bea asked.

They all laughed.

"I made my famous banana cream pie," Scarlet said. "I

know you love it. And wine, of course. Can't have poker without wine."

"And I brought quesadillas," Nelly said.

"I brought chips, queso, and guac," Birdie said.

Bea's mouth watered as the women placed their dishes on the counter and moved through her kitchen grabbing utensils and plates to get things served. Her eyes misted just a bit as she watched. They'd coordinated this. Cooking her favorite comfort foods and gathering here tonight. These women were the best defense against the crap that life tossed at you that a woman could have.

They all filled their plates and in their usual poker night format, headed to the table to eat first and talk. Then it was on to cards.

"Okay," Izzy said as they sat. "We won't beat to death the situation with Alayna because this night is about putting that to rest for a while. But just tell us if she's okay and if there's anything we can do."

"She's fine," Bea said. "The FBI doesn't think she's at any risk. She had a great security system installed at the beach house today and my renter next door, who is military, has taken an interest in looking out for her. As for what you can do, you just did it. A night of good food and great friends is just what I needed."

"Whose food are you calling good?" Scarlet asked. "My pies are legendary."

"Just like your boobs," Birdie said, and they all laughed.

Scarlet adjusted her well-endowed chest and gave them a sly smile. "Guess which one I've caught more men with?"

Scarlet had been married and divorced three times, each time resulting in a better payoff. The Jokers liked to tease her about thinking she was Delta Burke's character from *Designing Women*. Scarlet took it as a compliment.

"So who's up on the chopping block these days?" Birdie asked.

Scarlet gave a dramatic sigh. "I'm afraid I've been running solo for a while."

"What about that attorney on the mainland?" Nelly asked.

Scarlet gave her a mischievous grin. "He lacked the, um...*size* I'm looking for."

"Good Lord, woman," Bea said. "You're pushing sixty. Does that still matter?"

Scarlet waved a hand in dismissal. "*Wallet* size. You can work with the other."

They all howled. When they finally settled down, Izzy looked at Scarlet and shook her head.

"I don't know how you do it," Izzy said. "All those men. I just had the one and the thought of doing all that training all over again makes me tired enough to stay single."

At forty-eight years old, Izzy was the youngest of the group. She'd been widowed five years before when her husband Antonio had died suddenly from a heart attack. Given that he was a doctor, the shock had been huge for everyone, especially Izzy. Neither she nor Antonio had any idea that he'd had heart issues. There had never been any signs. Izzy was a physical therapist and had her own practice on the mainland.

"Honey, I don't know how *you* do it," Scarlet said. "A woman has needs, if you know what I mean."

"I have a vague recollection," Izzy said drily.

They all laughed again, and Bea felt the tension slip from her shoulders. It was hard to remain stressed and angry in the company of these women. Their regular talk and joking reminded her that this was just another blip on the radar. It too would pass, and life would be back to normal.

She hoped.

———

ALAYNA WATCHED AS LUKE ARMED THE SECURITY SYSTEM using the keypad by the front door and then showed her the app on her phone that allowed her to arm and disarm. Pete had left twenty minutes before after consuming what he declared to be the best meal he'd had in forever. Alayna was so grateful for all the work he'd put in with Luke that she was happy to feel she'd repaid it a bit.

"Now you try it," Luke said.

She disarmed the alarm and it beeped twice to let her know she'd been successful, then the lights on the system turned green. She armed it again and smiled.

"That's simple enough," she said. "When I saw all the boxes you carried in, I was a little afraid."

"That's because we put connections on all the windows and doors and cameras to cover every angle on the outside," Luke said. "Under normal circumstances, it would probably be overkill, but yours aren't normal circumstances."

"You can say that again."

"I guess you haven't heard anything else from Davies."

"Not so much as a text. But then, until they find Warren, there's really nothing to say. And I don't think he likes being bothered with me anyway."

"Well, that's his problem. He put you in the middle of this by arresting you along with Warren. They should have bothered to do their homework before they implicated you in something. Once they make that first move, it's all over. Even if they make a statement about your innocence later on, the damage is already done."

She sighed. "So true. I knew as soon as my arrest hit the news along with Warren's that my career in New York was over. There are simply too many restaurants—too many great options. If people don't want to be associated with someone who consorted with and might have aided a criminal, then it's not like they're going to be short on great food. And the best restaurants wouldn't hire me for the same reason. It might cost them business. Even the slightest downturn in a place like Manhattan can cost you your business."

He shook his head. "It's wrong on so many levels that you had to go through that."

"What happened to you was worse."

"Doesn't make what happened to you or what's happening now any better."

Her heart clenched at his words. He'd lost so much so young, and even though she'd lost her parents as well and the car accident was certainly tragic, it still didn't compare to what had happened to Luke's family. She wondered briefly if the FBI agents who'd pushed his mother to the breaking point had ever apologized or even felt guilty for their actions, but she didn't want to ask. What good would it do? Even if they were sorry, the damage was already done.

"At least I have people supporting me," she said. "Aunt Bea and her best friend Nelly, who's like another aunt to me, you, and even your buddies who don't even know me are pitching in. It's nice to not be alone this time even though it was my choice at the time."

"That must have been hard."

"It was. I had an attorney but besides being questioned by the FBI, I never left my apartment. The press was hounding me, so I avoided anything public."

He nodded. "And you didn't want to put Bea in the middle of it."

"Then or now. That's why I won't go stay at her house even though she's right about there being more lights, more people with eyes on the street, and all. But if anyone is coming for me,

I'm not going to risk her. I already feel guilty about everything she's having to do for me—her reputation is on the line too. I don't want her life to be as well."

"What do you mean 'her reputation is on the line'? Surely people here have known Bea long enough to know what she's about. I assumed she was well liked."

"She is by most people, but every place has its bad apples. You met Melody Whitmore."

He cringed. "Sure, but I just took her as a vapid fake. If I could figure that out in the twenty seconds that she accosted me, surely everyone else has caught on by now."

"Vapid fake is a very good description but unfortunately, her parents are the real problem. The Whitmores are island royalty. They have more money than God, and Mr. Whitmore runs the bank and is on the city council."

He shook his head. "And they use all that to run herd over people."

"Exactly. I mean, a lot of people just ignore them, but if someone has or needs a bank loan or owns a business that is dependent on the city council not passing a law that could bankrupt them, then they have a tendency to curb their opinion and kiss butt."

"I hate that kind of shit."

"So do I, but every town has its Whitmores. I've already decided that if Bea catches too much crap over my being here, then I'll leave."

"Where will you go?"

She shrugged. "What difference does it make? I've got to start over anyway. The zip code doesn't really matter in the big scheme of things."

The words came out of her mouth, but she didn't believe them for a second. The truth was being back on Tempest Island was the best she'd felt in a long time. Doing normal things like paddleboarding, sitting outside and reading a book, and having a drink with a neighbor were like having a million therapy sessions rolled into one. And that didn't even count seeing Bea again—having Chinese takeout or cooking her aunt a delicious meal. Even ice cream with Bea and Nelly was a happy event.

She had started to believe that life could be normal. And then it fell apart again.

She glanced at her watch and realized it was close to 10:00 p.m. They'd stayed at the dinner table for a while, talking about everything except her situation for hours after dinner. Finally, Pete had yawned a couple times, said his goodbyes, and headed out. Then Luke had begun showing her how to use her new system and she'd never realized how much time had passed. She glanced outside the patio doors at the inky black and tried to control the urge to draw the blinds.

"I, uh," Luke started. "I don't want to make you uncomfortable, but if it's all right with you, I'd like to stay the night. On the couch, of course. I know the likelihood of something happening is slim and even if someone tried to breach the cottage, the alarm would go off and I'd be here in seconds, but I'd just feel better staying until you're completely comfortable with the system."

Relief swept through her and then was followed by that familiar wave of guilt. Even though Luke was apparently very qualified to handle high stress and potentially deadly situations, that didn't mean *her* situation was his responsibility.

"Before you say no," he said, "consider that I'll probably spend all night on my deck or patrolling the beach to watch your house. The mosquitoes here can carry away a small child, so you'd be doing me a favor not to leave me outside. Plus, it's supposed to rain, and the deck doesn't have a cover."

"You've already done so much. Even if it's very low risk, I can't ask you to put yourself in the line of fire for me."

"You didn't ask. I offered. And my ability to retaliate to fire is far superior inside this house where I have cover than it is outside in the dark and the open. Besides, I'd rather know where you are if I have to fire."

She frowned, thinking about his words.

"I suppose I hadn't thought about it, but I'm running the same risk if I shoot," she said. "I might miss the bad guy and hit you while you're trying to come to my rescue. I couldn't live with that."

"Then it's settled. I'm going to head back to my place and grab a change of clothes—that is, if you don't mind my borrowing your shower."

She smiled. "As long as you don't use all the hot water."

———

BEA CLOSED THE DOOR BEHIND THE LAST OF THE JOKERS AND pulled the lock. It had been a good night. Exactly the medicine she needed with all that was happening. There were even moments that she forgot all the problems and actually laughed and enjoyed her friends and their time together. She was eternally grateful for these women. They'd come together one by one, looking for something to do to get out of the house every week, but they weren't interested in the "normal" things women's groups did. None of them knitted. None of them gardened as a passion. And Bea had a book club at the bookstore that met once a month.

The first couple times they'd gotten together, they'd chatted until there were lulls, then Scarlet had mentioned that she wished the casinos were closer because she loved playing video poker. Everyone else had agreed and they'd realized that was it. Their thing. So the Jokers were born. They'd had weekly poker night for eight years now. They'd supported one another through business challenges, divorces, issues with children, and death.

Bea turned around and started for her bedroom when a soft knock came at the door. Who in the world could that be? She looked out the peephole and saw Birdie standing there. Figuring she must have forgotten something, Bea swung the door open.

"Did you leave your keys again?" Bea asked.

Birdie stared down at the doormat for a couple seconds, not saying a word.

"Birdie?" Bea prompted.

"I...never mind," Birdie said, and turned to leave.

Bea reached out and grabbed her arm. "Something is wrong. Now, you can either come in and talk about it or you can go home and stew in it."

Her friend had never been the biggest talker in the group, but tonight, she'd been unusually quiet.

Birdie sighed and turned back around. "I don't want to burden you with anything else. You've already got so much on your plate. And I would have talked to one of the others, but they haven't known me as long and they're somewhat biased on certain topics and a couple of them will say what will make me feel better. I don't want that. I mean, I would like to feel better, but it's more important to know the truth. I know I'll get that from you."

Bea frowned and motioned her inside. "Good Lord, woman. This sounds serious. Get inside. I'll pour us some wine and you can tell me what's got you tied up in a knot. In all the years I've known you, I've never seen you this wound up."

Birdie followed Bea into the kitchen and sat at the counter while Bea poured them a glass of wine and then sat beside her.

"I don't know that I've ever *been* this wound up," Birdie said.

"What's going on?"

"I think Tom is having an affair."

Bea blinked. Of all the things that she'd imagined might come out of Birdie's mouth, that hadn't even been on the list.

"Okay," Bea said finally. "I'm not going to dismiss that as nonsense because clearly, there's a reason for you to make such a serious statement. Can you tell me why you think that?"

"He's been weird lately. He takes these trips to the mainland—for hours at a time—and when I ask where he's going, he says to the boat and tackle stores."

"Well, that's not unusual, is it? I mean, most men on the island can spend hours walking around those stores. And a lot of women we know, myself included."

Birdie nodded. "Of course. But he never comes home with anything. There are no charges on our credit card, and nothing new appears in his fishing gear."

"Okay, that's a little odd, but maybe he's just walking the aisles for exercise or meditation or simply because he's bored."

"Then why not just say that? 'I'm bored and I'm going to walk around a bit.' And that's not all. He's been preoccupied lately. I'll be talking and I'll look over and it's clear he's checked out of the conversation. When I ask him what's on his mind, he says the business, or his boat, or some other nonsense."

"Are there any problems with the business?"

"Lord no. We have employees we can trust and leave to handle things alone. The building's been paid off for years, and we make enough in the summer alone that we could close the rest of the year if we wanted to. But we have a steady business from locals in the off-season, which is all gravy. Besides, our retirement funds have been set forever. You know Tom. He likes quality but he likes it for the best price. We built our retirement quickly with help from the savings he finds us."

"I can appreciate that, and it's why I've asked his advice on some bigger purchases. He always manages to find the best deal." Bea shook her head. "Is there anything else that could be bothering him? How is Piper doing?"

"You know my daughter," Birdie said drily. "The house could be on fire and she'd never tell me. But as far as I know, she's doing fine. Still likes her job. Won't talk about her romantic life."

"Well, if she won't tell you if something's wrong, it's unlikely she'd tell Tom. I'm sorry, Birdie, but I don't know what to say. If you think Tom's behavior is off, then I have to believe you. After all, you know the man better than anyone else."

"I used to think so, but now..."

"Have you thought about following him?"

"Because I wouldn't stick out in the big Cadillac of mine. I'm no James Bond."

"You could borrow my car if you want to give it a try."

"Maybe. But if he is up to something bad, wouldn't he be paranoid and watching everywhere for anyone who might recognize him?"

"Probably so. Well, short of hiring a professional, I don't know what else to advise. I'm sorry, but I don't think I've been any help at all."

Birdie reached over and squeezed her hand. "But you have. It helps to get it off my chest, and you never once told me I was imagining things. Knowing that you believe me helps reinforce the fact that I'm not."

"I would never think that. You never have been one for drama. Now, if Scarlet had brought me this tale, that would be a whole different story."

Birdie smiled. "Scarlet's mother named her appropriately. Well, I'm going to get out of here. Tom's probably wondering why I'm so late."

"Tell him you stayed later to talk to me. He'll assume it's about Alayna."

"Good idea. Thanks again, Bea."

Bea followed her to the door. "You let me know if there's anything I can help with."

"I will."

Birdie waved over her shoulder and headed down the street to her house. Since Birdie and Nelly lived next door to each other and usually walked home together, Bea stood on her porch and watched until Birdie went into her house. Not that things happened much on their quiet street, but a woman should always look out for her girlfriends. When Birdie's front porch light clicked off, Bea went back inside and headed for her bedroom.

Birdie's worries troubled Bea. She couldn't imagine her friend's husband with anyone else but his wife. And Tom had never struck her as anything but the loyal type with a high moral code. But she supposed most divorced people had thought that of their spouses at one time. And it was possible he was hiding something, but not another woman. Not that it was any better if he was. If you had to hide something, then you were usually already in the wrong, it was just a matter of degree. Look at Alayna's situation. Warren hadn't been cheating but good Lord, it would have been so much better if that was all that had been going on behind her back.

Bea pulled off her clothes and left them right where they fell on the floor, then she grabbed her nightgown and pulled it on. She needed a shower but didn't have the energy for it. She'd take one in the morning and put the bed linens in to wash before she left for work. She climbed into bed and was asleep before she even remembered lying down.

———

ALAYNA HEADED INTO THE LIVING ROOM, HER WET HAIR wrapped up in a towel. Because Luke was staying overnight, she'd donned shorts and a T-shirt instead of the usual tank she slept in. He was sitting on the couch, watching the weather report.

"Looks like that storm is coming right for us," he said as she plopped down on the other end of the couch.

"No surprise on the island," she said. "It will blow over soon enough. Will the cameras outside be okay with the storm?"

"Absolutely. You should be able to watch a hurricane with those things."

She laughed. "Well, that would be the only way I'd watch one."

"Have you been through one before?"

"Yeah. I mean, nothing major, but if it's only a Cat 1 or even a 2 and not much chance of it getting bigger, most of the islands just lock up and stay put even if the county calls for an evacuation. Main Street sits higher than the rest of the island —about fifteen feet above sea level—and then most of the houses are built up some. You've got to get a pretty good surge to get inside them."

"What about these cottages? Seems like they'd be hit hard, especially being one-story and right here on the beach."

"Bea's had to do some work on the interior a couple times, but with the outside being cinder block, they're pretty bullet-proof for anything less than a Cat 4. With the smaller storms, the bigger threat is really tornadoes and wind damage that can cause leaking. And loss of power. That's no fun."

"I've been out in some pretty bad storms but never in a hurricane. Of course, the one good thing about them is you know they're coming and can prepare. Unlike tsunamis. They can sneak up on you and don't leave a lot of time to flee."

"Thank God we don't have those here. How does the weather look tomorrow?"

"All clear. Maybe we can hit the paddleboards again."

"That would be nice." She glanced at her watch and realized it was close to midnight. "Well, I guess I'll head to bed. Are you sure you're okay here? I have another blanket."

"No. It's warm enough and Lord knows I'm used to sleeping in places worse than on this couch."

"Okay. Well, I guess I'll see you in the morning then."

As she headed for the bedroom, there was a news break in the weather report.

"Fishermen from Staten Island got a surprise this evening when they pulled up a body with their anchor. The authorities remain tight-lipped, but the fishermen identified the man as Warren Patterson III, who escaped from FBI custody last night. Patterson, who was expected to go on trial..."

CHAPTER NINETEEN

ALAYNA SUCKED IN A BREATH AND FELT HERSELF SWAY. LUKE was almost immediately beside her to help guide her onto the couch. She tried to listen to the rest of the news report, but all they had to offer was information about the charges against Warren, not anything else about his death. Relief washed over her when her name never came up in the broadcast, and then she felt guilty for feeling relieved. When it was over, she looked over at Luke.

"I wonder what happened," she said.

He shook his head. "We have to assume that Rivera got what he wanted."

She took in a deep breath and slowly blew it out. "I knew this was going to be the outcome. I mean, the chances of anything else were practically nil, but it's still a shock, you know?"

"I imagine it is. No matter what Warren did, he was still an important part of your life at one time. All of this has to be incredibly hard to process."

Alayna nodded, not even sure what she was feeling or what she was supposed to feel. Anger, sadness, relief, fear? All of them made sense in a different way but they couldn't all be the right answer.

"I guess I should call Davies, right?" she asked.

"I would. The fishermen might have gotten it wrong but if anyone knows, Davies will."

She grabbed her cell phone from the bedroom and dialed. Davies answered on the first ring.

"I guess you saw the news," he said.

"Is it him?"

"Yes."

"How did he..."

"He was shot. And he was worked over pretty good before then. It was an execution."

"So Rivera wins."

"This round," Davies said, sounding beyond frustrated.

"What does this mean for me?"

"You're off the hook. We don't need your testimony against a dead man. It's over, Alayna. Get on with your life and forget you ever knew Warren Patterson."

He hung up before she could respond. She stared at her phone for a second before relaying what Davies said.

"He really needs to work on his communication skills," Luke said. "But Alayna, this is good news. Horrible, but good for you."

"I know. My mind is telling me that this is finally over, but..."

"You feel guilty."

She stared at him. "How did you know?"

"Look, you said you didn't love Warren. What he did made you rethink everything about your relationship and it probably didn't come out all that positive. But you're a good person, Alayna. You don't want to see people die. Not even people like Warren. Not even after what he did. Not even after what you lost."

Alayna bolted up. "Oh my God! I have to tell Aunt Bea. I don't want to wake her but if I wait until the morning, she might see it on the news."

Luke rose and took her hand in his.

"Call her," he said. "She won't mind. I promise."

She flung her arms around him and squeezed as hard as she could. "Thank you. Thank you so much for everything. For sticking with me even after I tried to run you off. For installing an awesome security system so that I could feel safe. For sleeping on my couch."

She released him and he smiled down at her.

"You're worth it," he said.

———

MATEO'S CELL PHONE SIGNALED THE CALL HE'D BEEN expecting ever since he'd seen the news. He grabbed it.

"Is it him?" he asked.

"Yeah," the client said.

"So you got the information?"

"No." The reply was short, and Mateo could feel the tension through the phone.

"What happened?"

"My associates got careless. Patterson managed to get loose from the handcuffs and grabbed one of their guns."

"He shot one of your associates?" Mateo was beyond surprised. He'd never figured Patterson had it in him.

"No. He shot himself."

Mateo blew out a breath. "So how do I proceed? Our previous plan isn't going to work. The neighbor is not only sticking close, but he spent the day with a buddy installing a security system and a ton of cameras. The stealth option is no longer viable. I say I proceed with elimination of the man and get what we want from the woman."

"Not yet. There's one last thing I want to try."

"How long?"

"Forty-eight hours. No more."

"And if it doesn't work?"

"Then you can proceed with your methods."

Mateo placed the phone on the table and smiled. From his slot in the marina, he could see the tiny dots of light from homes on the shore and knew that inside Alayna's cottage, there was probably a celebration going on.

Enjoy yourself now. It will all be over soon.

BEA PRACTICALLY DANCED INTO THE BOOKSTORE THE NEXT morning, surprised to find Nelly already making coffee. Nelly was a great friend, but mornings weren't usually her strong suit. And after the amount of wine and food Nelly had consumed the night before, Bea had figured she wouldn't come rushing through the door until opening time. And that wasn't for another hour.

Nelly looked over when she heard the door and gave Bea a huge smile.

"I started to bring champagne," she said, "but then I thought that was morbid. I mean, celebrating a man's murder, even though he did it all to himself. But I've never been as relieved as I was this morning when I saw it on the news. I'd gotten up to take some aspirin for my hangover and Harold had the news on. I dropped the entire bottle down the drain. Harold's having to fish it out now and was cussing a blue streak when I left. But it cleared my hangover right up."

Bea gave her friend a hug and smiled. "I felt the same way

when Alayna called last night. Lord knows, I was so wiped out I'm surprised I heard the phone. And then when I saw her name in the display, my pulse shot right into the stratosphere. Then she told me it was all over and my whole body collapsed. It was like I didn't even have bones anymore. I think I slept harder last night than I have in the last ten years."

"I bet you did. So what else did Alayna say? Did she talk to that FBI contact of hers?"

Bea nodded. "He said she's off the hook. There's no testifying against a dead man, and Alayna didn't know anything about his business or any of his associates so she's no use against Rivera."

"Oh, Bea! This is the best news ever."

Bea grinned. "Bet we don't have crowds of people in here today."

"No. The drama is over. Almost before it began, thank God. Now that girl can get on with her life. Bad enough to be starting over after all her hard work, but having all that still on her shoulders was making it next to impossible to move forward."

"I'm really hoping that she'll give my restaurant idea serious consideration now. I could see the wheels turning when she looked at the space. She knows I'm right. The location is perfect. The building is perfect. And if anyone can come up with a menu that has people flocking to the island, it's Alayna."

Nelly held up her hands with her fingers crossed. "Your mouth to God's ears. I am dying for a high-class meal. One that Harold has to dig out his slacks for. The only time the man dresses up is for a wedding or a funeral, and since I'm not a fan of either, I don't get much enjoyment out of it."

Bea poured herself a cup of coffee and took a sip. "I don't need to be drinking this. I'm already so amped up I'm ready to bounce off the walls."

"Why don't you shut down today and go spend some time with Alayna?"

"No. When Alayna called last night, Luke was still there, and I got the impression that he'd intended to stay the night."

Nelly's eyes widened. "Do you think..."

Bea shook her head. "No. Alayna is really careful right now with her feelings, and I imagine that goes double for any with romantic inclinations. But I'm hoping, now that this is over, that those two can do some regular stuff like normal young people. If I show up, I'll be right in the middle."

Nelly nodded. "Cockblocking."

Bea spit out her coffee. "What in the world? Good Lord, Nelly. What a term."

"I heard it on the MTV. I thought I was going to have to buy some pearls for Harold to clutch."

Bea started laughing and once she got going, she had to put her coffee cup down and drop into a chair, she was shaking so hard. But she couldn't stop the visual of Harold, sitting on the couch with his hand wrapped around a string of pearls. Finally, she sucked in a couple deep breaths and some of the heat began to leave her face. Nelly had just stood there grinning the entire time.

"It's good to hear you laugh," Nelly said.

"You keep watching the MTV and it could be a regular comedy show in here. Or I'll need oxygen."

"Have you seen the new paramedic?" Nelly fanned herself. "Worth passing out for."

"Uh-huh. And how old is he?"

Nelly waved a hand in dismissal. "That doesn't matter when you're window shopping."

"True. So I think the first part of your idea—shutting down the store today—has merit. But since you were planning to be here all day with me anyway, then I say the two of us get up to some trouble. What do you say?"

"I say we head to New Orleans—gambling, great food, interesting people..."

"That's a four-hour drive. If we go there, Harold won't get his dinner on time."

"He can eat a sandwich. Besides, I was thinking we could make it an overnighter. No sense going to NOLA if we're not going to have a Hurricane or two."

"So drive back tomorrow afternoon hungover and then open up the store on Friday?" Bea grinned. "Best idea ever."

————

ALAYNA PLACED HER CELL PHONE ON THE TABLE NEXT TO the chaise and smiled. It was a glorious day. She'd had a few hours of dreamless, restful sleep—the first in a long time—and then she'd fixed breakfast and headed outside to the deck where she'd been enjoying the sun and the smell and sound of the surf. Luke had stayed up with her for hours the night before, talking about everything that had happened. It felt good to finally get it all out and she'd never wanted to burden Bea with the details, knowing it would just make her aunt angry and heartbroken for Alayna all over again. It was a little strange talking to a man she was attracted to about the man she'd recently been in a relationship with, but Luke was a great listener and a sympathetic one as well. She'd never felt uncomfortable with the conversation.

She'd finally talked him into going back to his place around 2:00 a.m. While she appreciated his offer to stay, she knew they would both benefit from a comfortable bed and some quiet. And even though she had no intention of making a move on her attraction, and she didn't think Luke did either, she knew that just having him in the house would be a distraction.

Despite getting to bed so late, she was still up early enough to see the sunrise. It wasn't enough rest, but she awakened so energized that she knew it would be impossible to go back to sleep. Once the adrenaline wore off, she'd be able to put in more hours. Maybe catch up on all the sleep she'd lost the past five months.

Movement in front of her caught her attention and she looked up as Luke stepped through the marsh grass. He was wearing blue shorts, a white tee, and no shoes, and he looked gorgeous with his tanned, muscled skin.

"You look refreshed," he said. "You been up for a while?"

She nodded. "Couldn't sleep anymore. Too wired, I guess, but I feel good."

He smiled and took a seat at the patio table. "That's great. I will admit that I had a good round myself. Slept right past my usual waking hour and had two cups of coffee standing in the kitchen. Then I did some laundry and other household chores I'd been putting off."

Alayna smiled. "We wouldn't want you running out of boxers. You might need to apprehend another patio furniture thief."

He grinned. "I guess if that's the worst story people can tell about me, I can't really complain. Have you talked to Bea this morning?"

"Oh yes. She called as soon as she got up, talking about a thousand miles an hour."

"She's excited and relieved. I can appreciate that."

Alayna nodded. "I just got off the phone with her again before you walked up. I'm on Shakespeare duty today."

"Shakespeare duty?"

"Her adopted cat. He lives at the bookstore. Aunt Bea

decided to close for the day, and she and Nelly are headed to New Orleans for a day and night of debauchery."

"Maybe we should call New Orleans and warn them."

Alayna raised one eyebrow. "Have you ever been to New Orleans?"

"No."

"Let me just say that Bea and Nelly are so boring by New Orleans standards, no one will even notice they're there."

He laughed. "Maybe I need to plan a trip then."

"It's a wonderful city. So full of culture, and the food...such awesome food."

"Then I definitely need to go. If I have a chef of your caliber raving about the food, then it's a must. Maybe you could show me around."

She felt heat run up her neck. It was as if he'd read her mind. As soon as he'd said he'd like to go, she could picture the two of them there, dining on the best food the city had to offer. Then strolling through Jackson Square to see the artists. Taking in the many sights and creative endeavors that Bourbon Street had to offer. And then at night...

Hence the blush.

"I guess we'll have to see how long you're here," she said, not really asking the question she wanted to ask but hoping he'd divulge the information anyway.

"Yeah. Pete's been nagging me to check in. I'm pretty sure he's going to clear me for restricted duty."

"What does that mean?"

"It means I'm no longer a SEAL and I have a decision to make. I have a couple of options—all keep me stateside and out of the action—or I can leave when my time is up in about three months."

"If you left, what would you do?"

"I'm not sure. My buddy that I got the security system

from offered me a job. He has a branch that offers personal security—you know, escorting famous people, politicians, rich people, and the like. I have to admit the salary surprised me. I wouldn't make that much in the navy even if I stayed until retirement."

"So is that something you're interested in?"

He shrugged. "I don't know. I mean, the pay is great and I don't think the security part of the job would be that difficult. But when I think of the clientele I'd be dealing with... Let's just say I was on a mission once where we rescued a diplomat, and I was less than impressed."

"I can imagine that the personal element might be hard to handle. I hated when the big food critics came into my restaurant. Not because of the food. I knew I offered a good product and they either loved it or they didn't, but I hated trying to chat with them after the meal. They all want some personal tidbit and I'm just not that kind of outgoing. I didn't even have a picture of myself on the restaurant website."

"You should have. It probably would have gotten you even more business."

She laughed. "I doubt that, but it's a nice thing to say."

"So now that this is over, are you going to try again?"

"It's funny you should ask that. The other day, Bea asked me to meet her at the bookstore. She owns the building, and the top level has been leased to an attorney for as long as I can remember. Well, apparently, he expanded his practice and moved it to the mainland, so the space is up for grabs. But she never listed it. We took a look and she told me she wants me to open a fine dining restaurant there."

"That's a great idea. I bet you'd pull in a ton of regular business from islanders and the mainland. And that's not even counting tourist season. Once word gets out about your cooking, you'll be taking reservations for the next twenty years."

She felt heat creep up her neck. "Thank you. I have to admit, it sounded lovely when she pitched it but there was no way I could let her gamble her money on me. Not with all that hanging over my head. And I was afraid the situation would keep me from being successful and I don't want to cost her part of her retirement."

"But now?"

"I'll confess that I never really put the idea away completely. That was what all the notes I was making yesterday were about. I needed something to occupy my racing mind and thinking about food and the business was the only thing I could ever concentrate 100 percent on."

He smiled. "So you're going to do it."

"I, well...I want to look into it anyway."

"Excellent! That's great, Alayna. So how does one go about opening a restaurant? I assume you build out the space first, then what?"

"Actually, you do a whole lot at the same time. When I opened my place in New York, I found the space, then sourced my kitchen equipment. That dictated the layout and design for the kitchen, then the contractors went to work. While they were working, I sourced the furniture, light fixtures, and decor, designed the menu, and scouted for potential sous-chefs and a solid dessert person."

"Sounds like a lot of work."

"That doesn't even include all the cooking. You have to prepare the dishes over and over again to get the ingredients just right. You can't expect another chef to prepare your food without instructions."

His eyes widened. "So you have to cook all the things that you're going to put on the menu? Multiple times?"

"It's the only way to be certain."

"And when does that part start?"

She laughed. "As soon as I make a run to the grocery store, butcher, and fish market on the mainland."

"Do you need a lift?"

"Not just yet. I don't have the proper equipment to cook with. I have my chef's knives, of course. Bea gave them to me after I graduated from culinary school. And I brought my good kitchen appliances, cookware, and bakeware with me from New York, but I didn't have a lot. Limited space, you know? And once I got the restaurant up and running, I mostly tried out new recipes there. Ultimately, I never stocked my home kitchen as well as it needs to be to create a menu from scratch."

"So we're going shopping for pots and pans today?"

"Oh! I guess we could, but surely you'd rather spend the time off that you have left doing something fun."

"Hanging out with you *is* fun. And seeing you smile like this makes me happy and gives me hope that I can find a way to restart my life as well and be better than just content."

"Obviously you have a lot of talent or you wouldn't be a SEAL. I have no doubt you'll figure out what to do with all that ability so that you're challenged and fulfilled."

"I appreciate the vote of confidence."

She stared down at her feet for a moment, then looked back at him. "And I probably shouldn't say this, but I hope whatever you decide to do keeps you here."

He stared at her for what seemed like forever, and her heart pounded furiously in her chest. Then he cupped her face with his hands and lowered his lips to hers in a kiss so soft, so sweet, that it took her breath away. Even the slightest touch from Luke created a rush of emotion she'd never felt before, and she was still surprised to be feeling so much now. So soon after...

She pushed those negative thoughts to the back of her

mind. They had no right to dwell there anymore. That was the past, and it was finally laid to rest. From this day forward, everything was new.

"We'd better get to shopping," he said, his voice low. "Or I'm not going to want to leave."

CHAPTER TWENTY

ALAYNA STARTED TO TELL LUKE SHE DIDN'T WANT TO LEAVE either, but then her stomach clenched and she hesitated. Was she really ready? She was in the clear to move on with her life in every way possible but that wasn't a small step in the romance direction—it was a gigantic leap. And there was no point in leaping too soon. She had time. Maybe. If Luke didn't leave.

"Let me put on some tennis shoes," she said.

"Yeah, I suppose I should do that myself," he said. "I'll meet you out front. We can take my truck, in case you run across bargains you can't refuse and need the hauling space."

She laughed. "I don't think my credit limit will fill the back of your truck."

"Still, it's the least I can do since I'm going to be your menu test subject."

He gave her a grin and hurried back across the dune. Alayna went inside and grabbed her newest pair of tennis shoes, just in case they did a lot of walking, then stuffed her wallet and cell phone into a small cross-body purse. When she got to the front door, she paused. Did she set the alarm? She felt more than a little guilty that Luke and Pete had spent their entire day installing the system and now it wasn't even necessary.

And yet.

She bit her lower lip and stared at the alarm panel. Plenty of people had home alarms, she reasoned with herself. It was a smart thing for a single woman to have. The house wasn't like her apartment in New York that had restricted entry. Anyone could walk up to her front door or for that matter, her back deck. And Bea said she'd been meaning to install a system because the island was getting more crowded every year with vacationers and minor issues were starting to crop up, especially when houses stood empty. The cameras were recording no matter what, but if she was leaving for a while, she should turn on the alarm. It wasn't a step back. It was just a normal thing that people did every day.

Before she could change her mind, she punched in the code and waited for the beep to signal that she could leave. She stepped outside and locked the door. Luke was waiting by his truck and came around to open the passenger door for her. She was certain he heard the alarm arming, but he didn't mention it.

He walked around to open her truck door, which she thought was charming, and she hopped inside. Warren had never opened her car door, but then to be fair, his driver had opened the door for both of them. She buckled her seat belt and they headed out. As they crossed the long bridge that separated the island from the mainland, Alayna couldn't help but smile. When she'd crossed this bridge in the other direction, just days ago, she'd been in a completely different state of mind. It was amazing how time could change things.

And a death.

She pushed those thoughts aside. No matter how angry she

was with what Warren had done and all that it had cost her, she didn't like to dwell on the fact that her freedom had come at a steep price for another human being. Some would say he deserved it, but Alayna didn't feel that way. She did, however, believe that his actions held consequences. He'd just paid the ultimate price for his crimes.

"Look at the birds," Luke said, pointing to pelicans diving in the Sound.

"Looks like they're picking up lunch," she said.

"Seems like a good idea," Luke said. "Are you hungry?"

"I could eat," she said.

"Then direct me to a good lunch spot," he said.

"Oh, well, I haven't been here in a long time, but the Dock always had good seafood po'boys and the best crab salad."

"That sounds great."

She gave him directions and ten minutes later, they pulled up to a small weather-beaten building sitting right on the Sound. The buildings around it were new construction, but the Dock had remained intact.

"Looks like the rest of the neighborhood sold out," Luke said.

She nodded. "Bea said it's happening everywhere with a water view. People who had businesses thirty, forty years are retiring and cashing out to the big money investors with their fancy chain restaurants and stores."

"That's a shame. I mean, I'm not saying all chain food sucks, but the mom-and-pop places are usually better."

She nodded as she climbed out of the truck. "Chains have their place in the ecosystem just like fast food and hot dogs at convenience stores, but I wish there were more family restaurants sticking around. Still, it's a lot of work and finding qualified help is always a challenge. I don't blame people for wanting out after decades of juggling all those balls, especially if a big corporation offers them enough cash to head into retirement early."

Luke nodded. "Yeah, that would be hard to refuse. And I suppose if they got bored afterward, there's nothing stopping them opening another place."

"A lot of people do. It gets in your blood."

They walked inside and Alayna smiled. The place hadn't changed one bit. The same rustic furniture was still crammed in the small space and the nautical decor still hung on the walls. The smell of fried fish and shrimp filled the air and made her stomach grumble. A server collected a couple menus and asked if they wanted to sit inside or out on the deck.

"The deck sounds great," Alayna said, and Luke nodded.

The server sat them at a two-top near the railing and Luke looked out over the Sound.

"This is a great view," he said. "If the food is half as good, I can see why the place has been here so long."

"Alayna?"

A man's voice sounded behind them and Alayna looked over to see an older man with silver-and-black hair approaching.

"Hobart," she said and smiled as she rose to give the older gentleman a hug. "It's so good to see you."

"You too," Hobart said. "It's been a long time."

"It has. This is my friend Luke. I promised him the best po'boys on the mainland."

Hobart shook Luke's hand. "That's not a promise I take lightly coming from this one."

"How is Sean?" Alayna asked. Sean was Hobart's son and his only child. He was five years younger than Alayna.

"Doing great," Hobart said. "He's the head chef here now."

"You stepped out of the kitchen?" Alayna asked.

"I'm easing into retirement," Hobart said. "Got a lot of

years standing at that grill. It's time for a new generation to step up. He went to that same culinary school you went to."

"That's great," she said.

"I guess so," Hobart said. "Didn't need it, mind you. He could cook our menu in his sleep. Now that he's been to school, he's got ideas."

Alayna smiled. "That happens. But I'm sure he won't let your regulars down."

Hobart nodded. "He's smarter than that. Got a good head for the business side of things and a lot of people don't. Have you moved back or are you just visiting?"

"I'm back," Alayna said.

Hobart frowned. "I heard about that business in New York. I know Bea is thrilled to have you back, but I was really sorry to hear about your trouble."

Because she knew he was sincere and not looking for gossip, Alayna gave his arm a pat. "I appreciate that," she said. "But I'm putting it behind me. Time for act two of the Alayna Scott show."

"You thinking about starting something up here?" Hobart asked.

"It's crossed my mind," she admitted.

"It would be nice to have something ritzy," Hobart said. "I mean, I'm not trying to tell you what to do, but sometimes, a man wants a place to take his wife that doesn't allow flip-flops."

"Ha," Alayna said. "Well, if I move forward, it will definitely be the kind of place where people wear fancier shoes."

"You know," Hobart said, "that outfit two doors down from me hasn't been able to make it work. I heard they're closing up. The space wouldn't work for a high-end restaurant, but I saw the equipment when they brought it in. It's top-of-the-line. You should talk to the owner. You might be able to pick up some barely used equipment for a discount."

"Thanks!" Alayna said. "I'll go by there after lunch."

He squeezed her shoulder. "It's really good seeing you. I hope you make coming by a habit. It was nice to meet you, Luke."

They enjoyed the po'boys, which Luke agreed were the best he'd ever had, and he declared the crab salad just as good. Alayna tried to pay the bill but Luke grabbed it up first, so she insisted on leaving the tip. They waved goodbye to Hobart, who was chatting with a couple inside, and headed out.

"So do you want to see if that owner with the equipment is there?" Luke asked.

"I guess it wouldn't hurt. I mean, it's not like I have to buy anything."

They walked down the sidewalk and Alayna studied the menu that was taped to the front door. It was a decent menu, but there was nothing unique about it. Nothing that would cause people to make a special trip there just to try it. New restaurants had to offer something outside of the norm to get regulars to change up their routine.

The lights weren't on in the dining room, so she knocked on the door. She was just about to decide that no one was there when a middle-aged man wearing a ball cap and wiping his hands with a rag came out from the kitchen. He spotted her and frowned but as he stepped closer, he gave them both a once-over, then opened the door.

"Hello. My name is Alayna Scott," she said, and extended her hand. "I was talking to Hobart at the Dock and he said you might have some kitchen equipment for sale."

The man nodded and waved them inside. "I'm Michael. I haven't gotten around to listing it yet, but I need to. I gotta recoup some of the money I poured into this place. You thinking of opening a restaurant?"

"Yes," she said as they walked back to the kitchen. "I'm just at the planning stage, but as you know, kitchen equipment is one of the biggest costs, so I figured it wouldn't hurt to ask you about yours."

Michael waved his hand around. "It's all got to go. I've got about a hundred grand in it, including the walk-in freezer tucked around the corner."

Alayna took in the high-end equipment and tried not to smile. Hobart had been right. The equipment was top-notch, and it was barely used.

"How much were you looking to get for it?" she asked.

Michael shrugged. "I know it devalues a lot once it's installed and turned on, but I was hoping to get maybe sixty-five. I figure I could push for higher, but it would probably take longer to sell. The only thing going up around here seems to be chains and they have their own equipment suppliers."

"That sounds really fair," she said. "Can I talk to my investor and get back with you?"

"Sure." He pulled out his wallet and handed her a card. "That's my cell number. Just give me a call if you're interested. I was going to list it on one of the online sites in a couple days."

"Great," she said, and tucked the card in her purse. "My investor is out of town today, but I'll get with her as soon as she returns tomorrow."

He nodded. "Good luck."

They headed out and Michael locked the door behind them.

"I take it that's a good deal?" Luke asked as they climbed in his truck.

"It's an excellent deal," she said. "The equipment has barely been used. He could probably get eighty for it, but he's right that it might take longer to find a buyer at a higher price."

"So you're going to talk to Bea?"

She stared out the dashboard for several seconds, then blew out a breath. "I think I am."

He grinned. "That's awesome. I can't wait to see you in action. You're going to be a star. I just know it."

"I'll settle for making a good living and getting Aunt Bea's money back to her."

"I have a feeling you're going to be the best investment Bea ever made."

Alayna felt a rush of warmth and also worry at his compliment. "She's always said that. I'd just like for it to finally be true. Even though she tries to hide it, all of my stuff has been really hard on her. She deserves a break."

Luke reached over and squeezed her hand. "You both do."

———

NELLY TUGGED ON BEA'S ARM, TRYING TO GET HER TO hurry up and cross the street. They had arrived in New Orleans thirty minutes ago, full of energy and hungry enough to eat a horse. They'd made a quick check-in at the Marriott, which put them central to the casino and the French Quarter, and now they were heading to grab lunch at Crescent City Brewhouse.

"If you don't hurry, we're going to be waiting for second shift to get a table," Nelly said.

"If we load up on NOLA food, we're going to be calling Uber the rest of the trip."

Nelly waved a hand in dismissal. "We only need to hurry for lunch. After that, we can stroll leisurely everywhere we go. Besides, we're not here to shop. When we leave here, we're headed to the casino where we can sit on a stool and servers will bring us drinks. When we run out of money or can't walk properly, then we'll call Uber to get back to the hotel. Room service for dinner."

Bea laughed. "You've really thought all of this out."

"We don't get away often. I've had plenty of time to dwell on it."

"Maybe we can change that," Bea said. "At least in the winter, anyway. It won't hurt for me to close the bookstore for a day here and there."

"And now that Alayna's back, you have someone to check in on Shakespeare."

"I could have had one of the other poker girls stop by."

"But you never did. Just admit it, for all your grousing, you don't want just anyone seeing to the cat."

"Maybe," Bea said, not quite ready to agree.

"Hey, when tourist season is over, we should plan a girls' trip for the Jokers. Take a couple days and really do the town."

"I have a feeling the town may do us, but that's not a bad idea."

Nelly, who had been walking at a good clip, slowed and pointed across the street.

"Isn't that Tom?" she asked.

Bea looked over and saw a woman open the main entrance door to a condo complex. Then she reached out and hugged the man before he stepped inside.

"I can't imagine it is," Bea said. "Birdie said he was going to visit that Army buddy of his today."

"The one she doesn't like?" Nelly asked.

Bea nodded. "That's why Tom visits him instead of inviting him to their house."

"Ha. There's no moss on Tom. Well, I guess it's just one of

those things. You know, they say all of us have a doppelgänger somewhere in the world."

"Really? That's interesting."

Bea forced a smile but inside, she was at war. It was definitely Tom. She recognized the hat he was wearing because she'd been with Birdie when she bought it. And she knew the way the man looked from behind and the way he stood. But she didn't know the woman.

The much *younger* woman.

CHAPTER TWENTY-ONE

ALAYNA HAD ALREADY POPPED INTO THE BOOKSTORE TO feed Shakespeare on the way to the mainland, but she asked Luke to stop by again on the way back so she could attend to his litter box and play with him for a while with a fake mouse on a string. When he'd had enough, he climbed on top of one of the display cases and Alayna grabbed the keys for the second floor.

"Want to take a look upstairs?" she asked.

"Absolutely!"

They headed to the second floor and Alayna let them inside. Luke walked around a bit, taking in the area, then nodded.

"This is great for fine dining," he said. "All that exposed brick is perfect and those windows across the front...with the building across the street being only one story, you've got a great ocean view."

"I agree. It's the perfect space for upscale but without being stuffy."

"But do people have to come through the bookstore to get up here? How would that work?"

"There's an entrance on the back of the store where the parking lot is. See?"

She walked over to a window on the back side of the building and opened the blinds. Luke peered outside.

"That's a good-sized balcony at least," he said. "But what about ADA laws and that sort of thing? Do they apply on the island?"

"They apply everywhere, but in this case, it would fall under the impractical structure caveat, so nothing has to be done. However, Bea said there's a place on the mainland that makes outdoor elevators specifically designed to hold up in salt air. She'd been thinking about adding one anyway so she could get a higher rent for the space. From what I understand, they could install it right at the end of the balcony."

"That's cool."

She nodded. "I'd never heard of such a thing but then I guess I'd never had the need to check, either. So anyway, kitchen along the east side wall where there aren't any windows because I don't want to waste any of them."

She walked the space and described her vision to Luke, who not only paid attention but asked questions as they went. When she was done, he smiled.

"I can see it just like you described," he said. "This place is absolutely perfect. Please tell me you're going to go for it. For sure, I mean."

Alayna glanced around and blew out a breath.

"Look," Luke said. "This building is perfect, and your aunt already owns it—free and clear, right?"

She nodded.

"And the kitchen equipment you looked at today was well below what you'd have to pay for it new even though it is practically new. I don't know what the build-out would cost, but it sounds like Bea has the capital to make it happen. You have the hometown girl advantage, the perfect location and space, a good deal on equipment, and the talent to power two hundred restaurants, much less one. The universe is talking to you. Everything just fell into place."

"I...I guess I'm afraid it's all an illusion."

He frowned. "Like before?"

"I guess so. Logically, I know this isn't the same—not even close—but those nagging thoughts are still in the back of my mind. That it's not meant to be. That I don't deserve it. That I'm not good enough."

He put his hands on her shoulders. "I understand why you would feel that way, but you're wrong. You do deserve this. You've earned this. You have the talent to pull it off and make something really good for yourself and for Bea."

Tears pooled in her eyes and she sniffed. Was he right? She wanted to believe so much that he was, but her old friend, doubt, cuddled up against her so easily. It was hard to shed.

But that's exactly what she needed to do.

She pulled herself up straight and nodded. "You're right. I can't let the nightmare I lived ruin the rest of my life. I got past my parents' death and thrived. I can do it again."

He smiled. "That's what I want to hear. And Bea is going to be thrilled. I can't wait for you to tell her."

"Me either. Well, now that I've had a mini-setback and an almost-cry, what do you say I cook up some grilled scallops and shrimp and toss them into a pasta."

"Will there be garlic bread?"

"It wouldn't be a meal without it."

"I am your willing slave. Whatever you need—dishes washed, floors mopped, I'll even do windows."

She laughed. "I don't think that will be necessary. Maybe you can just open the wine and pour."

He took her hand in his and they walked out of the

upstairs space. Alayna couldn't believe how much her emotions could swing in such a short amount of time. But she knew one thing for certain—Luke Ryan was a positive force in her life. And she really wanted to keep him there.

———

BEA PRESSED THE BUTTONS ON THE SLOT MACHINE AND watched as the reels whirled with rainbows and unicorns and some puffy purple thing that she hadn't quite identified yet. Nelly was on a stool next to her, feeding credits into a slot with magical cats. The sounds coming out of them sounded like a frantic Disney movie.

"You know," Bea said. "I really miss putting actual quarters in and just having cherries and the like spin around."

Nelly nodded. "That's because we're getting old. Pretty soon we'll be yelling at kids to get off our lawns."

"I've been doing that for forty years," Bea said. "I don't spend weeks planting and caring for all those tropical plants only for kids to trample them when the beach is only a couple blocks away. They can throw balls and run in the sand where they only annoy the tourists."

Nelly laughed. "Definitely old. But I understand. We've been in a lull, if you think about it. When Alayna came to live with you, there were more kids on the island, but those kids have grown up and left while their parents remained."

"So you're saying the entire island is getting old?"

"In a way it is. Or was. Some kids never left and now grand-kids are starting to pop up. And some younger people have been relocating to the island in the past couple years. Mark bought the surf shop, and Alayna's back. And I heard Gary's grandson is going to come here and help him with the motel."

"Really? I know his daughter's husband is stationed overseas. I guess I figured after all that world travel, none of his family would be coming back."

"The scoop is the grandson went to school for hotel management but loves to surf. This way, he gets to indulge both his degree and his passion and hopefully, Gary gets someone who can help take some of the weight off."

Bea nodded. "That's great. Ever since Marie passed, he's been trying to do the work of two people."

"More like three since Marie did the work of two."

"True. I've been trying to convince him to hire someone forever, but he only gets some help in the summer and even then, it's not enough."

"Well, let's just pray that Seth, the grandson, is as smart as Gary says he is. That might be the answer to his problems. I know it's only been a day of freedom, but has Alayna said anything about the restaurant idea?"

"No, but I know that super-talented mind was thinking hard on it. As soon as we get home, I'm planning on revisiting it. Just have to wait for the right moment. I don't want to be too pushy and have her start considering other options."

"You don't think she was planning on leaving again when the trial was over, do you?"

"I honestly don't think she was planning anything at all a week ago other than getting the hell out of New York."

"And now?"

"Now, I just don't know. All this stuff with Warren has been super stressful. I hate to say it, but his escaping and dying was probably the best possible outcome for her. But with the trial no longer an issue and Warren no longer a threat, I was thinking she might decide to stick her toes in deeper water again. There's only so much she can do with a restaurant on Tempest Island, even a great one."

"I suppose it doesn't really compare to being a top chef in Manhattan."

"No. But I'm hoping being home reminds her of the differences in lifestyle and that sand and flip-flops win out."

Nelly held up her hands with both sets of fingers crossed. "And I'm really hoping that new future involves a fancy restaurant above the bookstore."

"You and me both."

Bea punched a button and watched the reel spin. Then it stopped on three rainbows and the whole thing set off with flashing lights and blaring music.

Nelly grabbed her arm. "You won the grand prize!"

"I did?" Bea stared at the machine. "What is it?"

Nelly started to laugh. "A week's paid vacation for two to their sister casino in Vegas."

Bea grinned. "Really? Looks like another road trip is coming."

————

LUKE DROPPED HIS FORK ON THE PLATE AND SLUMPED BACK in the patio chair with a groan. Alayna looked at him and smiled. Score another point for her cooking.

"That was incredible," he said. "I might not move for a week. What was that sauce on the pasta? It was awesome."

"It's a secret," Alayna said. "A very decadent, fattening, and scrumptious secret."

"I don't even care how fattening it is. If you cooked that every day, I'd just spend the rest of the day jogging to make up for it."

"Because you could get up and jog now?"

"Good point. Maybe jog all day, then have it for dinner."

"I'm really glad you enjoyed it."

"How could I not? I can't wait for you to get up and running and let everyone else in on this. I feel guilty being the only one who knows. Well, me and Bea."

"And Pete."

"That's right. Pete got in on it too. He was really impressed."

"Maybe you could invite him over again for dinner. Just dinner this time. No manual labor."

"He'd love that."

"I take it you guys are good friends?"

"As good as we could be. Pete was the medic for my team on two of our tours, but we didn't spend a whole lot of time in the same place. He's a fantastic doctor and a really good guy. The Navy is fortunate to have him. He could be making a mint in private practice."

"Some people find their calling and the money doesn't matter. I mean, don't get me wrong, it's awesome when you can have both, but if you can do what you love and still make it work financially, then maybe more people should be happy with that."

"So what you're saying is money doesn't fix everything."

She laughed. "Yeah, I have firsthand experience with that one. Warren had a huge trust fund and access to family properties in multiple countries. And my understanding from the FBI was that his legitimate business was very successful. Why he risked all of that to get involved with a drug cartel is at the top of the list of the things I don't understand. And apparently, I never will as he can't explain."

"All I can guess is that something was missing, and no one can say what except Warren. But the whole thing certainly seems like a waste. Still, I have trouble working up even an ounce of sympathy for him because of what it did to you. If he had even a bit of feelings for you, he should have never gotten involved."

She sighed. "Agent Davies said that people like Warren never think they'll be caught, so they don't consider the fallout their actions will have on other people."

"That makes sense, but it doesn't return your restaurant, your reputation, or your money invested."

"Oh, understanding doesn't mean I forgive him. I mean, I guess I need to at some point for myself. But it would never be about him."

He nodded. "I understand the sentiment. There are some people in my past who really set me back."

"Ah, do I sense a problem with a woman or two?" Something in his tone had her wondering.

"Just one. I guess you could say a second never got the opportunity."

"What happened?"

He frowned. "It's not a nice story."

"It can't be worse than being hauled out of your boyfriend's apartment in handcuffs by the FBI."

"No. It definitely wasn't that bad, although at the time, I'm sure I would have felt it was. It's a short and often-told story—I was a young SEAL, finally confident that I'd found my path, and that's when Serena appeared." He shook his head. "She was beautiful and charming and a complete fraud."

"What do you mean?"

"It was her thing—to pick out a young soldier, convince them she was their dreams in the flesh, then drain them for every dime she could get. I fell for her line of bullshit, even though my commanding officer had warned me about her. It was my own fault. I had limited experience with women and was just a little full of myself, and women like Serena could spot those characteristics as if they were lit up in neon."

"Predators know how to pick their prey. But you shouldn't be so hard on yourself. Like you said, you were young and had limited experience. And God knows, I'm preaching to you about things I have to remind myself of. People like to say that I have to forgive Warren in order to put this in the past, but I think what was really important is that I forgave myself."

He nodded. "I made peace with myself years ago, but I will admit, the entire situation combined with all the travel the Navy required has kept me from pursuing anything serious with someone else. I won't say I've forgiven Serena, because honestly, she's never asked and I don't believe she ever will. You have to be sorry to ask for forgiveness. But I've moved on. It's locked in a drawer in my past and simply no longer matters."

She studied him for a moment, then nodded. "I think that's a really good way of doing things. Then you're not forcing yourself to feel conciliatory when you're not. You're allowing that your feelings are valid, but they don't have to be part of your everyday life. I like that. Thank you."

He smiled. "Anything I can do to help."

"You've helped me tremendously."

He reached over and took her hand. "I know we haven't known each other for very long, but I feel a strong connection with you—like we've always known each other. It's a little off-putting because I've never had that before, but mostly it's exciting."

"And scary?"

"Yeah, I guess I can admit to that even though most men wouldn't."

"I know. I feel the same way. And it *really* scares me because I just made the worst choice ever and I'm still paying for it. So now I'm second-, third-, and fourth-guessing every move I make, every emotion I feel."

"Do me a favor," he said and leaned close to her. "Don't think about this."

He pressed his lips to hers and kissed her softly, lifting his hands to cup her face. His lips brushed hers so lightly but with so much passion that her entire body tingled. Without breaking the kiss, he rose and pulled her up with him, wrapping his arms around her and pressing his body into hers as he deepened the kiss. She moaned as he moved from her lips to her neck, trailing kisses along the sensitive nape then down to her chest, stopping at the collar of her T-shirt.

"I'd love nothing more than to take you inside," he said, his voice low. "But only if you're ready."

She nodded. For the first time in a long time, she was absolutely certain.

CHAPTER TWENTY-TWO

LUKE EASED HIS ARM UNDER ALAYNA, AND SHE TUCKED HER head in between his shoulder and chest. His heart was pounding in his chest and he wasn't breathing properly...and none of that had to do with physical conditioning. It had everything to do with the naked woman pressed against him. Never in his life had he felt so much in a single moment. It was overwhelming, exciting, and yeah, scary.

But one thing was certain—he was going to do everything possible to make Alayna Scott part of his future.

"I think I pulled a calf muscle," she said, and grinned up at him.

"You know how you fix that?"

"How?"

"More practice."

She laughed. "I think that's the best idea I've heard all day. I'm thirsty. Do you want something to drink?"

"Just water would be great."

She slid out of bed and his body instantly ached to have her warmth back against it. He watched as she exited the bedroom, not even bothering to don clothes or a robe. She was a goddess. He was convinced.

His cell phone rang, and he groaned. Whoever it was would have to wait until tomorrow. He wasn't about to do anything to ruin this moment. Alayna walked back into the bedroom and handed him the water before plopping onto the bed.

"You gonna get that?" she asked.

"I was thinking no."

"What if it's important? You should at least check and see who it is."

He sighed and reached over the side of the bed to retrieve his shorts and dig his cell phone out of the pocket. It had stopped ringing, so he checked the incoming call list.

"It was just Pete," he said. "Probably wanting to set up a time to get together. I'll call him back tomorrow."

Then his phone signaled an incoming text from Pete.

Got an emergency. If you're around, please call!

Luke frowned. Pete wasn't the dramatic sort. If anything, he was the opposite of drama. He showed Alayna the message before he called.

"Luke, man," Pete said as soon as he answered. "I got a situation here and I need some help. You're not with Alayna by any chance, are you?"

"Yeah, she's right here."

"Good. Put me on speaker."

Luke was confused as to what was going on with his friend, but switched the phone over to speaker as requested and told Alayna that Pete wanted to speak to both of them.

"So I went for my usual walk this evening," Pete said. "Today I walked west on the protected seashore and ended up way past your cottage. Well, I come up on this tidal pool and there's an old guy sitting in it with a scrub brush and soap and not wearing a lick of clothes. In fact, there's no clothes in sight so I don't even want to think about how he got here. He's insisting he's in a hot spring at someone's private ranch in Arkansas."

Alayna started giggling and covered her mouth with her hand. "Sorry. Ask him if he's Mr. Franklin."

"Give me a second," Pete said. "I walked off a bit because that's just not something a person wants to get a long view of, even a doctor."

They heard some muffled shouting, then Pete came back on the line.

"He says that's right. He's Mr. Franklin."

"Hold tight," Alayna said, and ran into the kitchen for her phone. She scrolled through her address book.

"I'm calling his son, Young Franklin," she said and dialed, then put it on speaker.

"Hello," Young Franklin answered.

"This is Alayna Scott, Bea's niece."

"Yes, of course. Bea said you were moving back. Is there something I can help you with? I hope nothing is wrong."

"There *is* something you can help with," Alayna said and explained the situation.

There was dead silence for several seconds.

"I don't even know what to say," Young Franklin said. "My father...well, you know my father. He wasn't the most reliable before you moved away and recently, he's gotten to be not only unreliable but quite, uh, colorful, shall we say. I hate to do this, but can you please ask your friend to keep an eye on him until I can get there? I don't want him wandering off into the surf, especially so close to dusk."

"I'll do better than that," Alayna said. "I'll head out there right now with a towel and a blanket. Maybe your father will remember me."

"That would be a huge relief," Young Franklin said. "I'm driving back from the mainland now, but it will be at least ten or fifteen minutes before I can get there."

"I'm on my way," she said. "Don't worry. My friend is a doctor. He's in excellent hands."

"Did you get all of that, Pete?" Luke asked as Alayna hung up.

"Mostly, and please hurry," Pete said. "He's saying something about ballroom dancing. I just can't..."

The call dropped and Luke stared at Alayna. "Is there some island information on this man that I need to know?"

"I'll tell you on the way," she said as she pulled on her clothes, then ran out of the room.

Luke got dressed and hurried into the living room where she was exiting the laundry room with a beach towel and a blanket. They locked up and armed the house and headed off, Alayna directing him to the beach path that she thought the man had used. As he drove, Alayna filled him in.

"So Old Franklin is Young Franklin's father," she said.

"No one uses their first names?"

"It's not really required. You see, Young Franklin is the island pastor and he followed in his father's footsteps. So they've always been Pastor Franklin. Locals just refer to them as 'Young' and 'Old' when talking to each other so that we know which one they're talking about."

Luke stared at her in dismay. "A pastor is bathing naked in a tidal pool on a public beach?"

She laughed. "He's either reached that age where nothing fazes him anymore and all sense of propriety has fled the building, or he's got more serious issues going on."

She relayed a story Bea had told her about Old Franklin losing his bathing suit and flashing the entire beach the week before.

"Exactly how old is this guy?" Luke asked.

"Ninety if he's a day."

A visual of his buddy on the beach with an almost century-old naked dude flashed through Luke's mind, and he started to chuckle. "I guess when I'm ninety I won't care either. But that means Young Franklin can't be all that young."

"In his late sixties, I think."

"Is there a Younger Young Franklin?"

She shook her head. "He had two daughters. One is the secretary at the church and married a congregation member, had three kids, and does needlepoint. The other had a falling-out with her father and I don't think they've spoken in decades."

"I'm almost afraid to ask why."

"She converted to Catholicism."

"Well, good Lord, that just means she goes to a different church. How is that a problem?"

Alayna grinned. "She's a nun."

"Oh. Well...I guess that's a bit different than spending eleven till noon on Sunday in different buildings."

"Just a bit. Pull off over here. There's a walking trail that leads to the beach. Tidal pools used to form a lot here, so hopefully this is where they are."

Luke parked, then grabbed the towel and blanket and headed down the path after Alayna, thinking this was the strangest follow-up to a romantic moment that he'd ever encountered. Naked was fine, but only if it was Alayna. A ninety-year-old man treating the beach like a bathhouse was well outside of things he ever wanted to experience.

They spotted Pete as they came through a patch of sea oats and Alayna called out. He looked over at them, his relief apparent. Old Franklin was out of the tidal pool and sitting on the sand next to Pete, glaring up at him. Pete was dripping wet and his shirt was missing. Luke glanced down and realized it was covering Old Franklin's lap. Mostly.

"Mr. Franklin," Alayna said, "it's Alayna Scott. Remember me? I brought you a blanket."

"Don't need it," Old Franklin said. "Warm enough out here already."

"If you catch a cold, then your son will be mad at me," Alayna said. "You don't want that to happen, do you?"

Old Franklin sighed. "Fine. But that boy is a trial for me. Always bossing. Always knowing better. I can't believe I raised such a stick-in-the-mud."

Alayna draped the blanket around him as he scowled.

"Thank God," Pete said. "He insisted he was going to rinse off in the ocean. I told him that it wasn't safe to go swimming in the surf right now, especially as the sun was going down. But he's surprisingly quick for an old guy."

"Who are you calling old, punk?" Old Franklin groused.

"So what happened?" Luke asked, indicating Pete's wet clothes.

"When I was talking to you, he jumped up and ran for the water," Pete said. "By the time I noticed, he was halfway there. I took off after him, but he made it in before I reached him. He was staring out at the ocean when a huge wave crashed into him and he crashed into me. I've got burns on my knees and elbows from being rolled in the surf."

"I've got burns in worse places," Old Franklin said. "If you hadn't gotten in my way, I could have dived right through that wave."

"You were standing upright and I was behind you," Pete said. "You were never going to dive into that wave and I'm the victim here."

Old Franklin waved a hand in dismissal. "Get off the cross. Someone needs the wood."

Pete's eyes widened, and Alayna burst out laughing. Luke tried to contain himself as he had a ton of empathy for what his friend had been through, but he couldn't help it and finally joined Alayna laughing.

"Sorry, buddy," Luke said. "But Alayna was explaining to me on the way over that Mr. Franklin is a retired pastor."

Pete stared at Alayna in disbelief and dismay as she nodded.

"This is wrong on so many levels," Pete said.

"His son is on his way," Alayna said. "He's the current pastor. He should be here any minute."

Voices sounded on the trail behind them, and Luke looked over to see an older gentleman wearing a suit and no shoes hurrying through the sand with a woman wearing a pretty yellow dress and no shoes right behind him.

"Dad, what are you doing?" Young Franklin asked as he approached. "We've talked about this. When you're outside the house, you have to wear clothes. At minimum, a swimsuit. And you can't go swimming this late and definitely not way out here. It's not safe."

"Wasn't swimming," Old Franklin said. "I was bathing. You know I love the hot springs."

Young Franklin glanced up at the sky and Luke guessed he was praying for divine intervention. The woman Luke assumed was his wife bent over, trying to coax Old Franklin up so they could take him home.

Old Franklin groused for a couple seconds, then flung the blanket off his shoulders and popped up, remarkably fast for someone with ninety-year-old knees and no muscle content to speak of. Unfortunately, Pete's T-shirt dropped on his way up and everyone averted their eyes. Young Franklin looked as if he wanted to take a long walk into the ocean and not come back.

Mrs. Franklin hurried to grab the blanket and threw it over his shoulders. "Thank you so much, Alayna. I'll get this washed and back to you. And maybe we can have a visit and catch up. I know Bea's thrilled to have you home."

As she started to lead Old Franklin away, Young Franklin stuck his hand out to Pete. "I assume you're the gentleman who kept an eye on my father. Thank you so much. When I think of what could have happened..."

"You're welcome, sir," Pete said. "I'm a medical doctor with the Navy. I hope I'm not overstepping if I say that you have a situation here that you need to address. Has your father been tested?"

Young Franklin nodded. "It's Alzheimer's. We've been trying to manage it but it's becoming increasingly more difficult—and you're right, unsafe. I've been putting this decision off for quite a while, but I know it's one I have to make soon. I'd never forgive myself if something bad happened and I could have prevented it."

"It's a hard place to be," Pete said. "If you need any help with your decisions, I know someone who specializes in elder care. She'd be happy to speak with you and let you know what your options are. No cost involved."

"I would be grateful," Young Franklin said. "Please get my number from Alayna and send me the information. Thank you again. I best get him home."

The three of them watched as they walked away, and Pete shook his head. "What a sad and frustrating situation," he said. "And so many find themselves between that rock and a hard place where a facility with experience with aging diseases is the most viable option but the senior is dead set against it."

Alayna nodded. "I imagine the guilt is overwhelming."

"And a former pastor would be well versed in how to dish out that guilt," Luke said.

"Sure," Pete said. "But when it reaches the point of being danger to themselves, then you have to let go of the idea that you can handle it alone, regardless of how bad it makes you feel."

"Not to mention that it's not the best idea to have your father flashing tourists when you're the pastor," Alayna said. She told Pete the boogie board story.

Pete cringed. "I desperately need a shower and a drink and not in that order. Would you guys give me a ride back to my place? And maybe join me for a round? I don't want to be that sad guy drinking alone."

Luke laughed. "You're just hoping you can bribe me with that expensive bottle of whiskey you bought so I don't tell everyone on base that you got rolled in the surf by a naked old guy."

Pete grinned. "Got me."

————

BIRDIE CLEARED THE DISHES FROM THE TABLE AND STARTED loading them in the dishwasher. Since Tom had gone to visit his friend out of town, they'd eaten later than usual. Dinner had been Tom's favorite—stuffed bell peppers. She didn't make them often and quite frankly, had expected a better reception than what she'd gotten. Tom had seemed somewhat pleased but clearly, his thoughts were elsewhere during dinner. She'd had to keep repeating herself. And he didn't even take seconds as he usually did. He'd just finished off what she'd put on his plate and said he was going to work on something in the garage for a bit before bed.

For a long time, Birdie had thought she was being foolish for thinking something was off, but that was no longer the case. When she'd finally worked up the strength to tell Bea about her suspicions, she was relieved that her friend didn't think she was being dramatic. If anyone was going to tell her she was wrong, Bea would. Bea had known Birdie and Tom for decades and wouldn't hedge on anything.

So Birdie was now standing firm in the fact that Tom was hiding something. And in her experience, hiding things rarely came to a good end. Look at poor Alayna and what had happened to her. She'd lost her entire life's work because she'd accidentally taken up with someone who was invested in living a lie.

Was the same thing going to happen to Birdie?

Would all the years spent building the business, paying off debt, and saving for retirement be thrown out the window? Together, they had a comfortable life. Split in half, things would be much harder for both of them. And how did they split the business? No way Birdie would be able to work with Tom every day if she was no longer married to him. And what about the house? It was paid for and worth a pretty penny given the lack of real estate on the island, but half of the sale price wouldn't even buy her a tiny cottage here now.

What if she had to move to the mainland? Get a job? Her only qualifications were running an ice cream shop and serving up treats. And at her age, how many would be willing to hire her? Businesses would rather invest in someone younger who wouldn't retire and leave them high and dry and who would likely be healthier and have more energy. Birdie knew the health and energy thing wasn't necessarily true as she could match any young person in her store, but the perception was all that mattered. It meant she had marks against her before she ever got into an interview, assuming she could even get one.

She sighed and turned on the dishwasher. This entire train of thought wasn't helping matters. She was worrying about things before she needed to and all it was going to do was lead to a night of restless sleep. Then she'd awaken in the morning feeling like crap and without a darn thing changed. All her life, she'd been able to keep her stress levels reasonably in check. She managed to convince herself that there was no point in dwelling on things she couldn't control.

But this time, she'd met her match.

Breaking Point

"Love is bigger than any tidal wave or fear." – Bethany Hamilton

CHAPTER TWENTY-THREE

ALAYNA OPENED THE DOOR TO HER COTTAGE AND DISARMED the alarm as soon as she stepped inside. Luke closed and locked the door behind them and then pulled her to his chest and gave her a long, lingering kiss that set her entire body on fire.

"I've been wanting to do that since we left earlier," Luke said.

She grinned. "Even while we were on the beach with Old Franklin?"

He winced. "Maybe not then. But the entire time we were having drinks with Pete, all I could think of was kissing you again."

"Just kissing?"

"I am on board for anything your heart desires."

"Right now, it desires another kiss."

He obliged her and she melted into his embrace. She could feel his heart beating against her chest and it excited and comforted her at the same time. She'd never felt so many things about one man. One moment. She'd fought the attraction at first because she didn't think she was ready, but there was no preparing for this anyway. It was like being knocked over by a tidal wave.

Her phone rang and Luke groaned. She frowned, wondering who could be calling so late. It was near midnight. She pulled her phone out of her pocket, expecting to see Bea's number and hoping nothing was wrong, but she didn't recognize the number on the display.

"Is it Bea?" Luke asked.

"No. I think it's from California, but I don't recognize the number."

"Probably a sales call or wrong number. Just let it go to voice mail."

Alayna frowned. Something about the call bothered her and she didn't know why. But the overwhelming urge to answer it rushed over her and she pressed the button.

"Hello?" she answered.

"Alayna?" a woman's voice asked. It sounded vaguely familiar, but Alayna couldn't place it.

"Yes?"

"This is Carrie Winston. We met last year at a charity event."

"Yes. Brad's sister. I remember."

"I...I got your number from Brad's phone. I don't know how to tell you this, but Brad has been killed."

Alayna sucked in a breath. "What?! How? Oh my God."

"The police said it was a robbery at his house here in California. I'd called him yesterday evening and he never returned my call and wouldn't answer this morning. So I went over to see if he was all right. The cops were already there. Apparently, his housekeeper found him and called it in. They wouldn't let me in the house, claiming it was a crime scene, even though I told them I could advise them on anything missing. Then I went to the morgue and they refused to let me see the body."

"Why would they do that?"

"They claimed it was because they had already established identity and it wasn't necessary to put me through the stress of identifying Brad. I told them that wasn't the only reason I wanted to see him—that our parents were going to want someone other than strangers verifying that their child was dead."

She choked up on the last few words and Alayna waited as she composed herself.

"Their refusal was so odd that I started calling in some favors, and I think I finally got to the root of it all," she said. "Because of Brad's ties to Warren's investigation, the FBI was notified. And according to a friend of mine at the morgue, they were given strict instructions that neither me nor my parents were allowed to view the body."

"But they can't do that."

"Apparently, they can. But my friend sneaked me in late tonight after everyone had gone home."

She paused for several seconds and Alayna heard her take a deep breath and slowly let it out.

"He was tortured, Alayna. That's why they didn't want me to see. I won't go into the details, but it's clear by the marks on his wrists that he was tied up, and I won't even describe the rest of the damage. This was no robbery. I don't have proof, but I know this has something to do with Warren. I would bet my inheritance on it. As soon as I got over my shock, the first person I thought of was you. If they came after Brad, then you're not safe either. Brad didn't know anything about Warren's dealings. I asked him about it over and over again and I'm certain he wasn't lying."

"I'm certain too," Alayna said. "He was blown away by all of it...just like me."

"You have to protect yourself," she said. "I don't know

what's going on and the FBI won't even return my calls, but tomorrow, I'm going to start raising hell. And trust me, they will regret the choices they made today. When I get answers, you'll be the first person I call. But please, *please* watch your back."

"I will. And thank you for calling me. I'm so sorry about Brad. He was a really good man."

"He was."

She disconnected and Alayna dropped her arm and stared at Luke. "Did you hear that?"

He nodded, his expression grim. "Brad was one of Warren's friends, right?"

"They'd been buddies since they were kids. Do you think Carrie's right about what happened?"

"What do you know about her?" Luke asked.

"She and Brad come from a wealthy family. I mean really wealthy—like Warren's—but they both work. Brad had several businesses—mostly to do with construction. Carrie founded and runs a nonprofit in LA that helps victims of domestic abuse get training and job placement."

"So she's levelheaded and has seen plenty of the dark side of human nature."

"I'd say that's probably true. I've only met her once, but she seemed very genuine and realistic." Alayna bit her lip. "So if she says Brad was tortured, then I believe her. But there's no reason to torture someone to rob their house. Why not just kill them and proceed at your leisure?"

"Maybe he kept a lot of money on hand—a safe maybe?"

"They wouldn't have had to torture him for the combination. Brad wasn't the sort who would have let pride stand in the way of his life, and there's no way that any amount of money he kept in his house could put a dent in what his family has. He would have given them anything they asked for."

Luke ran one hand over his head. "Unless he didn't have it."

"You think they were looking for something specific—something to do with Warren?"

"If the FBI is trying to cover it up, then I can't think anything else. They let the two of you, who were the closest to Warren, walk away with the reassurance that your lives weren't in danger. Then the son of a wealthy family is tortured and killed inside his own home and across the country from where Warren did his crimes, and the FBI has instructed everyone to go silent. They don't want that screwup to get out."

"Should I call Agent Davies?"

"Probably, but that conversation is a dicey one."

"Why is that?"

"Because you can't let him know that you're aware Brad was tortured, or you'll get Carrie's friend in trouble. And given what you told me about her organization, it's possible that 'friend' in the morgue was one of the people she helped at some point."

"Shit. I didn't think about that. He's just going to give me the whole 'it was a random thing and nothing to worry about' line, isn't he?"

"Since he didn't bother to call and inform you of what happened himself, I would bet money on it."

"So should I call?"

"I would. If they screwed up then maybe he'll throw some resources your way now, even if he just phrases it as them using an abundance of caution—or whatever ass-covering language he chooses. But I'd wait until morning."

She nodded. "That's smart. I'll have to tell him that Carrie is the one who told me because I have no other connection for getting that information. But if he knows she called me at midnight, then he'll know it wasn't a just-to-let-you-know call."

"Exactly. Carrie sounds like someone I'd like—especially

since she's not taking anyone's word over her own instincts and experience. I'm grateful that she called to warn you. I wouldn't want to create trouble for her."

"Me either. Especially since she's already got Brad's death to deal with. How do you tell your parents something like that? God, what a nightmare."

"I can't even imagine."

She sniffed and tears pooled in her eyes. "Brad was a nice guy. And it was real. He came to see me the day I left New York. He gave me five grand and insisted I take it. He felt guilty about what Warren had cost me even though he didn't know anything about Warren's crimes. But he wanted to do something to help. He wanted me to be all right."

And finally, the weight of the entire conversation hit her, and she started to cry.

Luke gathered her in his arms and held her tightly as all the forward progress she'd made slipped silently away.

————

LUKE INSISTED ALAYNA STAY AT HIS COTTAGE THAT NIGHT. It wasn't the best of evasive maneuvers, but she had to admit that it made her feel better even though she probably didn't manage an hour of sleep, if that. She hated the feeling that she was being driven out of her space, and the cottage had started to feel like her place. So had the island. She'd allowed herself to start to dream again about opening a restaurant, about menus and furniture, and now, she was almost bitter with disappointment that Warren's actions had ruined everything.

Again.

Luke claimed that it was his responsibility to cook breakfast since he was hosting her and his effort of eggs and bacon was appreciated, even though she wasn't really hungry. She stirred the food around and took a couple bites but was unable to finish even a quarter of what he'd put in front of her.

"I guess I need to call Agent Davies," she said when she finally pushed the plate away, done with all pretense of eating.

Luke nodded. "Just give him as little information as possible and ask the questions."

She pulled out her cell phone. "I'm going to put him on speaker so you can hear too."

Her hands shook a tiny bit as she found his number and dialed. He answered on the first ring.

"Davies."

"It's Alayna. I, uh, got a phone call from Carrie Winston. Is Brad dead?"

"Yes. Mr. Winston was apparently the victim of a robbery at his home in California."

"That's it? You don't think it had anything to do with Warren?"

"Why would it? Mr. Winston was no more part of Warren's crimes than you were."

"I know that, I just...well, it's a little unnerving when two people I was close to are now in the morgue."

"I can see where that might be upsetting, but I have no reason to suspect that you're in any danger. I sent one of my men to California to verify the police reports. But Mr. Winston's death, while unfortunate, doesn't stand out as something to be concerned about."

"You're sure?"

"I'm positive, Ms. Scott. If the situation changes—and I don't expect that it will—I'll notify you immediately."

"Okay, well, thanks."

She disconnected and looked over at Luke, who was frowning.

"He sounded irritated and not overly forthcoming," she said.

"Yeah, he's definitely unhappy about the situation."

"Then why isn't he saying something? Am I really so expendable that he could lose two people associated with Warren's case and thinks he won't answer for it? I think he's sadly underestimated Carrie Winston if he thinks that's the case."

"I agree. It's not the response I expected. I figured he'd advise you being more cautious...maybe even suggest you relocate for a while until they verify that things are as they would like us to believe."

A thought ripped through her mind. "Do you think they're watching me?"

Luke's jaw flexed. "If the FBI is using you as bait, they're going to have to answer to more than just Carrie Winston."

"Oh my God, I didn't mean as bait, necessarily, but I guess that would make sense."

"Sure. In a completely screwed-up FBI sort of way."

"So what do I do now? I'm not going to sit around waiting for someone to do to me what they did to Brad, and hope the FBI is watching *and* that they're good shots."

"I don't blame you."

She propped her elbows on the table and dropped her head into her hands. "I can't do this the rest of my life—looking over my shoulder every minute of every day, waiting for the other shoe to drop. And I can't put Aunt Bea in danger by staying here."

"Let's not make any hasty decisions, okay? You have to go to the bookstore this morning and feed Shakespeare, right?"

"Yes."

"Then let's go and take care of that and anything else you need to do today and then we can brainstorm this. Maybe call

Carrie and see if she's learned anything new. Bea's safe in New Orleans until late this afternoon, and no one is going to come after you in broad daylight, especially not with me standing next to you."

She nodded. "You're right. We don't know for certain what's going on. It's possible that Brad was targeted for something other than his relationship with Warren. He's wealthy and has a lot of pull in his industry, at least from what I understand."

"And I've always heard that with construction, you sometimes run up against people who aren't so interested in doing things lawfully."

She drew in a deep breath and blew it out. "Okay. So we'll go take care of Shakespeare and then we'll talk this out some more and come up with a plan."

And she said a silent prayer that the plan didn't involve her leaving Tempest Island.

Again.

CHAPTER TWENTY-FOUR

ALAYNA UNLOCKED THE BACK DOOR OF THE BOOKSTORE AND she and Luke went inside. Shakespeare must have heard them because he was waiting just inside, ready to inform them of how hungry he was.

"Stop faking," Alayna said as she reached over to scratch the cat's ears. "You don't get to eat this early when the bookstore is open, so I don't want to hear it."

Luke laughed. "How come Bea doesn't have Shakespeare at her house?"

"She tried. He came wandering into the bookstore one day when the weather was nice and the doors were propped open. Bea fed him and took him home with her, but every time she let him outside, he came right back here and sat at the front door until she arrived. So she started leaving him here and now he doesn't wander. I think he likes having all the high places to climb onto and observe from."

"Yeah, I guess a bookstore would be a sort of cat's paradise."

"That and he really likes people. I think he was bored at Bea's house all day."

Alayna headed for the storeroom to grab a can of Shakespeare's food but when she walked into the back room, she drew up short. Something was off.

"What's wrong?" Luke asked.

"I don't know. Something...maybe those boxes."

She walked over to the corner where she'd stacked the boxes containing the kitchen stuff from Bea's beach cottage and inspected them.

"These have been opened," she said. "You can see where the tape has been lifted."

"These were the boxes you used to move, right?" Luke looked confused.

"Yes. I packed up some of Bea's kitchen things because I wanted to use my own and didn't have room for both. But you can see where the first round of tape was, then where the second was lifted. The tape doesn't line up to either set of lines."

"You're sure you didn't un-tape it to add something?"

She shook her head and moved the two top boxes.

"Look," she said. "These are the same. Do you have a knife?"

He nodded and pulled it out of his pocket. She opened one of the boxes and shifted through the contents.

"All of this has been unwrapped," she said.

"You're positive about that?"

"Absolutely. I mean, whoever did it tried to duplicate my work but clearly, he never spent summers working in a bookstore and wrapping gifts for people. Even when I'm packing stuff for storage, I can't seem to get away from making the edges match."

Luke frowned at the boxes, clearly worried, and she sucked in a breath.

"You were right," she said. "He's looking for something. He

thought Brad had it, but he didn't. That's why he was tortured. And neither do I, but he's not going to believe me either, just like he didn't believe Brad."

The speed with which she spoke increased with every word until she was practically breathless when she finished. And beyond panicked. Luke took her arm and guided her to a wooden crate where she sank down onto it before her knees gave out.

"He's been in the cottage," she said when she got her breath back.

Luke narrowed his eyes at her. "Have you seen something suspicious?"

"No. It was a feeling. Right after I arrived. The night I ran into you in the pizza place. When I got back, things felt off, but I couldn't find anything wrong. But he was in there. I just know it."

She was getting worked up again, and he put his hand on her shoulder.

"I believe you," he said. "You've been neck-deep in this for a long time and your instincts are very developed now. If you think someone was in your cottage, then I believe they were. Did you feel unsettled while you were driving to the island from New York?"

"Yes, but I never saw anything. I just assumed it was my nerves, which are shot."

"I think your nerves are working just fine given the situation. I'm going to hazard a guess that someone has been following you and watching since you left New York. Think about it. He went through your cottage when you went for pizza but hasn't been back since we installed the alarm. And he had to have seen you transfer the boxes to Bea's bookstore and knew what they looked like or he would have trashed this place. Instead, he only disturbed the boxes you put here, right?"

She looked around the room. "You're right. Oh my God. He's been watching me this entire time. He could have put a bullet through me any time I stepped outside."

"I don't think that was on the agenda. I think he thought he was going to get his answer when he snagged Warren. But apparently, he didn't get the answer he wanted from Warren either." Luke shook his head. "And you know what, we're not stating this entirely correctly. There's no way the same person grabbed Warren in New York, killed Brad in California, and has had eyes on you in Florida."

"I'm sure Rivera has plenty of people to do his bidding."

"I'm sure you're right."

"But what is he looking for? I don't have anything. I mean absolutely nothing of Warren's. I sold all my designer clothes, handbags—everything he gave me—at consignment shops so I could pay rent. Anything personal of his, like his hairbrush or clothes, I threw away."

"Could anyone have searched your apartment in New York?"

She considered that for a couple seconds, then shook her head. "I don't see how. It was one of those buildings that you had to have a code to get in and there was always an attendant up front. You had to have a special key to get up the elevator."

"What about deliveries?"

"Left with the attendant. He'd call after they were dropped off and if it was a case of something like food delivery and you were ill or injured, then he'd bring it up to you."

"What about maintenance?"

"It was the same two guys the entire time I lived there. Both much older men and from chatting with them, they'd both worked in the building for over a decade."

Luke shook his head. "Everyone has a price, but given what went down with Warren, I can't see someone sticking their neck out to assist someone in entering your apartment."

"Which means he didn't have an opportunity to search my stuff until I came here. But now that he has, he knows I don't have anything of Warren's."

"I'm pretty sure Brad didn't either—especially in his house in LA. It seems like they're getting desperate. Taking Brad down in his own home was a huge risk."

"I'm next, right? That's the only logical conclusion. But why Brad before me?"

"If someone was in the cottage right after you arrived, then you were already on Rivera's watch list. He just made a move on the one he considered more likely to have what they're looking for. Brad, with all his money and connections, would be able to make use of information Warren could give him, whereas you wouldn't know what to do with a list of offshore bank accounts, for example."

"These boxes hadn't been tampered with when I was in here yesterday. That means he was in here last night. And since he didn't find what he came for, he'll be back. And he'll do the same thing to me that he did to Brad."

Luke knelt down and put both hands on the sides of her face. "That's not going to happen. Nothing is going to happen to you on my watch."

"I have to leave. If I stay here, he might go after Bea to get to me."

Luke started to shake his head, but she could see the uncertainty in his expression.

"If you leave, he could go after Bea to force you to return," he said finally.

"Shit!" She jumped up and started pacing, unable to remain

immobile. "Shit! Shit! Shit! I should have never come back here. I brought a killer to her doorstep."

"Don't panic. We can handle this."

"How are we supposed to handle this? I've got a target on my back and if I leave, then I push that target onto Bea. This is exactly the nightmare I worried about all those months in New York and that the damned FBI assured me wasn't a possibility."

"Yeah, well, you know how I feel about the FBI."

"You still think they have a traitor in the agency, don't you?"

He nodded. "Even more so now than before. Think about it. The FBI searched Warren's place, yours, his parents, Brad's, and your restaurant, right? And if they'd found anything, then Rivera would know that because his mole would have told him. The fact that he's still looking for whatever it is in your belongings and at Brad's place in LA tells me that he knows for certain the FBI doesn't have it and he thinks Warren hid it somewhere the agents didn't come across it."

"Then why didn't Warren just tell him what he wanted to know when Rivera had him? If they tortured Brad, then God only knows what they did to Warren. Why didn't he talk?"

"I can only speculate. Warren had to know that he was going to die either way, so maybe he figured he wouldn't give Rivera the satisfaction."

"Which only put them onto Brad and me."

Luke shook his head. "Maybe that didn't occur to him at the time. I can't imagine it was a situation where he had time for much critical thinking."

Alayna blew out a breath. "Okay. Then since someone was going through these boxes last night, they didn't get what they wanted from Brad either. Which they believe only leaves me."

"Could Warren have hidden something in your belongings?

It wouldn't have to be big. A tiny drive can hold a lot of account numbers."

"Sure. I mean, in theory. He was in my apartment plenty and it's not like I thought he was going to steal the china, so I didn't watch him every second."

"Then that's our next move. We go through every square inch of your things to see if Warren hid something."

"And if we find it?"

"Then we turn it over to the FBI."

Alayna stared at him, a little surprised, then she understood. "Because the traitor in the FBI will get word to Rivera."

He nodded. "And then the target is off your back."

————

MATEO LOWERED HIS BINOCULARS WHEN ALAYNA AND LUKE went inside her cottage. As far as he was concerned, he'd missed opportunities to wrap up this job, but the client had told him to hold off while he tried one last avenue, so that's what he'd done. Given that Mateo's contact in California had informed him that Brad Winston had been killed during a robbery at his home, he assumed things hadn't gone as planned. But that didn't change his directive. He'd been ordered to sit tight. Don't draw any attention. Just keep watch so that he knew the lay of the land when it was time to make a move.

All of this waiting was getting on his nerves.

Mateo was a man of action, not patience. A man of direct force, not finesse.

His cell rang and he saw the client's number come up. About time.

"Yeah," he answered.

"Do you have her in your sights?"

"She and the neighbor went to the bookstore for about thirty minutes but they're back now."

"And you're sure they haven't caught sight of you?"

"I cruise by a couple times a day to get the lay of the land, but I don't stay put. Every boat that wants to enter the Gulf has to pass this way, so there's plenty of traffic. I'm pretty sure she stayed at the guy's place last night. I could have searched then."

"No. He's military and on alert. He would have been watching for someone to make that move."

"He's going to be even more prepared awake."

"I didn't think you had a problem with such things."

Mateo frowned. "I don't have a problem with much of anything, but you've told me to stand down until you make the call, and I have."

"Well, it's time for me to change tactics. What I've attempted so far hasn't worked."

"You want me to move in and make it happen?"

"Not yet. I'm about an hour from the beach. I'll meet you there."

"Are you sure that's a good idea?"

"Don't worry about it. No one who can identify me will be alive to do so."

Mateo smiled.

Finally. It was time for some fun.

———

ALAYNA STOOD IN THE MIDDLE OF THE COTTAGE AND looked around, no idea where to start looking for the unknown item that might or might not exist somewhere among her belongings.

"Where do we start?" she asked.

"We don't have to consider everything. If Warren hid something among your belongings, he would only have put it in something that you were certain to keep. So that leaves things like clothes off the list straight away. Make sense?"

"Yes. So maybe start with pictures, knickknacks with sentimental value, that sort of thing?"

"Exactly. Which room do you want to start in?"

"I guess the bedroom has the most personal stuff but really, I didn't have a lot to begin with. Apartments aren't all that spacious in the city, so I didn't bring much with me when I left the island."

"Then this shouldn't take long."

Alayna said a silent prayer that they found something to give the FBI and headed into the bedroom. Until Rivera knew what he wanted was out of reach, her life would never be her own. And even worse, Bea's would no longer be either, because Rivera wouldn't hesitate to use her aunt to force Alayna to play ball if she ran. She was a sitting duck unless she could find whatever Rivera was looking for and get it to the FBI.

"I put some photo albums on that bookcase," she said. "As well as some pictures and a couple of keepsakes from the island and culinary school."

"So everything on the bookcase is yours?"

"Everything except for the seashells and the turquoise vase. They were already here. I'll take all the photos on the dresser out of the frames."

They went silently to work, only the sounds of shifting and disassembling items breaking the silence. After the third frame, Alayna realized she was holding her breath every time she removed the back and inspected every inch for something hidden. Finally, she'd gone through every picture in the room and she turned to look at Luke as he set a picture of her graduating from culinary school back on the shelf.

"Everything is clear," he said.

"Yeah, for me too."

"Don't give up hope just yet. This is just the first room."

"This place only has five rooms and one of them is the laundry room. Another is a bathroom just big enough for one person and a toothbrush. I don't have much more personal stuff to search. The majority was here in the bedroom."

He walked over to her and gently kissed her on the lips. "If this angle doesn't work, we'll figure out a new one."

Alayna nodded, but it was hard to remain optimistic when so much was riding on something that might not even exist.

"I guess the living room is next," she said and headed out of the bedroom. "The pictures on the side tables are mine. And the small quilt. It belonged to my grandma. She passed before I was born, but I like having something that was hers."

He nodded. "What about the pillows and the paintings?"

"No. Those are Bea's."

They made quick work of the living room, then headed for the kitchen. Alayna looked around and shook her head.

"I don't know how to approach this," she said. "I mean, everything besides the dishes and silverware is mine. But do we take a screwdriver to the blender? The mixer? Just in case something's taped inside?"

"I guess we should, just in case. I don't suppose you have a magnifying glass, do you? That way I could see if the screws had ever been loosened and we wouldn't have to open up anything."

She stared. "I'm not a detective. Nor am I that old. I've still got reading glasses to look forward to before I head for magnifying."

He smiled. "I think you still have a few years, but no worries. I have one over at my cottage."

"Why? You're a SEAL. I assume you can see a target in the middle of a hurricane at five hundred feet."

"I can, but I have this old map that I've been trying to decipher, and it's really deteriorated and has tiny print. I was trying to make some of it out."

"A map? Not like a treasure map."

"Maybe. I bought it off a guy when I was overseas. He claimed his great-great-grandfather was a whaler and had found the map in an old bottle."

"I hope you didn't pay a lot, because that sounds like a line of bull."

"I had it authenticated. The paper anyway. It's over two hundred years old."

"Really? Well, if you find a treasure, I'll apologize for thinking you've been had."

He laughed. "Be right back. Lock the door behind me."

She turned the dead bolt after Luke left and then studied the contents of the kitchen. There was no way something was taped to her cookware or she would have noticed. And besides, whatever it was probably wouldn't have held up to water and heat. Maybe she needed to think harder on this—apply logic to the situation. So what was the one thing that Warren would be sure she would never part with?

Her knives.

And he knew she washed them by hand. She went over to the stand and started going over every inch of the knives. Surely if he'd created a space in the wooden handles to hide a tiny drive, she would have noticed. And as she reviewed every square inch of the knives, she couldn't find even the tiniest of flaws in the pristine wood surface.

Then she locked on a dish towel hanging over the sink and she sucked in a breath.

Her mother's pot holder.

She'd told Warren why she kept the old, frayed pot holder, so he knew that no matter what, the pot holder would always be in her kitchen and would never be used for its intended purpose. It was just there for the memories. She went to the drawer with dishrags and pulled it out. The cloth was worn almost bare in some places and some of the sequins were loose —others were missing entirely—but the stitching on the edges was still strong enough to hold the quilted pieces together.

She ran the potholder between her fingers, trying to make out something that could be in between the layers of cloth. It wasn't easy to do with all the sequins but then at one corner, she saw thread that was barely different from the rest. It was a tiny bit darker, and she'd bet anything that if she looked at it with the magnifying glass Luke had gone to get, she'd see that it wasn't frayed like the original thread. Someone had cut that edge and re-stitched it. She grabbed her chef's knife and used the razor-sharp end to carefully slice the thread from the corner. Something hard and small was inside, resting in between sequins where it blended right in.

And that's when the first gunshot rang out.

CHAPTER TWENTY-FIVE

SHE LET GO OF THE POT HOLDER AND KNIFE AND DROPPED TO the ground behind the kitchen counter as glass from the patio doors exploded across the cottage. A giant rush of adrenaline coursed through her, making her momentarily dizzy, but when her mind cleared, it was only into panic.

This was it. This was how it all ended, on the kitchen floor of Bea's cottage.

There was no way out of the kitchen except the front door and if she ran for it, she'd be out in the open. Anyone standing in the living room could take her out with ease, and the knife, now resting on the floor under her mother's pot holder, was no use in a gunfight. Bea's pistol was in the living room in an end table, but there was no way to retrieve it when the shooter was clearly coming into the house through the patio doors he'd just blown away. She cursed herself for not having the gun on her and worried about what had happened to Luke as the first round of gunfire had been farther away than her cottage. Were there two of them? Or had the killer taken care of Luke before he came after her?

She heard footsteps on the broken glass, and her chest

clenched so hard she couldn't breathe. This was it—the nightmare she'd had ever since she'd learned about Warren's crimes was coming true. And just when she'd been about to buy her way into freedom. She clenched her hands as bitter tears ran unbidden down her cheeks. Why hadn't the FBI listened to her? If they hadn't dismissed her worries, she'd be safe. Luke would be safe and now...

"Give it to me."

A man's voice sounded from the living room.

"There's some money in my purse," she said. "Take it."

"That's not what I'm here for and you know it. Give me what Patterson asked you to hold for him."

"I swear Warren didn't give me anything," she said.

"Liar. You're going to tell me where it is. The question is, do you want to die swiftly and with minimal pain or do you want me to draw this out? Because I'm good either way."

"Is that what you told Brad?"

"Seems like sloppy work if the cops took it for a robbery. I'm not sloppy. When they find your body, they'll know exactly what happened."

A wave of dizziness washed over her, and her vision blurred. He was going to kill her no matter what. No way she was giving him what he wanted. She might die, but Rivera was not going to win.

"You can believe me or not," she said, "but I don't have anything. Warren never confided in me. I knew nothing about his illegal activities, or I would have never taken investment capital from him."

"Maybe that's true, or maybe you have it and don't know. Either way, I'm not leaving until I get what I came for, and I'm not leaving any witnesses. So you can come out from behind that counter, or I'll come to you. The end result is the same."

She heard a loud crack against the front door, and it flew

open, banging against the wall. She whipped her head around as Agent Davies stepped into the cottage and fired over the counter. She heard the gasp from the other man as the bullet hit, the cry of pain, and then a thud as he hit the ground. Davies barely glanced at her before hurrying past, she assumed to ensure the other man was unable to retaliate. Luke rushed in behind Davies, blood covering one sleeve on his T-shirt, and dropped down beside her.

He clutched her shoulders and looked over every square inch. "Are you hurt?"

She shook her head as relief washed over her.

"Take a deep breath," Luke said. "You're safe now."

"Except you're not," Davies said.

Alayna looked up to see the agent standing over both of them, his gun leveled at Luke. All the blood rushed from her head as she put everything together.

There wasn't an unknown mole in the FBI. Davies was the traitor.

"You," she gasped.

"Take that pistol out of your boyfriend's waistband and slide it across the floor," Davies said. "No fast moves. You can't aim and get off a shot before I pull the trigger."

Alayna looked at Luke, who gave her a slow nod.

She reached for the gun tucked into his waistband and slowly pulled it out, then set it on the floor.

"Now slide it this way," Davies said.

She reached to push the gun and deliberately faked losing her balance so that it slid across the floor and stopped a good ten feet from Davies. He gave it a frustrated look but since it was still closer to him than it was to Luke, he appeared only annoyed rather than concerned.

"I assume that other guy worked for you?" Alayna asked. "Is he an FBI agent too?"

Davies laughed. "Not hardly. Mateo was good at his job but a little too unpredictable. Since my other two attempts to get what I'm looking for didn't go as planned, I figured I better attend to the last stop myself. Now, hand over the drive."

"I already told your hired killer that I don't have it," Alayna said.

"I don't believe you," Davies said. "You're a smart woman... maybe a little too smart for your own good. You might not have known that Patterson left something with you when you fled New York, but I have no doubt you not only figured it out but located the prize. So do I have to put a bullet in him, or are you going to cough it up?"

"You're going to put a bullet in him anyway," Alayna said.

Davies smiled. "Maybe. Maybe not. Things are heating up for me at the FBI, and I'm afraid I might have drawn the wrong sort of attention. The contents of that drive will set me up for ten lifetimes, and I already have a way out of the country. Maybe I'll be so happy to get what I've been looking for all this time that I'll just let you live your sad little lives on this sandbar."

Alayna stared at Davies, his creepy smile making her skin crawl. She didn't believe for a minute he was going to leave her and Luke alive. Even if he got out of the country, he had to know Luke's background. The last thing Davies wanted was a SEAL coming after him the rest of his life.

"Okay. I'll get it," she said.

She leaned forward to rise and pushed the pot holder with the knife into Luke's knee as she rose. He glanced down as the knife connected with his leg and then looked back at her, their eyes meeting. He understood. They had to take a chance, and the knife was the only weapon Luke had within reach. Even if

Luke could only create a distraction, Alayna might have time to retrieve Bea's pistol. She walked slowly toward Davies, hands in the air.

"It's in my purse," she said. "In the living room."

"No sudden moves or I shoot the boyfriend," Davies said as she walked into the living room. "Show me the purse."

She lifted the handbag off the end table. It was too small to hold anything but the tiniest of guns, so no real threat to Davies.

"Good," Davies said. "Now put it back on the table and reach in with only one hand, keeping the other in the air, and pull out the drive."

She pulled open the flap of the purse and reached in with her right hand. Her cell phone was the first thing she came to and she pulled it out far enough to punch in her code and turn on the recording app. They might die here but at the very least, she was leaving the police with no doubt as to who the bad guy was.

"What's taking so long?" Davies asked, growing agitated.

"It's in a zipped pocket," Alayna said. "That's not easy to do with one hand. You're the one who took Warren, aren't you? It was never Rivera."

"Like I said," Davies said, "you're too smart for your own good."

"One of your own men got killed. That doesn't bother you?"

"It was an unfortunate situation. Only Rivera's men were supposed to go down in the exchange, but the rookie made a mistake and paid for it."

"What I don't understand is why you killed Brad. Didn't Warren tell you where the drive was?"

Davies's expression flashed with annoyance. "Patterson refused to tell—and my guys got a little overzealous. Things went too far and then getting the information out of Patterson wasn't an option."

She cringed, knowing that Warren had met a far more horrible fate than a lifetime in prison and said a silent prayer for his soul since he hadn't sent Davies directly to her doorstep. She reached inside the pocket and pulled out a small drive and held it up for him to see.

Davies smiled.

"Leave the drive on the table and come this way," Davies said. "Then you and your boyfriend can head into the afterlife together."

The joy at locking eyes on the drive was Davies's undoing. Before Alayna even realized what was happening, Luke flung her knife at Davies, and it embedded right in his neck. He screamed and dropped his gun as he stumbled backward, clutching his neck. Blood gushed through his fingers, and he stared at them in disbelief that turned to horror before he collapsed onto the floor.

Luke had kicked Davies's gun away as soon as he'd dropped it, and he now stood over the agent, staring down with a level of hatred and disgust that was only matched by what Alayna herself felt. Then relief coursed through her and she grabbed the back of the couch to keep her balance. Before this moment, everything had been played out in slow motion. Every excruciating second had seemed like an eternity. But suddenly, it all rushed in like the tide.

But this time, she was clear of the break.

"Are you all right?" Luke asked.

"Yeah, I think. Just overwhelmed."

She walked into the kitchen, skirting Davies's legs, and stood next to Luke.

"He's dead, right?"

"Definitely. That is a *really* good knife. Perfect balance."

Alayna looked down at her knife, protruding from Davies's throat and frowned. "I suppose we have to leave it there."

"Don't worry. I'll clean and disinfect it with medical grade cleaner as soon as the cops release it. But right now, we have a bigger problem."

"We need to call the police."

"And lawyers. You have a dead mercenary in your living room that ballistics will show was killed by Davies's gun, and a knife in Davies's jugular with only my prints and yours on it."

She sucked in a breath. "It will look like Rivera sent the mercenary and Davies saved us. Then we killed Davies."

He nodded. "Unless the FBI was already onto him, like he insinuated, they're not going to accept our word that Davies was dirty. They'll start digging into everything, but we have to hope that he left a trail somewhere. We need to prepare for an uphill battle."

Alayna stared at him then threw her arms in the air and spun around. "My phone!"

She ran to the living room and grabbed her phone, then hurried back to the kitchen to show a clearly confused Luke the display. "I turned on the recorder when I reached into my purse. That's what took so long, not the zipper. I figured that at least if we died, someone would check my phone and they'd know it was Davies that did it."

Luke's jaw dropped. "That's why you asked him those questions."

She nodded. "I had to get him to admit to at least some of it so that they'd have a place to start."

Luke grabbed her in a hug and spun her around. "You're the most incredible woman I've ever met."

She laughed as he put her down. "Stop. The recorder is still on."

"Good. Then hold it up and make sure all of this is clear—I

love you, Alayna Scott. From the moment I met you, I knew there was something different between us. Something bigger than either one of us. I want to stay on the island with you and watch you open your restaurant. I want to eat dinner with you every night, and I promise to do the dishes. You're the last thing I want to see before I close my eyes at night and the first thing I want to see when I open them in the morning."

Alayna's heart was beating so hard she thought it would jump out of her chest. This was it. This was what real love felt like. Long-lasting love. Love that was bigger than life or death.

"I love you, too," she said.

He drew her into a kiss so passionate that all of the tension left in her body drained away so quickly that it left her light-headed. Thank goodness, his strong arms were wrapped around her to keep her safe and steady. When he released her, she turned off the recorder.

"Now that we've decided on the rest of our lives," she said, "I guess we need to call the police. The sooner we get this circus over with, the better. But I want to contact some more people as well. I'm going to call the FBI and the DA, and I want you to call Pete and your buddy with the security business and ask them to get over here right away."

Luke looked confused. "Can I ask why?"

"Because Davies might have had a partner in this. I need your buddy to make copies of Warren's drive for me. And I want Pete to witness everything along with the island police. If there are more dirty agents, I want to give them too many people to have to kill to clean up this mess."

Luke stared. "That drive you showed Davies was the real thing? Where did you find it?"

She shook her head. "If I'm not mistaken, that's a drive with pictures from a party at my restaurant last year. I didn't even realize it was still in my purse until I looked for lip balm yesterday."

"Then where is Patterson's drive?"

She bent over and picked up the pot holder and placed it on the counter, then pushed on the edge where she'd removed the stitches until a tiny drive popped out.

"Your mother's pot holder," Luke said in amazement.

"I'd like to think that somehow she was watching over me."

Luke put his arm around her shoulders and squeezed.

"I think she was."

———

NELLY FANNED HERSELF WITH A MAGAZINE AND SHOOK HER head as Bea tapped on the computer, putting in her inventory order. It was the day after the big showdown at Alayna's cottage, and Bea had closed the bookstore so that she and Nelly didn't have to dance around a conversation the FBI said they weren't yet allowed to have. Half the town had already walked past the front door that morning, and Bea figured the rest would make it by that afternoon.

They had returned from their New Orleans trip at the same time the island police tore through town to answer Alayna's 911 call. Bea had sensed something was off with Alayna the entire drive home and had taken years off Nelly's life with her speed. She'd followed the cops to the cottage, and she'd almost fainted with fear and relief over what had transpired. Nelly had been so overwrought the paramedics had given her oxygen.

THEY'D BOTH BEEN GOING STIR-CRAZY SITTING IN THEIR homes trying to ignore phone calls, so finally Bea had suggested they pull the blinds and hide in the store where at least they could dillydally with inventory.

"When I saw that dead man on Alayna's kitchen floor, I thought I was going to pass out," Nelly said.

"Please, you weren't even close to passing out until you laid eyes on that hot new paramedic."

Nelly laughed. "Yeah, you got me there. Lord have mercy, when did they start making men who look like that? It was as if he stepped off a magazine page and into an ambulance."

"He was awfully pretty, but so young."

"When you're our age, everyone is young."

"Not Old Franklin."

"Old Franklin played marbles with Jesus. He doesn't count."

Bea laughed. "I think Jesus kept all the marbles, because Old Franklin has clearly lost his. I bet Young Franklin is feeling older than his father these days."

Nelly shook her head. "He is in a rough position. I really hope my body goes before my mind."

"What the hell are you talking about? You haven't been normal since I've known you."

"I'm not strolling naked in public."

"Not yet."

Nelly put down the magazine and stared at Bea. "Hey, have you talked to Birdie lately?"

"Not since poker night. Why do you ask?"

"I saw her last night in her backyard watering flowers and we chatted some about what happened. She'd already gotten the gossip that's going around and understood that I couldn't give details. Mostly she just wanted to make sure that Alayna and Luke were all right and that you were holding up okay."

Bea nodded. "I got a text from her checking in last night, but she said she didn't want to bother me, just let her know if there was anything she could do. I did the 'thanks but nothing at the moment' thing and told her I'd see her soon and hopefully be able to talk openly about everything, but that was it. Did she say something last night that's bothering you?"

"No. But she was off."

"How do you mean?"

"Distracted. Don't get me wrong, this business with Alayna is the scariest thing this island has ever seen short of a Cat 5, and she was clearly worried about the two of you. But I got the impression there was something else bothering her...something she wasn't saying."

Bea frowned as the image of Tom hugging the woman in New Orleans flashed across her mind. "Maybe something's going on with Piper."

Nelly nodded. "Maybe so, but that girl has always been so private I can't imagine her telling her mother if anything was wrong."

"But a mother still knows. It's something in their voice."

Nelly considered this for a moment. "You're probably right. Birdie's picked up on something and Piper is being her usual close-lipped self so it's making her worry. Well, hopefully it's nothing big and Birdie will work it out soon."

"I'm sure she will," Bea said and turned back to her computer.

But she wasn't sure at all.

CHAPTER TWENTY-SIX

Two weeks later

With her phone, Alayna took some pictures of the space that would eventually be her new restaurant. She needed the pictures for her files, not only to capture the before and after, but to get the correct hue on the bricks for when she started choosing light fixtures and furniture. Then there was paint and flooring and artwork and the million other things she had to address. It was overwhelming and also very exciting.

Luke looked out the big front windows at the Gulf, then turned around and smiled at her. She couldn't help smiling back. It had been two weeks since the showdown with Davies at her beach cottage. The week after had been filled with interviews with the FBI and the local DA, but this time, Alayna had Warren's files and her phone recording to back her up. No one even gave a hint of suggestion that she and Luke were anything but the wronged parties.

And those files had contained exactly what Luke thought they would. His security buddy made a copy and cracked the encryption on the files, so that they could see what the FBI was seeing. It was all bank account numbers and passwords to offshore accounts. A quick check revealed the balances in the accounts totaled over a hundred million. More than enough for Agent Davies to get away and disappear.

If he'd been successful.

The FBI was being tight-lipped about their investigation into Agent Davies—no surprise there—but the DA had assured her that once they started poking around into Davies's side interests, they had accumulated plenty of evidence against him, including his role in Warren's escape from custody. They'd also found information on the man Davies had hired to get to Brad and had arrested him trying to cross the border into Mexico. Between Davies's attempt to kill Alayna and Carrie Winston calling in favors with every senator and congressman her family knew, the FBI had put every available man on tracking down Brad's killer, and Alayna had no doubt he'd spend the rest of his life in prison.

"This restaurant is going to be so great," Luke said. "I can see it all just like you described. What happens next? Zoning?"

"No. We're lucky on that one. All the Main Street properties are zoned for any type of commercial business with a few exceptions."

"Exceptions?"

"Pawnshops, strip clubs, that sort of thing."

He nodded. "So anything that isn't family-friendly and doesn't suit the island vibe. When is the kitchen equipment going to arrive?"

"I have some movers bringing it tomorrow. The contractors will have to move it around a bit while doing the build-out, but it was too good a deal to pass up."

He turned to face her and gave her a soft kiss. "I have some news of my own."

Her breath caught in her throat because she knew Luke had been on the base the entire week, talking with Pete about his medical release and who knew who else. Had he made a decision about his career?

"I've been cleared for service again," he said. "Just not with the SEALs. I've talked with several of the commanding officers on base and have decided to take the trainer position. So I'm staying with the Navy and will be permanently stationed here."

Alayna's pulse ticked up, and her face almost hurt from the ear-splitting smile she wore.

He matched her grin. "I take it that means you're happy?"

"I can't believe how happy I am. When I came back to the island, I never thought I'd ever be normal again. Happiness wasn't even on my list. I think, sometimes, that I thought I didn't deserve to be happy because of what happened. But being here, I was finally able to get past that. I didn't have anything to do with Warren's actions, and I'm not going to feel guilty any longer for not realizing what he was doing."

"Considering the FBI didn't know what a supervising agent was doing, I think it's a good idea to cut yourself a break."

She laughed. "I hadn't thought about it that way, but you're right. If Davies could play the entire FBI, then a chef didn't stand a chance against a very seasoned and intelligent criminal."

"Ultimately, the chef proved to be the smarter one. And speaking of the devils, have you heard anything else from the FBI?"

"Not for a couple days now, but they told me last time that they had everything they needed and to call if *I* needed something. I took that to mean they were done with me."

Luke put his hands together like he was praying and looked up.

She laughed again and playfully grabbed his hands. "You

keep doing things like that and Old Franklin sees, he might get ideas about your career."

He stared at her in dismay. "Now, why in the world would you bring that man up? I'm here relishing a glorious future, in a beautiful place, with the woman who cooks food I could only dream about, and now all I can see is that unfortunate shirt of Pete's in an even more unfortunate position."

She wrapped her arms around him and gave him a sexy kiss.

"I can probably change your thinking," she said.

"Are you offering to cook?" he asked, then laughed as he dodged off.

She swatted him on the rear as he hurried away, and her heart skipped a beat when he looked over his shoulder at her and grinned.

She'd found real.

———

THANK YOU FOR READING, AND I HOPE YOU LOVED TEMPEST Island. Do you want to know more about the island and its residents? Are you curious about the mystery brewing between Tom and Birdie? Will the Whitmores cause problems for Alayna and her new restaurant? Look for *Adrift*, coming soon. To receive notifications when new books are available, sign up for my mailing list on my website janadeleon.com.

EMMA TURNER HAS SPENT YEARS RUNNING, HIDING, DODGING... limiting her short stays to bigger cities where she could easily avoid questions and get lost in the crowd. But when she steps onto Tempest Island, something changes. The tiny island speaks to her in a way no other place ever has, and over the past eight years, she's been to plenty of them. Suddenly, she finds herself breaking one of her many rules and applying for a job at the Island Surf Shop.

Since his wife's death a year ago, Mark Phillips has done the best he can to put life back together for himself and his five-year-old daughter, Lily. Now, he needs to turn some attention to his somewhat neglected business so that he doesn't have to worry about their future. Emma Turner has all the qualifications he's looking for, but the beautiful brunette is also keeping secrets.

And the life she left behind years ago is about to catch up with her.

IF YOU ENJOYED THIS TALE ABOUT STRONG WOMEN AND LOVE action and a lot of humor in your stories, try my Miss Fortune series – a New York Times, USA Today, and Wall Street Journal bestseller. This mystery series features a multi-generational cast of exceptional women and is set deep in the bayous of Sinful, Louisiana.

The first book is entitled *Louisiana Longshot* and is available for free in ebook format from all retailers. For a longer description, excerpt, and buy links, check out the book details on my website janadeleon.com.

CPSIA information can be obtained
at www.ICGtesting.com
Printed in the USA
LVHW010931230821
695886LV00001B/72